THE FULL

The womar
let the your
take her breasts.

'Violence is your therapy,' she said. 'Violence can purge you, make you clean, cure you. The humiliation and impotence are nearly over.'

She held him for a moment, then gently lifted his head to her eye level. On the huge screen that dominated the room, bestial images continued to glow.

'RFK,' she whispered.
'RFK,' he repeated automatically.
'RFK must die. RFK must die . . .'
'RFK must die. RFK must die. RFK must die . . .'

She guided his hand. They were chanting now – 'RFK must die . . . RFK must die . . . RFK must die . . . RFK must die . . . *RFK must die!*'

That night the doctor would be able to report to her employers that the first stage of the operation had been a success . . .

The Killing of RFK

DONALD FREED

SPHERE BOOKS LIMITED
30/32 Gray's Inn Road, London WC1X 8JL

First published in Great Britain
by Sphere Books Ltd 1977

TRADE MARK

Set in Photon Times

Printed in Great Britain by
C. Nicholls & Company Ltd
The Philips Park Press, Manchester

For Virginia,
Walter,
Virginia,
Bob–
Barboura
and Hugh

Saul and Jonathan, sweet and
beloved in their lives; nor in their
death were they divided; swifter
were they than eagles, braver than
lions . . .
DAVID'S LAMENT, SAMUEL 11:1

ACKNOWLEDGMENTS

Jack Kimbrough's early enthusiasm was important both to this book and to the film of the same name. Critical help and new information came from Paul Allan and a network of prison researchers led by Rusty Rhodes, Lake Headley, Robert Hyde, and Vladamir Zatko. Linda and Sue Valentino and Carolyn Keller were very resourceful and able in manuscript research and preparation. Walter H. King, my attorney, was of constant support in this difficult venture. Theresa Christenson, a very brave young woman, brought forward new information of what happened in the Ambassador Hotel that night in 1968.

Some of this country's greatest researchers and intelligence analysts continue to be generous with their time and expertise: Mark Lane, Professors Peter Dale Scott and Richard Popkin, George O'Toole, Victor Marchetti, William W. Turner, Lillian Castellano, Mae Brussell, Rod Larson, and members of the Fifth Estate and the Committee to Investigate Political Assassinations.

Finally, author and readers owe deep thanks to police and federal investigators formerly assigned to the assassination investigation of Senator Robert F. Kennedy – who were willing to talk, off the record, and cut through the official cover-up.

PROLOGUE

'. . . NNNNNNNNN . . . !'

Every day, at approximately one o'clock, the exotic Arabic name was chanted down the corridor of Death Row, with the *n*'s sustained so inhumanly that the name had the effect of being an echo of itself.

Earl 'Fresno' Thomas, a migratory farm worker who had been sentenced to die for the murder of his employer, was the man calling. Thomas drowned out his own thoughts by constantly reminding the diminutive political assassin that he, a foreigner, an *A*-rab, had taken the life of an American-born citizen.

The assassin never answered, never even came to the bars, silent and invisible in the terrific and echoing chamber.

'. . . NNNNNNNNN . . .'

The wild echolalia of the resonation smashed into their eardrums.

'Thomas, you're about the sorriest motherfucker that ever shit between two shoes. If you gotta do something, think about your mother and jack off.' The answering taunt came from Jesse James Gilbert, a cop killer who had rid himself of all belongings, including hope, except for a volume of the complete works of William Shakespeare. As he joined his voice to the din of the dozens, he continued to read from his beloved text:

'. . . how these weak vain nails may tear a passage through the flinty ribs of this hard world, my ragged prison walls . . .'

'. . . *NNNNNNNNN* . . .'

'Why don't you get on the dummy, Thomas. There ain't nobody wants to hear your shit.'

'How am I gonna get on the dummy, when your mama's already on it?'

'You white boys are something else. A nigger invents a game called the dozens. Now you motherfuckers play it like it belongs to you. You rob us of everything . . . even our profanity.'

'So what? A white man invented watermelon, but you eat it, chump.'

In his cell Edward 'Mr. Smooth' Carter grinned. Of the 140 men on Death Row in America, 60 percent are black, and at least one is a black revolutionary. Edward Carter's mind had been honed to a razor's edge on Marx, Lenin, Mao, George Jackson, and Huey P. Newton, but he maintained the classic strategy of a ghetto dweller. 'Let me tell you chumps something. Before this here moratorium was put into effect, there wasn't none of you suckers had anything to say. Now that you're living under an umbrella and the slave master ain't gonna kill you for at least another couple of years, y'all lay up here fat-mouthing one another. Y'all like a bunch of shack bullies – when the odds are with you you're tougher than a keg of ten-penny nails, but let 'em take their chickenshit moratorium off and you'll *all* fall down on your knees praying.'

'. . . *NNNNNNNNN* . . .'

'Yeah, Thomas,' Mr. Smooth said, 'that's right, get on his case. You found somebody you think's even lower than you. But what you're doing is picking on the only chump up here that ain't got a prayer. For him, the moratorium's over. He's got a twenty-five-grand contract on his head. Twenty-five big ones. In dollars-and-cents value, that makes him *better* than you.'

There was a chorus of 'Amen,' 'Hallelujah,' and 'Tell it like it is, Brother Smooth'; then Death Row fell silent as the first smell of food reached the tier. But Edward Carter knew it would only be momentary – too close to the dinner hour. Blood sugar was running low, and the men were restless. Some, like himself, would do pushups, but most of them would be back up to the bars in a minute, yelling their heads off.

Carter stretched out on the floor and with slow precision began a set of one hundred fingertip pushups. One . . . two . . . three . . . four . . . five . . .

Mealtime. Two officers, one on each side of the cart, work their way down the corridor. Stopping at each cell, one asks the occupant which of the two entrees he prefers – roast beef *au jus* or the Mexican Plate – while the other dishes up the order with stainless-steel ladles.

At dinnertime Death Row is quiet as a church. The condemned men keep their mouths busy with food. There is a long night ahead, and they chew slowly, using up the hateful time, killing it.

The men on Death Row, unlike the other inmates, are not afraid of the guards. These men, already legally dead, are treated with a kind of grotesque respect by the authorities; their food is the best in the prison; their mail is delivered promptly.

The guard called out the strange Arabic syllables.

The convicted assassin stared up from his bunk, the huge black eyes betraying nothing. The guard slid the letter through the thirteen-bar cell door.

Later, the silent prisoner fingered the thick stamp-covered envelope as if it were a booby trap; then he slipped it, unopened, between the mattress and the steel surface of his bunk. The sound waves of the after-meal noise began to rise up around him like another wall.

Three days later, he tore the envelope open.

FROM: The Committee to Investigate Political Assassination
RE: The assassination of Senator Robert F. Kennedy
Dear Sir:

We are an independent group of citizen-investigators who are working on your case. Our intent is to present your case to the public in the light of the following new or little-known information:

1) Los Angeles County Coroner Dr. Thomas P. Noguchi testified before the Grand Jury that the bullet that killed Senator Robert F. Kennedy was fired from no more than 'two or three inches behind the right ear.' All witnesses, as you know, put you no closer than several feet in *front* of Senator Kennedy during the shooting.
2) On July 1, 1968, William Harper, Chief Criminalist for the Pasadena, California, Police Department, and a charter member of Erle Stanley Gardner's famous 'Court of Last

Resort,' stated: 'Based on my background and training, upon my experience as a consulting criminalist and my studies, examination and analysis of the data related to the Robert F. Kennedy assassination, I have arrived at the following findings and opinions . . . 1) Two .22-caliber guns were involved in the assassination. 2) Senator Kennedy was killed by one of the shots fired . . . by a second guman. 3) It is extremely unlikely that any of the bullets fired by your gun ever struck the body of Senator Kennedy.'

3) Witnesses testify that when apprehended you were trembling and your eyes were glazed as if you had been hypnotized. . . .

JUNE 7, 1968

New York City, New York

> Your Eminences, your Excellencies, Mr. President. On behalf of Mrs. Kennedy, her children, the parents and sisters of Robert Kennedy, I want to express what we feel to those who mourn with us today in this cathedral and around the world . . .

There was a terrible beauty about the head and face. A halo of chestnut hair framed the youngest, last living Kennedy brother. Now he, the finest orator in the nation since the assassination of Dr. Martin Luther King, Jr., fought to pitch his strong and resonant New England voice above the level of sobbing.

> We loved him as a brother and as a father and as a son. From his parents and from his older brothers and sisters, Joe and Kathleen and Jack, he received an inspiration which he passed on to all of us . . .

From the church pews or on the television screen, in the tear-dimmed view of the mourners that day, and forever afterward, the face and head and voice of the youngest Kennedy man appeared for a moment to be a composite of all the brothers. As if it were a trick of the light, when they looked at Edward Kennedy Bobby's sharp, intense features were immanent for a moment, and then, more diffused, Jack's. The image was more than mere remembered grief or nostalgia, just less than a ghost – except for those who had hated or feared this American royal house, and saw in their heir apparent a revenant that had returned to haunt their conscience, or their bloodlust.

Beneath him near the altar lay the closed mahogany coffin of his brother Robert, surrounded by an Honor

Guard of enlisted men in dress uniforms, standing at attention. Near the altar stood the President of the United States, Lyndon B. Johnson, and the two remaining major candidates, Richard M. Nixon and Hubert H. Humphrey. Behind them stretched the overflow that filled the vast cathedral of St. Patrick's. Without exception, even those who sobbed quietly hung on the great funeral oration that was being delivered by the Senator from Massachusetts for the fallen Senator from New York, who, until his murder, had been the major standard bearer for the insurgent wing of the national Democratic Party in its campaign to capture the Presidency.

> He gave us strength in time of trouble, wisdom in time of uncertainty, and sharing in time of happiness. He will always be by our side.

Outside the cathedral were massed more than a half million people straining to hear history over loudspeakers.

> Love is not an easy feeling to put into words. Nor is loyalty or trust or joy. But he was all of these. He loved life completely and he lived it intensely.

And across the wired nation the radio and television images of the final rites fell on the population as if from some exponential Delphic Oracle. In the ghetto bars, the grape fields, the factories, the veterans' hospitals, the dormitories, prisons, houses, tenements, and apartments, they listened to the voice from the machine.

> A speech he made for the young people in South Africa on their Day of Affirmation in 1966 sums it up best, and I would like to read it now: 'There is discrimination in this world and slavery and starvation. Governments repress their people. Millions are trapped in poverty while the nation grows rich and wealth is lavished on armaments everywhere. These are differing evils but they are the common works of man.'

At Fiftieth Street and Fifth Avenue in New York the television networks' second units fed the pictures of the stunned and silent masses into the cables and then out around the world, sending simultaneously a corner of the fabled *mise en scène* of the American Empire in its hour of darkness: the rich architecture and soaring sculptured spires and towers of Rockefeller Plaza, with its statue of Atlas.

Inside, the cameras focused on Edward Kennedy at the podium, and on the faces of the great, humbled on this day by terror and pity. The Kennedy women were in black, the girls in white. Four of Robert Kennedy's sons served as acolytes; eight other young Kennedys bore the bread and wine toward the altar. The next generation of the tragic house passed under the sad, stern eyes of the matriarch Rose, watching like Hecuba, listening to her last son.

> It is a revolutionary world which we live in. . . . Some believe there is nothing one man or one woman can do against the enormous array of the world's ills.

St. Patrick's Cathedral, known as 'the powerhouse' to the political elite, was built in the 1850s on the upper meadows of Manhattan, and opened its doors in 1879. Now its spires were canceled out by massive piles of stone being erected on every side.

> Yet many of the world's great movements of thought and action have flowed from the work of a single man . . .

Crammed in at the back, behind the notables, was a black man named Paul Woods who looked like an All-American halfback – which he had been – dressed immaculately in a light gray suit and black tie. A look of the most terrible grief and rage was set on his face, as if he would never again relax his Greek mask of tragedy into a human countenance.

Standing next to him, clutching his hand, was Judith Shankland, a tall, slim young woman whose tailoring and grooming made her a candidate for that clan of beautiful people who had dwelled for a time in Camelot. Except that she stood at the rear holding the hand of a black man.

These two, Paul Woods and Judith Shankland, formerly with the Robert Kennedy presidential-campaign staff, stood there listening to the eulogy: she with her eyes closed as if against a harsh light, he staring with that look of irreconcilable hurt and rage – and remembering: the procession from St. Matthew's Cathedral to the Capitol Building Rotunda in Washington, D.C., five years before; the flag-draped coffin of John Fitzgerald Kennedy surrounded by guards from all the services; a black-veiled Jacqueline Kennedy and the children, escorted by Robert Kennedy; the band playing the sorrowful Navy hymn; the drums; the great black horse, Blackjack, riderless and rearing, following the caisson of the fallen president; the brothers, Robert and Edward, in the funeral cortege; he himself, younger then, the first black Secret Service agent, moving through the crowds with a coded insignia pinned to his lapel. He thought of all this, and of the special suffering of black people on that day just eight weeks ago, when they had buried his friend Martin King in Atlanta.

Edward Kennedy had moved into the peroration of his eulogy, straining for lucidity while the entire body politic trembled on the brink of madness and blindness and astonishment of heart.

> It is from numberless diverse acts of courage and belief that human history is shaped. Each time a man stands for an ideal, or acts to improve the lot of others, or strikes out against injustice, he sends forth a tiny ripple of hope, and crossing each other from a million different centers of energy and daring, those ripples build a current that can sweep down the mightiest walls of oppression and resistance . . .

They all dreaded the silence, more than he who would now wear the mantle of America's once and future king. But the end was near; the great voice had begun to quiver slightly; choking sobs began to sound at the back. Judith Shankland was one of those who began to sway as the broken voice passed its limit.

> That is the way he lived. That is the way he leaves us . . . My brother need not be idealized or enlarged in death beyond what he was in life. He should be remembered simply as a good and decent man who saw wrong and tried to right it, saw suffering and tried to

heal it, saw war and tried to stop it . . . Those of us who loved him and take him to his rest today pray that what he was to us, and what he wished for others, will some day come to pass for all the world. As he said many times, in many parts of this nation, to those he touched and who sought to touch him: 'Some men see things as they are and say why. I dream things that never were and say why not.'

They were all standing. Out of the terrible and final silence the singer, Andy Williams, began the haunting verse of 'The Battle Hymn of the Republic', the first Protestant song of protest. Then the congregation began to flow like a dark wave out into the massed sea of humanity that spread from Fifth Avenue out over New York as far as the television-camera eye could see.

Paul Woods and Judith Shankland sat wordlessly as the funeral train made its way from the Hudson to Washington. At each stop and crossing they could all hear the refrain of 'The Battle Hymn of the Republic' starting again and again in an endless funereal round. Then silence and patches of open country, gaps in the line of mourners and curiosity seekers. A margin of industrial and human waste like century-old scar tissue across the face of the East. They just stared through the dusty train windows at the almost unending ranks of people standing in small groups or by the thousands on every hill and bridge and station, eight hours and two hundred twenty-five miles of people down the great industrial corridor: New Jersey, Pennsylvania, Delaware, Maryland.

On the train, Judith Shankland felt the powerful arm under her hand go rock rigid before she was aware of the announcement from the small portable television in the railroad car. The millions staring into the electronic eye that stared back at them in their homes watched as the anonymous image of Eric Starvo Galt, a.k.a. James Earl Ray, materialized on their screens, superimposed by the networks' news chiefs. Over the flowing, moving images of the lonesome train and the sidings heavy with the hymn-singing mourners the mask of the petty thief who the FBI claimed had shot Dr. Martin Luther King, Jr., hung disembodied and demonic. The voice of a special broadcaster, sounding like an FBI spokesman, announced that the slayer of the civil rights leader had been apprehended in London.

On the train, Paul Woods seethed. He had stood next to Ramsey Clark earlier in the day in a Justice Department office as the young Attorney General first tried to explain and then order his FBI liaison, over the long-distance telephone, to inform J. Edgar Hoover that no announcement concerning the King case would be made until after the funeral ceremonies – finally shouting into the receiver that any premature FBI exhibitionism or intervention into the proceedings would be outright insubordination. Now, once again, Paul Woods raged inwardly. The incredible superimposed image of James Earl Everyman mocked them from the tube. The real power had spoken.

The people who had loved him and his brother were weeping and singing as the train rocked past them. In shuttered rooms millions upon millions huddled around their television sets as if for warmth. The lonesome train, like the train that had carried Abraham Lincoln, moved like destiny across the miles toward the Capitol.

The lonesome little people watched slack-jawed: the generations who had worked, had paid for the wars with money and men, had lived through the Great Depression but now had lost the confidence and hope that once had sustained them, and whose offspring were the children of assassination and riot and conspiracy and could believe in neither the past nor the future. An endless human chain singing the old song as they stood there waiting patiently in their cheap clothes with their tired, shapeless bodies and their big-eyed, frightened children; standing there numb and dumb, but for the song, as the beautiful princes and princesses from Camelot passed in their mystery along the dusty road that led to Washington, the city of lies.

As they sang on the public highway or watched in secret, they wept for themselves as much as for all those who had been cut down by the decade of death. For they feared for themselves and the children they clutched to their legs, feared that *they* – whoever *they* were – who had conspired to slay their leaders were now conspiring to slay them as well.

MARCH–APRIL 1968

March 16 *Washington, D.C.*

The pale gunmetal-grayish-blue eyes of William A. Must, Jr., shifted from side to side behind the lenses of his dark glasses. He could see the fanglike turrets of the Watergate complex in the distance as he threaded his way through the garbage-choked streets of the Columbia Road pocket, a small fraction of the huge Washington, D.C., ghetto surrounding the stage-set props of pomp and power that the public watched on their television news every evening.

Despite its picture-postcard image, the nation's capital is very much a colonial city. More colonial than a Southern town, with rather sharp class and caste distinctions among the occupying army of the white senior bureaucrats and their political managers; the 'colored' lesser bureaucratic strata and service-industry employees; and, at the bottom, the sprawling, impacted black enclaves of misery where the wretched and damned of the Empire seem to hide in the shadows, spying on the stage set of historic buildings and monuments.

William A. Must, Jr., would never have allowed himself to be caught in this forbidden native territory, any more than any other white official in the town, if it were not for the fact that he had decided that he required a circuitous and clandestine route from his Georgetown flat to the safe-house apartment available to him at the Watergate, which he sometimes used for days at a time. He had never trusted anyone. He lived in a perpetual state of war. He always assumed that he was followed, his telephone tapped, his mail read; he believed in the game of total surveillance, and whether he was hunted or hunter did not matter. It was the game that gave him a pleasure that he could feel, as now, in his blood, bones, bowels. So he had chosen a devious path – one along which any white man tailing him would be immediately visible among the dark people who glared at Must as he passed by quickly.

Two prostitutes leaning out of a window to catch a little warmth on this clear March day studied the white man as he crossed the street with a military stride. They noted the polished black brogans and the rich, conservative tie and soft button-down white shirt under the lightweight black raincoat. As he passed under their window, the fast-moving legs clad in a bureaucratic gray showed a flash of his black, garter-controlled hose. The prostitutes knew something about the peculiar tastes of some of the white men in Washington, but this powerfully-built middle-aged man, already blurring into the chaotic middle distance of the next block, was quite obviously just passing through.

Must felt trim and dry as he strode purposefully. The police positive revolver in the belt holster felt good under his snug raincoat. He was certain now that he had not been followed. He paused in front of an ancient cigar store. Bookie joint, he noted mentally as he glanced at a newspaper. Black capitalism – cockroach capitalism. He rolled the words around silently to himself as he used up time with the newspaper.

He scanned the lead stories:

BLOODY BATTLE FOR
KHE SAHN CONTINUES
VIET WAR LEGAL, U.S. TELLS COURT

NATION'S POSITION
UPHELD BY BRIEF
IN SPOCK CASE

HIGH SCHOOL, COLLEGE
DEMONSTRATIONS ERUPT

and in a sidebar:

243 REDS KILLED
IN STRUGGLE FOR
SAIGON OUTPOSTS.

Farther down, beneath the fold, was:

JOHNSON REAFFIRMS
TIES WITH LABOR,
GOALS IN VIETNAM.

He started to turn to the saturation coverage inside of the RFK TO DECLARE CANDIDACY TODAY article when a wire-service filler caught his attention: 'In a legal first, in a murder trial here today a jury was allowed to see films of defendant Antonia Thomas made while she was under hypnosis. . . .'

Must threw change down on the pile, rubbed his neck hard, and tucked the paper into his coat.

He moved on, graceful for a fifty-five-year-old man built like a professional football fullback, stepping with precision around and above the minefield of dog waste that only a clear eye could distinguish from the general debris underfoot. Something about the man made two otherwise self-possessed street bloods step aside casually as Must loomed up in the middle of the sidewalk, where they had been talking. He did not look like an aging professional athlete to them; he looked like a cop. But not the kind of cop they had known and would know for as long as these streets prevailed. He was big but not gone to fat; the clothes were not only expensive but in very good conservative taste; the face, despite the brutality suggested by the dark glasses, was neither corrupt nor drink-stained; the neat brown hair was long enough to part near the center, and showed only as much white as a man in his middle forties might admit to.

When he was within a pistol shot of the toothed turrets of the Watergate, William A. Must, Jr., checked his watch and slowed his step; he did not want to arrive at the meeting more than ten minutes before Antony 'Black Man' Prince. Prince was not black at all, only a very swarthy and hairy Italian-American from Bridgeport, Connecticut, who, Must knew, would get lost in the labyrinth of the Watergate, looking for Must's suite.

Antony Prince had arrived at the Watergate via Teamsters Union limousine, but now, as he cursed his way through the huge complex, hopelessly lost, sweating in his new $350 suit, he felt like who he was: Antony Petrocelli of Bridgeport, Connecticut, and Leavenworth, Kansas, #97440771, with a rap sheet that wound through three decades all the way back to Chicago and the still unsolved murder of Tony's old boss in the United Waste Handlers Union. Now he felt like a bum. He had wanted to meet Must and this other guy at the usual place in New York. He hated Washington, it was always too hot. The coloring was rubbing off the handle of the fake cordovan briefcase that kept bouncing off his knobby, bowed legs and staining his fat, manicured hands. He hated this faggot town, as he always referred to Washington.

Prince had gone into the hotel by mistake, then had to walk down Virginia to New Hampshire Avenue to the Watergate Apartments. He paused now to scrub his imitation-leather-stained hands with an elaborately monogrammed linen handkerchief.

The extensive complex, consisting of two office and three apartment buildings and the hotel, gives the impression of an updated medieval fortress looking down upon its less formidable surroundings, such as the plebeian red-roofed Howard Johnson's Motor Lodge across the street. Tony did not know, of course, that the bridge between Watergate East and Watergate South is suggestive of a Bridge of Sighs, an American flag high atop, or that the whole neofascist pile of concrete and plastic was designed by an Italian architect. His fat mod sideburns were filling up with sweat, and in the heat Tony felt like crying, or killing somebody.

With the exception of the two office buildings, the whole complex is ribbed with rows of what appeared to be stony turrets of teeth, but which in fact are the balconies which open off nearly every room. These even gray-white incisors projecting from the strange, swollen, elliptical, wedgelike, and semi-circular shapes of the building units suggest a mythic sea creature, or perhaps a shark. To assure utmost privacy, the balconies are separated from each other by what appear to be cement fins. Tiny pebbles pressed into the cement give the 'fins' a scaly effect.

Almost nobody can be seen on the balconies, which are the main architectural feature of the complex. The sense of this being a high-security fortress is augmented by the lower-level passages, known as malls, but which are more like labyrinths. In these labyrinths one can buy anything from groceries to air tickets, for, as the complex brochure proclaims, the idea was to make Watergate as secure and self-sustaining as possible – as though it were under siege.

Upstairs in the austere, anonymous apartment, William A. Must, Jr., had changed glasses, hung up his raincoat and suit jacket, brushed his hair with the twin silver military brushes, poured a double Scotch, neat, and flicked on the television console. The main room of the small suite was clinically cold, the off-white walls bare except for the framed Green Beret motto over the portable bar: GRAB THEM BY THE BALLS AND THEIR HEARTS AND MINDS WILL FOLLOW.

The TV picture bounced into focus. The scene was the chandeliered and Corinthian-columned interior of the Senate Caucus Room. There, as his brother before him had done, Senator Robert Francis Kennedy was declaring his candidacy for President of the United States.

> I run because I am convinced that this country is on a perilous course and because I have such strong feelings about what must be done that I am obliged to do all I can . . .

As the camera panned the crowd of poised journalists, Must looked for John R. Martin III, a thirty-year-old Ivy League boy. Must, who had worked his way through Brown University during the Great Depression, instinctively mistrusted anyone from Cornell, and half expected Mr. John Randolph Martin III to blow his research/press cover before the campaign even started. Must noted Ethel Kennedy and at least nine of the ten Kennedy children. The unmistakable Kennedy voice, not yet used up on the throngs that awaited his coming, began, as always, to literally get under Must's skin.

> I run because it is now unmistakably clear that we can change these disastrous, divisive policies only by changing the men who made them. For the reality of recent events in Vietnam has been glossed over with

illusions. The report of the Riot Commission has been largely ignored. The crisis in our cities, the crisis on our farms and in our ghettos, all have been met with too little and too late . . .

Must's heavy, symmetrical jaw set grimly as the camera swept the long, green-felt-covered table at which the young Robert Kennedy years before had sat as a counsel for the old McCarthy subcommittee – and, later, at the same table for the Army hearings, which had brought the Wisconsin Senator down and driven him to drink himself to death. William Must's ice-cold eyes went out of focus for a moment as he remembered his friend Joe and the most vital and meaningful period of his own life: the early to mid-1950s.

The Muzak medley in the elevator was featuring 'Sweet Georgia Brown' as Antony Prince finally reached his destination. He could hear the television being turned off abruptly as he knocked lightly on Must's door.

'*Buon giorno, Antonio. Che se dice? Como estar?*' Must had a slightly hoarse and resonant voice. It could stroke and it could cut.

'What do you say, Bill. Hey, is the kid here yet? I got something –'

With his finger to his thin lips, Must pantomimed the possibility of the presence of a listening device, and then motioned his visitor to the bar. Tony nodded sagely as Must turned on the radio to an all-music station. Mozart flooded the room, making Tony wince. He felt more comfortable in the spotless bathroom, where Must was turning on the shower full force.

'Got your drink? "Remember the Pueblo," ' Must proposed by way of a toast. They drank. 'Got something for me, Tony?'

'Yeah. Our contact with the feebies says this here is hot.' Tony sat his squat bullet of a body on the closed toilet seat, lit an Antonio y Cleopatra, and rummaged through the briefcase. Must waited, sipping his Scotch and studying his hard, regular features in the mirror.

'Here it is.'

FD-302 (Rev. 3-3-59) FEDERAL BUREAU OF INVESTIGATION

1 Date 12/2/63

LEOPOLDO RAMOS DUCOS, Supra, advised that ANA MARIA DEL VALLE voluntarily appeared at his office on November 26, 1963. She related information that MIGUEL CRUZ told her, 'We killed KENNEDY and the next will be RAMOS DUCOS.' RAMOS DUCOS had no additional information concerning this statement.

RAMOS DUCOS also related the following:

RAMOS DUCOS formerly was an Organizer of Local 901, Teamsters Union, from 1960 until March, 1962. During this period he heard FRANK CHAVEZ, Secretary-Treasurer of that Local, mention the name of one JACK RUBY as someone connected with Teamsters Union.

Sometime in about September, 1961, FRANK CHAVEZ told RAMOS DUCOS that CHAVEZ had an appointment to meet RICHARD KAVNER, International Vice President of Teamsters Union, and JACK RUBY as well as a third Teamsters official whose name RAMOS DUCOS could not recall. The meeting was to be in San Juan, but RAMOS DUCOS could not furnish any further details. He had neither seen nor talked to JACK RUBY who allegedly killed LEE HARVEY OSWALD in Dallas, Texas, on November 24, 1963.

on 11/26/63 at SAN JUAN, PUERTO RICA File ♯DL 44-1639 by Special Agent ROYAL L. BLASSINGAME-gi Date dictated 11/27/63.

In 1967, Puerto Rican Teamsters chief FRANK CHAVEZ allegedly flew to Washington intent on assassinating SEN. ROBERT KENNEDY, WALTER SHERIDAN and their prime witness against HOFFA, ED PARTIN. KENNEDY'S men learned of the assassination plot and asked the F.B.I. for help. They were told, however, that the F.B.I. had no jurisdiction. In the end, HOFFA dissuaded CHAVEZ, and the would-be assassin docilely surrendered his pistol to HOFFA. A few months later, CHAVEZ was slain by one of his own bodyguards.

Must scanned the stolen document wordlessly, frowning, rubbing a cancerous-looking mole just above the collar line on his thick neck. Before he could speak the door chimes sounded. 'Take it easy with this punk,' he whispered. 'I've got his pants off, but he's not in bed with us yet.' Prince showed brown teeth and hissed a laugh. Must had assured him that their young visitor would be signed on as a White House junior aide or researcher if Nixon won. 'We have to talk about these *and* your L.A. man, Brading, afterwards.' The report secure in his own attaché case, Must opened the door to an obviously nervous John R. Martin III, who was clutching several large art-board 10 × 10 displays wrapped in brown paper.

'John R.! Come in, old boy. You don't drink, do you? Have a soft drink. You've met Mr. Prince? Come in, come in.' The veteran agent-handler's voice was hoarsely hale above the Mozart. The scrawny Ivy Leaguer was putty in his thick hands. The music had the opposite effect on John R. Martin III than it had on Tony Prince, and he smiled weakly as he tore the brown paper off of his displays.

'Here, sit out here in the air while I put Tony in the picture regarding these really champion charts of yours.'

John R. Martin III had been signed on for the Nixon campaign by 'Big John' Mitchell himself after Nixon's law partner had been shown a sample of his Master's-thesis political-science graph by a Yale alumnus in the Nixon, Rose, Mudge, Mitchell firm. His first job in Washington had been as an 'ethnic specialist', working at a desk in a cramped hallway in the campaign headquarters on Pennsylvania Avenue. His rise through the hierarchy of bright young men was dramatic. He would make statements like 'There is a conservative revolution coming – the Democratic party will not carry Oklahoma again for the rest of this century!' Then he would open a desk drawer and produce surveys made among seventh-graders in Tulsa and Oklahoma City, and senior staff men would slap him on his tense shoulder with pride.

Young Martin III soon replaced a computer that had been doing the semantic-differential study of which words should be used to best market the candidate – the 'Ideal Presidential Curve', it was called. By March, Martin's memos were zipping right through to the top echelon and he had been switched to Media Liaison and introduced to William A. Must, Jr,. by the head of security for the Nixon campaign.

Martin sat, at ease now, chewing his ice cubes on

Must's sunny terrace, enjoying the view and the music. Inside, the two older men studied Martin's charts, which Must had arranged in order on a tripod. Felt-pen poll charts, just another pre-campaign research assignment, strictly legal, Martin reassured himself – just like all his other tasks. As he chewed the ice and hummed along with the Mozart, only an occasional phrase from the adjoining room reached his ears.

'... Wallace and Kennedy or ... Tony, your people ...'

'Kennedy, *period*!'

Martin was proud of his multicolored poll mockups based on computer readouts; he pictured them in his mind's eye as Must and Prince bent over them and the concerto spun into the final movement.

NIXON	33%	NIXON	40%
McCARTHY	39%	HUMPHREY	36%
WALLACE	10%		
NIXON	34%	NIXON	35%
HUMPHREY	35%	KENNEDY	45%
WALLACE	12%		
NIXON	35%	NIXON	41%
KENNEDY	41%	LBJ	39%
WALLACE	8%		

'No one has these but us. Roper, Gallup, nobody. What's their story? "Nixon trails *all* the Democrat front runners except when Wallace is in." But RFK has the big lead, *and* he cuts into the Wallace vote.'

'... gotta look like some kinda red ...'

'Yes, you notice on this chart how the Wallace vote shifts over to ...' Must paused in mid-sentence as the music stopped. 'Let's take a break.' He smiled as he poured fresh drinks and led Prince out onto the terrace to join Martin, who jumped up from his chair helpfully as the older men walked to the balcony rail to take in the vista of the cherry blossoms and the buildings below. Martin was startled when the radio interrupted their reverie.

> We will continue with our all-Mozart concert in a moment. Now for the news highlights on the half-hour ...

'I am announcing today my candidacy for the Presidency of the United States. I do not run for the Presidency merely to oppose any man but to propose new policies . . .'

Irritated, Must left the balcony to turn down the second coming of the bad news. Prince followed, cursing, 'That little prick controls the fucking press.' As Prince spoke, Must motioned him back out to the relative security of the terrace.

'I'm telling you, Bill, the boys won't buy another Dallas.' At the mention of this taboo word they both turned to look at Martin, who swallowed the last of his iced Coke. Now the Mozart program was resuming, but even after Prince and Must had returned to the bar to continue their conversation, because of the lower radio volume, Martin could hear what he told himself later was nothing but a theoretical diatribe, of the sort that old hands like Must often indulge in. But he did wonder why Must had not dismissed him, and why, lately, he was being introduced to a rogue's gallery of police types like Antony Prince. Did they want him to hear? Up until now the only act he had been asked to commit that gave him any anxiety was to bring the polling and computer results from the Committee to Elect the Next President to Must first. Must himself had urged him to play by the rules and kiss every ass on the committee so that after the election he would have a crack at the White House staff, and Must had insisted that he take $7,500 for his wife's psychotherapy bills. And his wife was crazy about Must, so why feel nervous . . .

Despite the fact that there was no photograph or biography of Must in any of the usual *Who's Who*'s or media morgues, Martin had researched enough about his mystery-man benefactor to know that he was indeed an old hand: spying behind the lines in World War II; working under cover of the Marshall Plan after the war with the narcotics and fascist underground in France to undermine the leftist trade unions; propaganda and 'destabilization' in Italy and Greece to block the rise to power of the postwar popular-front movements; and, vaguely, 'dirty tricks' of some kind in Latin America and the Caribbean until the purge that tore the Central Intelligence Agency apart after the Bay of Pigs disaster. So he did not take too seriously what he overheard from the other room.

'See, Bill, the boys figure we shouldn't oughta make no move until after California –'

'Look here! You tell *them* that *I'm* the man in the field with his life on the line. In this kind of operation I've got the action veto over any politico lying on his ass in some executive suite.'

'Yeah, but the fuckin' Agency –'

When he leveled with Prince, Martin noticed, Must's voice and manner took on a coarse, cold quality quite foreign to the Ivy League patois that he was accustomed to hearing from his mentor.

'Don't worry. The Agency's gone soft, soft as mush . . . Look at the Pueblo, look at –'

'But you said before –'

'– and the Arrow Shirt boys over at the White House will cover automatically to save their own, ah, skins. Nobody's concerned with, ah, "details" once the goal is determined from the top.'

'You keep leavin' out LBJ. If he runs –'

He slid out another of Martin's elegant mockups. 'This is projected on the RFK declaration that he made today. And, Tony, this data was stolen from the Democrats! When they showed it to LBJ he had a fit. Beat up his valet.'

'No shit!'

They gave guttural laughs and pounded each other on their broad backs.

March 15, 1968

	Kennedy	Johnson
March	44%	41%
Early March	44%	45%
Jan. 68	40%	52%
Dec. 67	43%	45%
July 67	44%	47%
May 67	39%	52%

'He won't run. He can't after today.' Instinctively both men glanced out at Martin, who was still pretending to look at the view. Must turned the Mozart up full again, creating gaps in the dialogue.

'I wouldn't trust those pricks as far as . . .'

'. . . Don't worry about afterwards, Tony . . . para-military *always* controls the political . . . when I was in Greece we . . .'

'I'm a soldier, Bill, you know what I . . .'

'. . . words from us in the proper places . . . *and every tree in the forest falls!* . . . I saved Dick Helms's ass after Bay of Pigs . . .'

'I'll tell 'em that in California, Bill, but the . . .'

'Tony, L.A.'s easier than Dallas. The LAPD's "Red Squad" is my . . .'

Must's gangster argot was putting pressure on Prince. 'Put 'em in the picture, Tony. Tell 'em this Coast guy, Brading, better be a stand-up guy. Tell 'em not to bust my balls, Tony. Make 'em see that a Kennedy candidacy means *Rockefeller* could go all the way . . . Say that we plan to use a *Cubano* or –'

'A nigger!' That word and the burst of heavy male laughter that followed was the last thing that John R. Martin III could decipher as the Mozart escalated toward its apotheosis of mathematical glory.

March 31 *New Orleans, Louisiana*

For a split second the Saturday-night bedlam of the bar was suspended, except for the sound of one drunken prostitute sucking an oyster off the half shell. The balance of the regular crowd in Sam's Original Oyster Bar stared at the wavy picture on the insect-splattered TV screen.

> . . . accordingly, I will not seek, nor will I accept, the nomination of my party for another term as your president . . .

The club, three quarters black, let out a kind of collective whoop, and hands began to slap so that it sounded like cap guns going off along the whole length of the scarred and heavy old bar. On the screen the lips of the fallen president continued to move, unheard in the racket. A man dressed to kill in the style of a big-time pimp sang out, 'Lynchin' Baines Johnson!' in a heavy bass, and two whores – one black, one yellow – swung off their stools and started a stylized careening among the tables, doing a dance called the Dog.

The bartender switched channels, looking for some other image to replace the face of the man from Texas who had followed John F. Kennedy and who had now been driven from office. The dewlapped jowls of the sad and vulgar power broker, broken, were on every working channel of the ancient bar console, so the lips continued to move mechanically, unnoticed in the more or less sustained hysteria of the Original Oyster Bar.

Most of the hustlers, pimps, prostitutes, and police characters, not only in this archetypal New Orleans joint but across the entire French Quarter, had long since been convinced that President Johnson had either murdered his young predecessor (whom they had loved) or had covered up the killing. In either case, since the death of their prince the level of humanity in the Quarter had slipped, they thought. Most of those who could would never vote again unless it was for the brother Bobby, and even that would not be the same. So now they screamed and shouted and laughed louder than ever in order to beat down and drown out all the old ghosts that had tried since Dallas to get out at them from inside the TV tubes.

From their booth in the darkest corner of the bar, William A. Must, Jr., and Melvin Gibson leaned forward, straining to at least read the lips of the ghost on the television screen. Must gave up first. Sinking back into the corner of the booth bench, he studied Gibson's coffee-colored face, turned partly away toward the bar, and reflected on the vulnerability of the other man. Then, as if to intercept the fantasy that he knew was coming, of smashing the unprotected head of the other man, he slowly removed his glasses and began to polish them with a dollar bill from the change on the table. When Gibson finally turned back from the TV, what he saw were the soft, unfocused blue eyes of his old spy master. Gibson shook his head in disbelief and waited for Must to comment.

The two men dressed in tennis shoes and old raincoats could have been working undercover for the vice squad, or killing time waiting for their mob connection, or both; the ancient hustler who brought them fresh beers could not have cared less.

Must looked like he might say something after the waiter left, but instead he just smiled emptily at the other man and scratched at the black mole on his neck.

'The King is dead . . .' Gibson tried tentatively. Must continued to smoke and started his beer, and when he did speak it was clear that he did not wish to discuss the fortunes of Lyndon Baines Johnson. Gibson leaned toward him. Must was talking under instead of over the jukebox and its fake Dixieland. '. . . only got about twenty minutes. You using two covers?'

Gibson shivered slightly. It was damp outside the big bar's pool of light and animal energy. People staggered past them through the shadows toward the toilets behind their booth. There was no trace of Negro or Southern dialect in Gibson's speech pattern as he leaned in, pushing the beer aside to give his hands room to move. 'One: It's a Muslim hit. Two: That cover falls and the hit will be blamed, finally, on RAM, the Revolutionary Action Movement.' The nervous hands stopped their shuffling. Gibson waited for his 'case officer' to react to the bureaucratese word-salad for violent death and its cover-up.

Must, smiling like a fish, answered in a heavy Kingfish vaudeville voice: 'Right on!'

Burning inside, Gibson poured beer carefully. When the familiar spasms of humiliation had passed, Gibson jerked his head toward the bar. 'What do you think of my man?' His voice had slipped slightly into a Southern register.

Must's empty blue eyes shifted to the middle distance to study the lean figure of a black man costumed in pimp finery. The man, with two whores in tow and his hands stuffed with money, was dancing in slow motion around a fat, drunken white customer who could hardly keep his head off the bar. From their booth they watched the action, unable to hear the hustle as the thin man waved the money hypnotically around the nodding head of his mark.

'He looks like a pimp.'

'Believe me, I know *my* man.' Gibson's accent was even thicker now. He stared right back at Must.

'Sure you do. But, ah, don't give him any real cash in, ah, advance . . . you, know . . .'

'No, suh, Boss. Ah sho' won't.'

APRIL–MAY, 1968

April 1 *Langley, Virginia*

Judith Shankland studied Paul Woods's profile as he steered the yellow '67 convertible, one-handed, along the scenic palisades. Her round brown eyes took in the fine modified Afro, high forehead, long curly eyelashes, prominent Adam's apple, the quiet but expensive tie, and soft blue shirt and Harris tweed sports jacket. Her gaze followed the outline of powerful thighs under the charcoal-gray slacks. The spring air was delicious and the Potomac glistened; she felt better than she had at any time since New Hampshire. Even the guilt feelings that had ravaged her after she had left the McCarthy for President campaign were temporarily cleansed in the whipping Virginia breeze. Just as she started to speak, a sign on the Parkway caught her eye: FAIRBANK HIGHWAY RESEARCH STATION.

'What's that?'

'What?'

'The Fairbank Highway –'

'Oh. That's the "Company." '

'The what?'

'Sometimes known as the CIA complex.' He slowed to about 20 mph and looked over at her with his wide, warm eyes; eyes that she was beginning to need to see every day, eyes that reminded her of a phrase from an early Sumerian myth that she had studied at Mount Holyoke: 'He looked at her with the eyes of love.' But she asked, 'The Central Intelligence Agency? Why does the sign say the Fairbank –'

'Fun and games. Inside the joint they've got a sign that reads – I'm not fooling – "And ye shall know the truth and the truth shall make you free." '

'April Fool.'

She swiveled back to stare at the complex of buildings

barely discernible from the cleverly landscaped trees that grew back from the highway. Woods watched her, enjoying the way her cashmere sweater tightened over her breasts so that the pattern of the nipples suddenly became visible.

'I didn't realize it was so big,' she said, turning back to face him, self-conscious suddenly as he watched her, pulling at the short plaid skirt in a vain attempt to cover a bit more of the long, tennis-tanned legs.

'It's big,' he said softly, 'no one knows how big, eighteen-some-odd thousand officers alone and God knows how many "contract agents." ' Then, in a mock-conspiratorial tone: 'It's a secret.' He sped the car up, and the wind caught her long hair again.

She grinned. 'You have a secret yourself.' He relished the timbre of her intelligent, well-educated Eastern Seaboard voice. 'You still haven't told me how you arranged for me to be invited to a party at –'

'No secret. I simply told the Senator –'

'Is that what you call him? The –'

'I simply told the Senator that I knew a beautiful young lady who could help him raise a million bucks for his campaign'

She laughed heartily. 'My father wouldn't give Nixon a *hundred* dollars, and he thinks Nixon's the American Dream incarnate.'

But Woods was peering into the rear-view mirror at a black limousine about to overtake them. The larger car's horn blared as it screeched around and in front of them. Now Woods was answering with his horn and pushing the accelerator hard. A shirt-sleeved arm was waving crazily at them from the window of the speeding Cadillac as it pulled away. She realized that Woods was shouting something over and over: '*Bobby!*'

Woods's usually quiet, rich voice was high and happy – like a kid's, she thought in the near silence that came as the limousine disappeared around a bend. His whole muscular body had surged with energy as he half leaned out of the convertible, waving and calling. Now he chuckled happily, more open and vulnerable than he had ever let her see him in the month that they had known each other.

'You really love him, don't you?'

'He's a credit to his race.' And he squeezed her wrist in his big cleat-scarred black hand.

Before she could respond, he had slammed home the brakes and blocked her body with his shoulder and arm to keep her from hurtling into the dashboard. The tires screamed as he shot the vehicle into reverse and gunned backwards, his entire torso twisted toward her. As their car ground to a stop, Judith finally saw a blue 1968 Ford sedan wheel out from behind a clump of trees and roar off in the opposite direction. All she could comprehend was that the sedan had plain tires, a license plate she did not recognize, that one of the two men in the car was wearing sunglasses, and that, obviously, Paul Woods assumed that the men had been in hiding behind the trees.

In the sudden silence, she was aware of bird song and Paul's heavy breathing. He turned front and began to straighten his shirt and tie. The look on his face warned her not to speak to him now. Then she noticed the sweat pouring out of his hair and down his face in the cool air of the late Virginia afternoon.

Judith inspected the gathering, scattered about the Kennedy grounds, from a chair that she had moved half behind a bush so that she would not have to talk to anyone. The incident on the highway had shaken her. Paul had not said a word until he began introducing her to other guests after her arrival. She had asked him to go ahead and 'take care of business,' as he always put whatever he was doing. She now was on her third glass of champagne and still behind a bush, tousling a big Alaskan-type dog that she had never seen in any of the picture layouts of the Kennedy clan. As she drank, the guilt returned. An uninvited guest at Camelot, the revels of Camelot, she thought bitterly.

The next time she looked up for a champagne cocktail, Paul Woods was standing there grinning. 'Do all these beautiful people give you the blues, lady?'

'Where were they when we needed them in New Hampshire?'

'Here in Vuhginuh. Let me take care of business. As a public-relations aide, let me introduce you to some of the notables here today – hush up, I mean introduce you from the vantage point of this bush behind which we are both now hiding –'

'Public relations, social relations –'

'Sexual relations. I will return with champagne if you will promise not to do anything to embarrass the Senator.' She stuck out her tongue, but he sensed the threat of real anger in her, and he moved away slowly.

Without knowing the names of the fabled company gathered here at Hickory Hill, she recognized, at least, the categories of film stars, novelists and journalists, astronauts, mountain climbers and other sports heroes, ambassadors and military men. Schlesinger, Sorensen, Salinger, that crowd from 1960 – she had heard Gene McCarthy talk about them: Philistines, hypocrites, cold-war liberals . . . she could not remember what else. But she felt good and hateful now.

On the other side of her bush, three men were discussing the Wisconsin primary. It was being held tomorrow, April 2 – why wasn't she there? She let her head hang. The men were saying that McCarthy would win by 25 points and that Reagan could not dent Nixon's 80 percent. Then they cursed George Meany for throwing the AFL-CIO behind Hubert Humphrey when 'the Hump finally waffles into the race.'

The voices moved away and she returned to spying on the passing parade. The dog ran off in pursuit of a Kennedy child. She should not be in this peaceful, secure setting; she should be on the barricades, in Wisconsin, risking something. She began to pick out celebrities again, the way a nervous woman, like her mother, might pick at her beads. Then there are, she thought, the attendant lords, where I would find my niche. And she identified the speechwriters and aides like Paul Woods, the secretaries and drivers and assorted camp followers and groupies. Then she started to count the ten Kennedy children and the dogs, cats, goats –

'Here's your champagne, lady.'

'"We are closed in, and the key is turned on our uncertainty." Yeats.' She squinted up at him, smiling humorlessly. 'You knew I was an English major, didn't you? More poetry: "Jack was nimble, Jack was quick –"'

'"But Bobby makes you sick." I know. An English

major? I thought you said you were majoring, or minoring in "private relations" while I was sleeping through public relations.'

'Right on.' Her voice was tight. 'I learned that "all protoplasm displays irration" and that "tissue is erectile." '

'Why are you acting like a bitch in heat, Miss Judith, ma'am? Don't drink that so fast. Just a minute, Doctor Feelgood is going to analyze you, and I'll take my fee out in trade later. Whoops.' She shot a sad little smile up at him. He sank to one knee, talking quietly.

'I was in New Hampshire on a fact-finding trip for the – you know who – remember? We *met* there. I saw you all in your shiny leather boots, your miniskirts and sleek ponytails. You had all the A students in your "Youth Quake" –'

'And you've got all the B's.' It bothered her that he was forcing himself to believe so much in 'the Senator.'

'I'm going to let that go. And all those guerrillas with tenure from Columbia and Yale and Dartmouth and Cornell and all the "toughs of the tender left" – you didn't know I could quote Sartre, did you – you all went "clean for Gene." '

She opened her eyes at this and interrupted him. 'So? You know what Mary McGrory wrote? That Kennedy thinks that American youth *belongs* to him. And that when we went off with Gene McCarthy he reacted like a ruthless Victorian father – like *my* father – whose daughter has run away with a dustman.' She arched a golden eyebrow.

'Mary McGrory is in *love* with McCarthy,' he answered.

'She is not!'

'Who am I? The dustman?'

'What? I didn't mean –'

'You didn't know that Bobby went with the UAW man Paul Schrade to pray with Cesar Chavez and the Farm Workers when some of his senior aides from the JFK days told him not to, that it would hurt his image? You didn't know that, did you? Or that neither Big Labor or Big Business is supporting him?'

'Then why –'

'I know all about it.' He was bearing down a little now. 'Listen, will you! You were magnificent, you all were beautiful in New Hampshire. You went door to door in the snow, you froze your cute little ass standing at factory gates at six in the morning, you lived on cocoa and sandwiches from January to March. You were part of the great Amherst-Smith-Mount Holyoke crusade. And – with a little help from the Vietcong and the Tet offensive – you and your "man for all seasons" won! You turned the country around, you slew Lyndon the king of the cowboys, you even forced *the* Senator to "reassess his position." Your battle cry was "Never trust anyone over thirty!" Now you look around at all this tits and ass and gold braid that has co-opted your movement and it makes you sick.'

'It makes me . . . sad.'

He dropped the half-mocking tone and dashed the dregs of his champagne onto the green lawn. 'Look, Judy – Judith – you may think that Bob Kennedy is just barely the lesser of two evils, but I've got news for you. He's good news for my people – penned up in ghettos like cattle – and for the stoop laborers, and the old people, and the kids in this fucked-up country.'

He kneeled close to her and drew out his wallet. He opened it and took out a piece of print copy. 'This is going into a brochure I'm working on. The one I hoped you were going to help me with. Remember?' His movements were brusque as he handed the copy over to her, but he never stopped watching her high-colored, aristocratic face as she read.

> He always talked about poverty. He said, 'Charles, is poverty really that bad in Mississippi?' I said, 'Bobby, words can't express it.' He said, 'I'm coming down.'
>
> He and the committee came down in the spring of 1967, and we sat there at night, and we talked, and he listened. The next day he said, 'I want to go see it.' We went into one of the worst places I've ever seen. There was no ceiling hardly; the floor had holes in it. There was a little stove over in the corner, and a bed that looked like the color of my arm – black as my arm – and it was propped up with some kind of bricks to keep

it from falling. The odor was so bad you could hardly keep the nausea down.

Bobby went in with a little child and looked in the kitchen. This lady came out and we spoke to her, and he told her who he was. She just put her arms out and said, 'Thank God.'

This little child – must have been about three or four years old – came toddling out of the back room. His tummy was sticking way out just like he was pregnant. Bobby looked down at the child, and then he picked him up and sat down on that dirty bed. He was rubbing the child's stomach. He said, 'My God, I didn't know this kind of thing existed. How can a country like this allow it? Maybe they just don't know.'

Roaches and rats were all over the floor. We stayed there ten or fifteen minutes, just sat there talking, and then he said, 'I'm going back to Washington to do something about this.'

The man cared. You could see it in his eyes, and in the expression on his face. When he got really concerned, his hand would quiver. Or, if he was riding in a car, he'd just slump down and sit there and stare.

—Charles Evers,
civil rights leader

'That's not the "politics of joy"! See, he's good news for my people. And Tricky Dick Nixon is bad news for everybody – including me certainly and you probably – who can be crammed into a concentration camp. Now that sounds extreme, doesn't it, paranoid? Well, lady, I was once a member of what we laughingly call the intelligence community, and I want you to know that there are some people in this country that could have blended right in with Adolf and his gang and never looked back. And Bob Kennedy can win. And between Camelot – no matter how phony – and Buchenwald, I have no problem *at all* making my choice.'

He stood and walked away then, just a shade more bulky than when he had been an All-American left half-back at Northwestern in 1958 and '59, favoring his left knee just a little the way he had told her he had to when he was tired. Watching him, the remorse began to flow to the surface of her feelings, began to turn from guilt into shame. She did not have the heart to remind him that Dr. King was still supporting McCarthy.

In the distance a football was being tossed. Robert Kennedy passed her on his way to join the famous politicians and writers who were already choosing up sides for the contest that symbolized the coming campaign. Kennedy was smoking a cigar and had one of his children by the hand. His eyes met hers for a moment, and she saw in them an unexpected awareness and vulnerability. She thought, This is the man who defused the Cuban missile crisis and prayed with the Farm Workers and buried his brother when I was an undergraduate in college – who in the Christ am I to judge him, she thought, and stood up to say something, but he was past her, running across the green lawn toward the game that had been waiting for him all his life.

April 2 *The Virginia Border*

He let her sleep in the car until he had returned from the motel office with the key to their cabin.

She laughed. 'I've been to a motel before, but, my god, Paul, I mean – a "motor hotel." I mean, this is Art Deco.' Her laughter rang out in the dark and empty parking lot.

'Shh. That Boston accent is going to give you away as a white girl. This is still Virginia, child. Shh! Art who?'

'Deco. You know, *moderne*. There'll be a picture over the bed – painted by hand!' She screamed with laughter, felt his shoulders shaking with suppressed mirth.

'Listen –'

'I know,' she choked, 'we mustn't embarrass the *Senator*!'

They stumbled through the cabin door. She was weeping and coughing with inebriated mirth. Paul finally found the switch for the thirty-watt bulb. As he turned from the wall, he narrowly missed stepping on her, on her hands and knees, convulsed with silent laughter. Woods stood there for a moment looking down soberly at the shaking splayed body that, if he had not known better, could have been a woman in mortal grief, like those Vietnamese women and their dead babies that they both had to watch every night on television.

He picked her up carefully and walked her the two steps to the double bed that was half the size of those in the Howard Johnson's that he usually frequented. 'Yeah,' he murmured, trying to bring her out of the hysteria, 'it's *moderne*, all right.'

She stopped shaking and stared at him in the dim light. He had lost his tie somewhere, and his powerful black neck seemed to rise before her eyes like a sculpted column. She watched, rather than looked into, the kind eyes – bloodshot now, too. He had to lean over to hear her: 'Is this what they call falling-down drunk?'

He reached up a big hand and brushed back her long brownish-red hair, straightened out a tangle, touched her ear with his fingertips. He tapped her forehead. 'What's going on in there, Judith?'

'Judith?'

'That's your name, isn't it?'

'But who am I?'

'That's what I'm asking you, lady. How old are you?'

'Twenty-five. There's nothing for me to tell you. It's like you said. Mount Holyoke, Cambridge, New Hampshire, the pill, the bomb.' Paul saw her eyes fill with tears and a tremor pass through her body.

'Cold?'

'Paul, do you think that what you're – *we're* doing has any meaning? I mean, half those people at the house . . . are parlor, you know, pinks.'

Paul chuckled humorlessly at the dated epithet and shifted his heavy shoulders. 'Judy, you laugh, you cry. You go to New Hampshire for Gene McCarthy, you go to Indiana for –'

'I don't think I –'

'You go to Indiana for *me*, and we'll go to D.C. for the Poor People's March. I don't want you to do anything for the – for Bobby, until it means something to *you*. Look, whatever you may think, I do not believe the man is a saint. What can I tell you? The Kennedy men mature late.'

'Does that include making it with movie stars and –'

'It includes shooting rapids, climbing mountains, hiking forty miles, whatever – playing football, chasing women – not like you hear, but yes, it's a physical thing. Then as they, uh, mature, there's some kind of transfer, from physical to moral or political courage. They're men who can grow. They grow. They grew – that's all.'

They sat there in the gloom, too tired to say any more. Paul kicked off his shoes finally. 'I think I'll take a shower. If this place has one. Go to sleep.'

The water was only lukewarm, but Paul was grateful for the uneven tepid tattoo, and he closed his eyes and let the muscled body remember a thousand football games and practice sessions and a thousand locker-room showers. The noise of the water on the old-fashioned tin siding was too loud for him to hear her step in beside him, but he felt her presence and opened his eyes as she said, 'Are you asleep?'

She reached past him to turn the water pressure to full. They stood there grinning at each other like two kids caught in a warm and sudden summer downpour. 'Hi.'

She handed him the thin bar of motel soap and turned her back. 'Come on.' Paul hummed softly as he began to work up a lather on her back, pale in contrast with her tanned neck and limbs. Her shoulders slumped with fatigue, and she swayed gratefully under the pressure of his powerful hands as they kneaded and soaped her shoulders and back. Paul felt a rush of tenderness canceling, for the moment, any sexual excitement. She turned. 'Now you.'

'Just a minute.' He could see her neck start to mottle as his hands slipped around her breasts, pale and firm, with the nipples already erect. He was touched for some reason when he saw that one breast was just slightly smaller than the other. Her breathing became more rapid as she took the soap from him and began to soap her curly pubic hair. Spreading her legs slightly, she began to move her hand over her thighs and between her legs. Then she reached out to massage his swelling member with the soft suds. 'You know, Paul, this is my first time with a –'

'With a black man?'

'No.' She whooped. 'With an uncircumcised man!'

They slipped into the bedroom, both chuckling, shaking water like dogs. She was glowing when he finished toweling her. 'You smell good, lady.' He kissed her toes, moved his lips to her arched hip, gently pushed her over on her stomach and began to kiss her on the back and waist and buttocks, cupping her firm cheeks, then slipping his tongue into her cleft.

He guided her up on all fours with her head resting on the pillow. As he kissed her from every angle, she made little moans and moved her hips slowly in the air. Then he lowered his taut, sculpted body down alongside her, lifted one of her legs, and slid his head under her hips, and she lowered her passion-full lips over his sex. Then quickly, after kissing like that, they were together and he was touching her and she could see his dark shaft moving in and out of her in the dim light.

Later, they lay on their sides staring at each other like children. As their pulses slowed they could hear the music of the crickets and frogs. She touched the thick tufts of black hair on his chest, ran her finger over the swelling pectorals. 'You're so black,' she said, her sensitive, intelligent face full of wonder. Studying the strong, fine hair, selected over the ages through evolution for survival in Africa. Yet here he was, a descendant of the survivors of the twenty-five million slaves who had died on the passage from Africa to the Americas. Here, and putting those surviving genotypes in her. She smiled to herself, and at the wonderful predictability of the crickets.

'Black?' He laughed softly. 'Lady, I'm so black I'm blue.'

'Paul, did we do what they call, uh, sixty-nine?'

'I think so.' He smiled, touching her ear.

'You're so tender.' She tickled his breast. 'Paul, will it be this good in Indiana?'

April 4 *Indiana*

Judy tried to inch her way through the throng without spilling the cartons of orange juice and vanilla milk-shake, which Paul Woods lived on each day. Rarely could the two of them find a passable restaurant open after ten at night in this flat Midwestern state that seemed so alien to her after the great adventure with Gene McCarthy in New Hampshire.

So much had happened to her since then that she felt as if history really was a tide, and that it was sweeping her along toward an unknown ocean. Only together with Paul late at night after another eighteen-hour day did she come back to earth, clinging to him as if he were a rock in the whirlpool of the campaign; falling asleep in his arms afterward, not knowing that he held her while she moaned and twitched in feverish sleep, replaying each night the swirling events of the past day.

The Indiana campaign was a film montage in her dreams. She had to travel on the 'Zoo', the plane used by the less important press, while Paul had to work in the Senator's private jet with the senior aides and the famous authors and reporters for the major media.

In the Zoo she rewrote and typed press handouts and grew to feel a kind of existential tenderness or, rather, solidarity for the already exhausted reporters, who still had months to go. They drank too much, ate on the run, talked the political gossip that their editors would not let them write, and made love to the stewardesses, standing up behind the curtains at the back of the plane.

Then at the next stop she and Paul would try to shout to each other over the pandemonium at the airport. Later she would join him at the rally with the orange juice and milkshake, and they would stand there quietly as the girls squealed, 'There he is, there he is!' and 'Bobby, Bobby, Bobby, *please*, Bobby!' Pulling him down and out of the car, once breaking a tooth and cutting his lip. In the midst of the hysteria senior aides huddled over notes, saying, '. . . no, we now have 1,273 delegates *committed* . . .' as the Senator – as she now called him, unselfconsciously most of the time – emerged from hotel or open car.

The crowd would close on him, the girls leaping up and down in near orgasm as their older sisters had done for Jack Kennedy, everyone trying to touch him, squeezing, yelling, bouncing, weeping. It frightened Judith every time it happened, and that was every day, every hour on the hour. Kennedy security men whirled desperately in the crush. She and Paul waited for the speech, no matter how many times they had heard the same words. At least then the mob would settle slightly, become individuals again as he called out in the hoarse and poignant accents:

> I was the chief law-enforcement officer of the United States. I promise if elected I will do all in my power to

bring an end to this violence. We needn't have to expect this violence summer after summer.

The Ku Klux Klan was still strong in Indiana – he had to talk like this, Paul kept telling her, his face glistening with sweat, his second shirt of the day soaked through.

An endless exhausting round that made her New Hampshire efforts seem a pleasure cruise by comparison. Fifteen, sixteen speeches a day, separated by bumpy plane rides. Bored reporters and technicians, growing slightly more mad each day, throwing sweet rolls and film cans at each other while the Zoo plane was in the air. The inevitable McCarthy supporters at every airport to haunt her. Always the song playing as the plane doors opened: 'This Man Is Your Man, This Man Is My Man,' lyrics by Theodore Sorensen, whom she distrusted as a closet hawk – 'CIA,' she told Paul Woods flatly. He shook his head in mock sadness and asked her, 'Now who's paranoid?'

Then the airport speech slightly softened by the man's sardonic delivery and vitality:

> . . . I talked to my brother Edward [*ripple of laughter*] and asked for some campaign buttons. Fifteen thousand arrived [*small laugh*] and they all had his picture on them [*big laugh*], and I told him he couldn't do that, I was the candidate [*small laugh*], and, besides, people would say he was 'ruthless' [*huge laugh*] . . .

Then, with passion, Vietnam. What she had been waiting for. Poised above the crowd, shy and abrupt, smaller than they had expected; his words chosen carefully for hawkish Indiana but the pain and anger over the war unmistakable:

> I'm not in favor of unilateral withdrawal from Vietnam, that would hurt us in Southeast Asia. But we have the right to expect an honest government in South Vietnam, we've got the *right* that out of every three dollars for refugees that are taxed from the people of Indiana, more than one of those gets to the pockets of the refugees. We've got the right to expect them to draft their eighteen-year-old boys if we're going to draft our

eighteen-year-old boys – that's what I'd do, I'd clean up that government of South Vietnam.

Then the wind-up. Always the same, always thrilling to Judith despite her suspicion of his compromises, and the psychology of mobs. 'Will you help me?' '*Yes!*' 'Do you know how?' '*Yes!*' 'Then if you know how, what are you college students doing here listening to a politician make a speech when you should be out canvassing?' And then the closing line from George Bernard Shaw, and Judith and Paul would look at each other with the start of tears in their eyes. Shaking their heads at their own incorrigible childlike trust and sentiment, the two would kiss quickly and Paul would dive into the roiling mass again the way he had on Saturday afternoons at Champaign-Urbana, or Ann Arbor, Madison, Evanston, or South Bend. And she would stand there alone, still hearing Bernard Shaw's words carved out in the hoarse Kennedy accents that concluded every speech and made her believe in him again despite the fact that he had cut his hair shorter for the Middle West.

Some people see things as they are and say: Why? I dream things that never were and say: Why not?

America is hard to see, she said to herself more than once, quoting John Kennedy's favorite poet, Robert Frost.

Then on to the next stop, riding a sea of radical rhetoric – war, race, crime – that made this campaign the most volatile since 1936.

April 5 *Indianapolis, Indiana*

I have bad news for you . . . for all of our fellow citizens and people who love peace all over the world . . . and that is that Martin Luther King was shot and killed tonight . . .

In the dark, the dark faces seemed to split open in grief and immemorial mourning. 'Oh!' 'Jesus, Lord!' 'Have mercy!' They had been waiting for the Candidate, had not heard the news yet about Dr. King. Kennedy's blue eyes were dark, his voice strangled.

Martin Luther King dedicated his life to love and to justice for his fellow human beings, and he died because of that effort . . .

Paul Woods leaned momentarily on one of the rented campaign Fords. His eyes were scalding again, and he had to use his fingers to blow his nose. The words hit him like bullets.

For those of you who are black and are tempted to be filled with hatred and distrust at the injustices of such an act, against all white people, I can only say that I feel in my own heart the same kind of feeling. I had a member of my family killed, but he was killed by a white man.

The hoarse, sad voice was like a soft trumpet on the night air over the stricken people. Cursing, Woods walked away as fast as he could on his throbbing knee, the voice following him.

. . . Or we can make an effort, as Martin Luther King did, to understand and to comprehend and to replace that violence, that stain of bloodshed that has spread across our land, with an effort to understand with compassion and love . . . So I shall ask you tonight to return home, to say a prayer for the family of Martin Luther King, that's true, but more importantly, to say a prayer for our own country, which all of us love – a prayer for understanding and that compassion of which I spoke.

A low sound was beginning to rise from the poor black people who had come, joyously, to touch him, to touch Robert Kennedy, and enter again the communal dream that had been born with his brother John and forever linked in their minds: the Kennedy brother and Dr. Martin Luther King, Jr. The sound rose, part anger, part illimitable anguish and immemorial despair.

Let us dedicate ourselves to what the Greeks wrote so many years ago: 'to tame the savageness of man and to make gentle the life of this world.' Let us dedicate ourselves to that, and say a prayer for our country and for our people.

Only a few began to move out, the sound of grief and rage low and timeless. At the back of the crowd two black men watched. One of them, Louis Osgood, dressed in a cheap white suit and fur-topped plastic half boots, snapped on a transistor radio:

> Cities across the nation were reporting widespread rioting tonight, in the wake of the assassination of Dr. Martin Luther King. From New York comes a report that –

As people in the crowd began to turn toward the hateful sound of the radio, the other black man jerked the radio out of Osgood's hand and shut off the noise. Melvin Gibson was dressed in a neat suit and tie – he could have been a professional man. Now he steered Osgood by the elbow away from the light and people. The raffishly dressed younger man pulled away, bouncing along angrily in his streetwise walk.

'No, man, I'm going back to New Orleans,' Osgood whined. 'You all must be crazy –'

'Cool it, brother – just *cool* it.' Gibson's voice was calibrated carefully to Osgood's street lingua franca of slurred sibilance. 'Later, brother, later.'

'Brother? I ain't yo' goddamn brother! Man, you must think I ain't got good sense. Sheet! You dealing with a back-stab artist when you do business with me. I come up here without no goddamn money and you set me up in a motherfuckin' cross. Sheet! I ain't no Lee Harvey Oswald!'

Gibson hurried him toward the motel, scanning the dark cars in the lot, thinking, That motherfucker Must is spooking around here somewhere watching my ass.

Gibson tried to talk as Osgood kicked open the dilapidated motel door. 'Slow down, Osgood. Say, Os, we've laid a lot of bread on you, Os, and we've got a contract, my man.'

'Sheet!' Osgood was turning up the bottle of Cutty Sark.

'Os, I keep telling you, this King bit is not our action. You really think we'd –'

'Off Martha Luther King.' mispronouncing the name as usual. 'Sheet! You'd shoot your mama –'

'Now you listen –'

'– like a motherfuckin' dog –'

'Osgood!'

'– for a *dime*!'

Osgood's stare was murderous. He drank again and flicked on the TV and sprawled on one of the twin beds, staring sullenly at the set as America burned in full color while the sound sputtered incomprehensibly. Gibson sat on the other bed, soft-talking. 'Brother, I'm only trying to tell you –'

Osgood rose to smash the empty bottle in the waste basket and light a Kool. 'You trying to jive me! Man, I know you ain't no Black Muslim. You ain't working for no *niggers*!' The TV crackled like electricity as the images of carnage alternated with the pale faces of officials and commentators. Osgood fumed. 'You listenin' to me? You a sad-ass chump, you know that? You didn't know they was fixin' to kill King, did you, sucker? We both been crossed so beautiful, man – they settin' us both up!' The older man had begun to sweat. Osgood yelled after Gibson as he went into the toilet. 'How somebody gonna off Bobby right after King been hit? Huh, chump? They gonna have wall-to-wall pigs from now on, *brother*!' Osgood kicked open the bathroom door.

Gibson flushed the toilet and washed his hands and face. Then he reentered the room purposefully and swung open the closet door to reveal an array of expensive leather and suede coats, complete with 'militant' hats and boots. 'My partner brought these while we was eatin'.' Gibson turned off the static, leaving the pictures of the black uprisings to flicker in pantomime as Osgood stood inside the closet examining the goods. Gibson's voice was velvet now.

'Look here, baby, it's all set up. You hit Kennedy and every pig in the country be lookin' for the Revolutionary Action Movement. We goin' out in a helicopter, and from that to a Lear jet. Blood, we'll be long gone while every one'll be lookin' for them cats from RAM.'

He paused to breathe, Osgood's face was lost in the gloom of the closet as he stroked the leather. Gibson started on him again. 'We layin' a trail of clues a mile wide. You goin' be layin' in yo' pad in the Caribbean, blood, with a go'geous fox suckin' yo' joint, smokin' that Panama Red, droppin' pills, talkin' yo' talk, doin' yo' thing! Os?'

Osgood stepped out and began to model a floor-length black leather coat and rust suede cavalier hat with a fat yellow feather that curled upward like a scimitar blade.

Gibson, pretending calm, handed him a roll of bills, then turned his back and began to fool with the TV while Osgood posed before the bathroom mirror. Suddenly the sound focused.

> This bulletin from our studios in Washington, D.C. Attorney General Ramsey Clark has just announced that the FBI has the lone assassin on the run. Stand by for a direct report from the nation's capital.

Gibson was already turning as the door slammed shut with terrific force. He emerged in time to see a yellow feather and a flying fur-topped boot tearing around the corner of the building. Osgood, coattails flying, beat Gibson to the Christ The King AME Baptist Church, three blocks away, by a hundred yards.

He stood panting in the double doorway. The church was full tonight with mourners and the sound of mourning. Osgood could hear Gibson coming up the steps behind him. Osgood had his second wind now, and, like the consummate hustler and virtuoso actor and survivor that he was, he began his tragic lament in a piercing, resonant voice as if on cue in a script written by some illiterate gutter Euripides. 'Brothers and sisters, listen!' He was striding down the aisle now, the long coat flapping, prophetlike, the hat and feather and high-heeled fur boots sending his lanky height up to six foot six. The congregation stared at him as if he were a messenger from the inner sanctum on this night of bloodshed.

'Listen! We got to get off our knees and fight! They done shot Dr. King down like a dog!'

Osgood neared the podium, the people in the pews beginning to mumble as the rhetoric fell on them like a lash. He knew that Gibson was leaning against the back pew, watching the performance, appalled.

'Just like they murdered brother Malcolm X and tried to blame it on black folks – and Medgar Evers and John F. Kennedy, JFK. Just like they gonna murder his brother poor Bobby, or anyone that stands up for the black man!' A volley of 'Amen' and 'Preach, Brother' rang out in perfect dialectic between the mourners and the inspired *agent provocateur*. Gibson stood half collapsed in the doorway, as if he had been shot. Osgood had blown his cover. Gibson was helpless.

'These vicious honky pigs gonna pen us all up in concentration camps' – half the crowd was on its feet and shouting now – 'they playing the Nazis, but we ain't gonna play the Jews!'

A storm of 'Amens' made the old church shake. A wave of nausea swept Gibson. He had lost more than the man and the money. He turned out of the din into the darkness, gulping air. Before he could descend the old cracked steps, he saw the unmarked blue sedan with the New York license plates waiting for him across the street – parked under a street lamp, he realized, so that he could not help but see it.

James Jerrold, trying to look like James Bond, chewed on the ends of his fluffy blond mustache, then asked Must in his man-to-man voice if he should run this loser over. Jerrold, who was thirty, and had spent his adult life as a Green Beret in Vietnam and later a CIA contract agent in the States, saw the world in terms of winners and losers. When he thought he smelled a loser, he felt the urge to kill him or her. In Saigon, after a rare drinking bout he and a CIA man had actually stuffed a beggar into a sewer manhole. Jerrold always behaved, Must noticed, as if he were an actor in a very weird movie.

When a partially bald, gray-haired man had been identified by Latin American CIA photoanalysts as the legendary revolutionist Che Guevara in disguise, a group of the agency's special-ops experts had brought in a gang of former Vietnam killers from a secret U.S. base in Panama. James Jerrold made his mark in the manhunt that followed over the Bolivian countryside. When Guevara's head and hands were shipped back to the CIA after the unequal hunt had ended, Jerrold was given a medal. He had quit then, one year ago. Nothing in Latin America could ever match the glory of that adventure.

Back home in America, he found black rebellion, bombings, flag burnings, police-militant shootouts, drugs, treason, debauchery. 'Help me stamp it out, Jim!' Must had challenged him. 'Yes,' he had sworn, 'I will.'

'Mm . . . that's an idea, Jim,' said Must, who enjoyed the sheer animal energy of his lithe blond Green Beanie killer. 'I have an appointment, also at a church, as a matter of fact, so we need the car, but by all means consider it a contract, but start with that zoot-suit low-rider, Osgood. Gibson you can deal with at leisure.' Jerrold, who was not familiar with the term 'zoot suit,' chortled with real admiration for the older man, to whom he looked up as a spiritual father, his own deceased father having been a definite loser.

Gibson was almost to the car, starting to wave, when Jerrold launched the machine at him, going full force. Gibson, lying in the street, knew that the purpose of a miss that near was to suggest that he blow his own brains out at the first opportunity. He lay there listening to the sound of the congregation singing 'We Shall Overcome,' and the distant police sirens wailing in the silent night.

April 6 *Washington, D.C.*

The big priest still looked like the assassin he had been in the old country, when he had tortured or broken the backs, outright, of other Yugoslavs during World War II in his capacity as a militant agent of the dreaded Ustaci. He was big-boned, green-eyed, his dry white skin mottled and veined as if the secret Croatian fanaticism had seeped through the capillary walls to proclaim itself at last all over his fat face.

The Ancient Orthodox Church – Overseas Mission was empty except for the priest, who sat eating a bowl of oatmeal in his food-stained cassock, watching the funeral of Dr. Martin Luther King, Jr., from the Ebenezer Baptist Church in Atlanta. He ate and stared dry-eyed as the cameras panned and cut in the stifling, jammed church from Richard Nixon to Robert F. Kennedy, Hubert Humphrey, and all the other notables. Even Nelson Rockefeller, the priest noted with that blank outrage that only deepened the incarnadine hue of the white flesh and the watery width of the pale green eyes. Rockefeller, and then there it was, a shot of the grieving black madonna, Coretta King, and kneeling in the aisle next to her, physically comforting her, Stokely Carmichael.

He turned at Must's soft footfall. Both men were rough and bulky in stature, but Must's firm and symmetrical countenance was not ravaged like the priest's. Both were heavyweights, but Must was a solid 215, while the cleric was a dropsical 260 pounds.

They shook hands wordlessly, as two 'real men of the clandestine services' will do at a reunion. Then they turned to watch the huge funeral procession, two hundred thousand strong, which had now moved out into the grueling heat of the streets of Atlanta to follow the mule-drawn coffin for five miles from Ebenezer Baptist to Morehouse College. The camera picked up Robert Kennedy, walking in his shirt-sleeves. People were crowding around. trying to walk with him, their last hope now. Must leaned forward to study the faces near the vigorous but somehow forlorn candidate – which of those near him were security? The audio picked up the singing of the marchers under the hot Georgia sky, and Must turned and walked through a door and down a flight of stairs to a basement storage room, empty except for a triple row of old wooden filing cabinets.

The porcine priest put his hand in his pocket so that he could scratch his testicles through a hole in the material as he watched the news coverage cut away to scenes of 'looting and arson' in Chicago, Washington, Pittsburgh; then back to Atlanta, where they had stopped singing 'We Shall Overcome' and started in on

We shall not be moved
Just like a tree that's planted near the water
We shall not be moved.
Martin's gone ahead
But we shall not be moved
Martin's gone ahead
But he shall not be moved
Just like a tree that's . . .

The priest stood there scratching, waiting for William A. Must, Jr., to finish and get the hell out. He chuckled. There was that Mrs. Martin Luther Coon, snubbing Dick Nixon as the politicos and black athletes streamed out of the old church. Romney, Rockefeller, Jacqueline Kennedy . . . The killer priest scratched, studying the spectacle, impatient to get to the toilet for his morning bowel movement.

The mule-drawn sharecropper's cart and coffin passed the helmeted, machine-gun-armed state police of Georgia Governor Lester Maddox, who had refused to close schools or lower flags for the funeral. The priest sucked his teeth and waited for the cops to do something.

Must could barely hear the mourners singing as he riffled the dusty dossiers. Under 'T' for 'Trans-Jordan' he found a list of names; then, list in hand, he cross-filed to 'S' for 'SOE', the designation for World War II British clandestine intelligence. The sound of the singing stopped for the moment as Must dug out a folder which proved to contain a typewritten uncoded memo and three photographs, of poor quality, of an Arab family.

Must glanced at the memo, speed-reading the entries, which dated back to the '40s. One member of the family had caught the attention of the unknown intelligence recruiter who had summarized the dossier. Must slowed down:

> . . . This twenty-four-year-old subject is a slim, well-muscled individual, alert and physically strong and active; weight 106 lbs., height 5′4″.
>
> Born 1944, Jerusalem. Arrived U.S. at age 13. Father worked for British until 1947; for U.S. after 1950.
>
> Religion: Lutheran–Greek Orthodox
>
> Sexual adjustment: Subject is . . .

He brushed the dust from his fingers with his blunt thumb. After dropping the folder into his attaché case, Must fingered the files until he found 'V' for 'Venezia Guilia', the artificial Italian province that the fascists had carved out of Yugoslavia in the late 1930s. The file was almost four inches thick, and Must searched for almost five minutes before he found the dossier marked 'HRB'. Finally he located the memorandum, to which was attached a picture of a distinguished-looking middle-aged man; this too went into the attaché case.

He wiped his hands with a handkerchief and prepared to mount the stairs as the singing sound of the civil rights anthem that he hated so, drifted down into the basement again. As he reentered the lounge, the big priest turned off the TV and moved to the liquor cupboard.

While the priest poured the Scotch, Must jotted a name on the back of a card and handed it to the other man.

'Bottoms up, Bill.' His Eastern European accent was as thick as ever, Must noted. 'What can I do for you?'

'Set up a meeting for me with this woman, soonest.'

As he drank, the priest studied the name Must had written, then turned the card over. As he read the embossed legend, he showed his big yellow teeth in his version of a friendly grin.

H
O
A

William A. Must, Jr.
Public Relations Consultant

HAYES-OGDEN ASSOCIATES

71926 Santa Monica Blvd.
Los Angeles, Calif.

Phone
(213)826-5870

'Yes, my dear old Kvaternick,' Must murmured, draining his glass and measuring out another drink, 'we shall overcome.'

April 7 *Indiana*

It was during her second week in Indiana, on a Sunday, that Judith Shankland told Paul Woods that she would go all the way to California with him. Robert Kennedy had given the single most devastating critique of the Vietnam war and the culture of death yet made by any Establishment political leader. Months later she would play the words back on her portable tape recorder, and that is how she would always remember the speech, always turning off the tape with the roar of the crowd rising as her own broken voice in the midst of the sound told Paul that she loved him and that she would stay until the end.

She had turned the tape machine on because the Candidate – as bored as the staff with the same Vietnam speech that he had to repeat as often as six and seven times a day – had, in desperation, started to give rare vent to the slashing wit that had to be kept hidden from most of middle America.

> . . . the problem was that the President and I couldn't agree who should be on the Commission. I wanted Senator Mansfield, Senator Fulbright, and Senator Morse appointed to that commission. And the President, in his own inimitable style, wanted to appoint General Westmoreland, John Wayne, and Martha Raye . . .

Then the gallows humor, through some alchemy of fatigue and free association, slid suddenly into the philippic.

> If our colleges and universities do not breed men who riot, who rebel, who attack life with all the youthful vision and vigor, then there is something wrong with our colleges. The more riots that come on college campuses, the better the world of tomorrow. I am concerned that at the end of it all, there will only be more Americans killed. More of our treasure spilled out . . . so that they may say, as Tacitus said of Rome: 'They made a desert and called it peace.' I don't think that is satisfactory for the United States of America. I am willing to bear my share of the responsibility, before history and before my fellow citizens. But past error is no excuse for its own perpetuation. Tragedy is a tool for the living to gain wisdom, not a guide by which to live. Now, as ever, we do ourselves best justice when we measure ourselves against ancient tests, as in the *Antigone* of Sophocles: 'All men make mistakes, but a good man yields when he knows his course is wrong, and repairs the evil. The only sin is pride.'

First the crowd and reporters were stunned. Then they let out an animal cry of guilt and long-accumulated pain and rage. Somehow the tense, embattled man standing on the red leather back seat of the convertible, by accepting responsibility for the long crime, was able to translate the hidden and impacted guilt into an anger and shame that could be vomited out in that mass roar. For the first time they let themselves hate the war more than they hated the demonstrators.

'You're a sucker for those old-timey quotes, ain't you, lady.' She could taste the salt of Paul's tears as she kissed him there in the middle of the street throng.

The rest of the day was like a dream. For nine hours they skimmed across northern Indiana on a carpet of excitement and sound. At South Bend, the trees and telephone poles had signs on them reading ROBERT KENNEDY WILL PASS THROUGH THIS WAY AT 2:00 P.M.; at 3:30 they were lined four deep, still waiting hopefully.

At the Gary city line, two men climbed into the open car to flank the lean figure. One was Gary's black mayor, Richard Hatcher, and the other was a saint in the white ethnic wards, Gary's indomitable former middle-weight champion, Tony Zale. The crowd was four and five deep as the three men passed through the traffic din. The flesh-and-blood message was completely clear: The deadly racial enmity between black and white blue-collar Americans somehow was being reconciled by this boyish man with the shock of unruly hair, with his arms thrown around the waists of the two symbols of the new political power base that John first built and now Robert Kennedy was leading.

April 8 *Gary, Indiana*

The rundown motel on the outskirts of the city literally shook as the motorcade roared by. As James Jerrold swung open the door to make his athletic entrance, the sound waves of the demonstration seemed to enter with him and hit Must physically where he stood drinking Scotch from the bathroom glass.

'The telegram came, Mr. Must.'

The older man kicked the door shut and tore open the yellow envelope, reading, ' "Your jockey is a winner." '

'Your jockey?'

'Yes. The, ah, Palestinian candidate.'

'Oh, the one you told me about? Who had the accident with the horses?'

'That is correct, James. And *he* is a real winner.'

April 11 *Lansing, Michigan*

The young Kennedy aide had no difficulty spotting Paul Woods in the middle of the hotel lobby. He could see the strong sculpted head that was at least several inches higher than those of the exhausted journalists milling around him trying to snatch press handouts and schedules for the Michigan appearances. The aide needed to tell Woods something before the police arrived. 'Paul, can I see you a minute, *Paul*!' Then, speaking low and fast: 'It's probably nothing, Paul, but Tom Gross, the AP man, just had a report of a possible sniper on a building across the street and –'

'Find security right *now*. Stay away from the local police. I'll check out the Senator's suite.' He was in the elevator before the reporters could sense anything out of the ordinary. As soon as he had turned the corner of the corridor on the fourth floor, Woods saw the man twenty-five yards down leaning casually against the wall, so just as casually he walked the few yards to the empty press room and entered with his key.

He was breathing deeply, his mind focused. He unlocked his briefcase in the closet luggage rack, took out his old service revolver, and began to move like a big black cat through the always unlocked doors of the connecting rooms of the Kennedy campaign suite. When he reached the third door, the Senator's private quarters, Woods paused to slip off his dark loafers. Then, moving low and smoothly, he pushed silently into the empty drawing room and froze, listening. From the bedroom, over the sound of his heart's thuds and street noise from below, he could make out the sound of someone moving.

He maneuvered like a man under water to the door jamb of the sunlit bedroom. Woods watched a lean man with light brown hair, in his late thirties, dressed in brown coveralls, kneel down next to the Senator's night table and begin to unscrew the mouthpiece from the telephone receiver while with his elbow he held down the bar of the instrument, which otherwise would have run through to the hotel switchboard. After about thirty seconds Woods saw the intruder's back stiffen. The man held a miniaturized device of some kind up to the light, replaced the receiver in its cradle, and started to swivel around toward a small tool kit next to the bed.

'Don't turn around. Lie on your face and spread your arms.' Woods's voice was like ice. The man complied with the order instantaneously, and he did not move a muscle as Woods bent over to pat him down. Only when Woods had rolled him half over to locate and remove his service revolver did he whisper up into the tight black face, 'I'm FBI.'

'You're what?' The man's response to Woods's growl was to point to the telephone with his head, indicating that the bug was live. Woods gestured to the prone figure to rise and precede him into the drawing room and sit down on the sofa. Woods closed the connecting door softly, then leveled the revolver at the other man's chest.

'My name is William Thurman, Jr., Special Agent, Federal Bureau of Investigation.' He quickly started to reach into a coverall pocket, but changed to a slow-motion pace as Woods followed his movement with the revolver. Then, carefully, he lifted out his identification and tossed it up to Woods.

'So?' Woods barely glanced at the plastic folder.

'FBI. Can't you read?'

'Phony credentials are a dime a dozen. You better talk fast, mister.'

William Thurman, Jr., stared at the powerfully built black man in the elegantly cut glen-plaid suit. FBI special agents were not accustomed to being talked to in that tone of voice. The telephone – specially installed by the telephone company and not connected to the switchboard – jangled. Woods moved to take the call, punching the lighted button, still watching Thurman.

'Senator Kennedy's suite.' As he spoke he measured the other man. He looked FBI: tall, WASP, short haircut, Boy Scout attitude. He reminded Woods of a bigger, younger version of the actor Richard Widmark. 'Peter? Okay, fine. Get the press to play it down . . . yeah, a false alarm. They'll understand. Peter, ask our FBI contact down there if he's ever heard of a . . . wait a minute . . . a William

Thurman, Jr., T-H-U-R-M-A-N, Junior. Right.' Woods stared the other man down while he held, waiting. 'He has. No, nothing. No, no problem. I'll be down there in five minutes.' He hung up and tossed the ID back to Thurman. 'Okay, Mr. . . . Thurman.' On an afterthought, he unscrewed the mouthpiece of the outside telephone in a quick check for a surveillance device. None. Thurman was studying Woods openly now that he had pocketed the gun.

'It *is* Thurman. You're Paul Woods, aren't you? Used to be Secret Service, then got fired after the JFK thing, right?'

'I'm listening.'

'Because you demanded to testify before the Warren Commission that you had knowledge of some kind of conspiracy in Dallas. Sure, I –'

'Just what in hell were you doing in the Senator's bedroom?'

'Paul *Woods*. Sure, I remember.' He paused. 'I'm here under orders, Mr. W–' Woods had reached into his pocket for the revolver.

'Mr. Thurman, I don't give a goddamn if you're FBI, CIA, DIA, or 007. I'm here to protect *this* Kennedy. Now I asked you a motherfucking question!'

Thurman's eyes flared up, then wavered. 'All right, I'm part of a surveillance team assigned to the candidate.'

'Why?'

'I don't know.'

'You don't *know*? You do know that Meyer Lansky and the Mob had a million-dollar contract out on him in 'sixty-six, don't you? Or do you people still deny the existence of the Mafia?' They stared at each other, both breathing deeply. '*I want an answer!*'

Thurman cleared his throat. A police siren from the streets below rose and fell in the silence. Woods noted with satisfaction a bead of perspiration just starting to gleam at Thurman's hairline.

'For what it's worth, Mr. Woods, the Bureau may be doing some good for your man. Did you know that we're rousting hell out of the anti-Castro Cubans, keeping them out of commission until after the election?'

Woods's eyes widened slightly. 'Very interesting. Very. Keep talking, Mr. Thurman.'

'Look, Woods, I work in the Technical Division. My orders are to provide continuing surveillance and protection. That's all I know.'

'Protection. You had Dr. King "protected" with a bug for four and a half years, and they just slaughtered –'

For the first time Thurman's voice rose slightly. 'That bug on King was ordered by your –'

Woods leaped to his full height. 'Bullshit! After JFK was hit, ol' pussyfoot Hoover wouldn't let up on Bobby about King and the "Communists", so Bobby – and he *admits* it was wrong – Bobby gave permission for a device for four *weeks* – you understand – and Hoover keeps it on for four *years*, and when you all got caught you tried to blame it on –'

Thurman stood too, his hands open in a placating gesture. 'Yeah, okay. So the bugs don't do any good. I just –'

'You just follow orders, don't you? Friend, you're blown! You have "embarrassed the Bureau."' Thurman was bathed in sweat now as Woods breathed in his face. 'All I have to do is pick up this phone and you go to Siberia.'

Thurman began to talk fast, almost wringing his hands. 'I don't know anything, and I don't know if I believe all this paranoid conspiracy crap. But I'll tell you one thing – while I was installing my bug, I found that someone had beat me to it – with a device that's sophisticated as hell. Yeah, I disconnected it. Look, I've got a family and –'

Woods shook his head and sighed, then handed back Thurman's revolver, walked to the desk, picked up a pad, and tossed it to the FBI man. 'I'm not going to get you fired. But before your buddy on lookout wakes up and starts acting crazy, put down there where I can get a hold of you – day and night. I want you to get me some information, and I want the identity of the Bureau's informant – don't argue with me! I want it!' Woods rode roughshod over the other's pleading look.

Thurman wiped his forehead and began to write thinking, This Woods was a crack Secret Service agent, of course he knows there was a goddamn informant. 'I'll do what I can.' He paused, still looking at the pad. 'I wouldn't vote for the man but I don't want to see him killed. Look, the rumor is the informant contacted our New Orleans office. Why not start there?'

Woods barked a humorless laugh. 'You want me to visit the FBI in New Orleans?'

'Well – maybe not, but you might check with the DA there – you know, Jim Garrison? I don't know if he's crazy or not, but the man *does* have connections.' He handed Woods the notepad.

The Kennedy man spoke more softly as he studied it. 'Look, if you get anything, contact me directly. Don't go through the campaign security.' He jotted a number down for Thurman.

'You're not security? You sure as hell act like it.'

'No, I'm public relations, believe it or not. But I do a little moonlighting – you know how it is.' The two men knew enough about each other now to drop their guard slightly. Woods offered Thurman a cigarette. They both lit up, and Thurman's wary green eyes seemed to come into focus for the first time.

'Yeah – I know. Look, this was a black bag job, I was putting in a suicide tap. Which means if you report me they'll deny everything. So leave the tap in and I'll find out what I can. Okay?'

They smoked in silence for a minute. Woods followed Thurman into the bedroom and helped him clean up his tools. Before leaving, Thurman quickly unscrewed the receiver mouthpiece and pointed out the FBI bug and, next to it, the other, smaller, more sophisticated device. Then, without shaking hands, he left, leaving Woods sitting on the side of the bed smoking, the sweat running down his face now.

April 12 *Santa Ana, California*

James Jerrold adjusted the telescopic lens of his Nikon camera and started shooting. The slat he had removed from the breeding-farm tackroom gave him a clear view of his subject.

The telephoto mechanism worked at 200 mm., but that was not elegant enough for one of the men who had tracked the immortal Che. Jerrold's innards churned pleasantly; the blood rushed toward his skin and into his muscles. He was ready. He set the Nikon on 'motorized';

now he could shoot this Arab loser at three frames per second.

A slight young man, leaning on a cane, watched two horses being exercised on the practice track. As the exercise boy passed, the young man with the cane gave a wave. The exercise boy turned away, and the man with the cane limped off at a fast pace. In the tackroom Jerrold stopped shooting and relaxed his sphincter muscle.

April 14 *New Orleans*

The Easter Sunday church bells rang out in the hot air for first mass as Paul Woods walked through the French Quarter toward his early appointment. He had always favored New Orleans, and now again he wished that he could spend a few days in the Quarter with Judith Shankland instead of having to fly out that afternoon to rejoin the campaign in Indiana. He had not even been able to tell her where he was going. She would have liked the mixture of church bells and Dixieland still oozing from a jazz club somewhere deep in the Quarter, all mingled and concentrated under the low, rainclouded sky. New Orleans was a Southern town, though some denied it, but they could have found some place to stay. The truth was he simply did not trust her enough. This is wrong, he told himself, you can't sleep with the woman and then shut her out of the center of your life. You know you're wrong, he worried to himself.

As he had been promised, Woods found New Orleans District Attorney Garrison's outer office open. Hearing a deep voice from an inside room, he continued down the office hall to find three young men watching film on a makeshift screen. The man running the 16-mm. projector was a giant – more than six and a half feet tall – with a deep voice that Woods knew could quote entire Shakespearean soliloquies from memory. He watched the screen as Jim Garrison narrated in sonorous tones.

'These are frame-by-frame blowups we had made from film taken at the scene . . . Notice carefully what happens to the President's head as he is hit from the *front*.'

Paul Woods felt the blood rush to his head. There on the screen was the film he had seen only once five years ago – a dim 22-second, 8-mm. record of the assassination.

He had not, then, been able to look at it for more than a few seconds.

Now Garrison had a clear 16-mm. copy running on the screen in slow motion and with stopped frames. There was President Kennedy's open limousine, code name 'Lancer', breaking Secret Service regulations by turning 120 degrees onto Elm Street and the death trap in front of the School Book Depository. The frame froze with the President lifting his hands as the first bullet tore through his throat; then the chest shot striking Texas Governor John Connally, sitting in the jump seat in front of John Kennedy.

This was the film that amateur photographer Abraham Zapruder had taken of the motorcade while standing to the right front of the President's vehicle on a grassy knoll in front of a picket fence.

Woods's body was rigid, waiting for the final explosion to register visually on the silent film. There it was: an unseen assassin obviously firing from the right front blew off the skull of John Kennedy. The men in the room gasped as a puff of smoke seemed to explode from out of the President's head. With the force of a sledge hammer, the victim was driven backward and to his left against his wife.

Woods's eyes widened in horror. Garrison's copy of the film, unlike the one Woods had seen years before, was sharp enough for the viewer to see clearly that Jacqueline Kennedy was drenched in a nimbus of her mate's blood and that as she crawled up and out on the trunk of the stalled Lincoln she was actually trying to retrieve parts of her husband's skull, exploded on the rear of the limousine.

Woods sagged against the wall as the sequence was rerun at normal speed – first shot, Connally shot, last shot and the puff of smoke. Woods knew that the two motorcycle police officers riding to the left rear of 'Lancer' had had their full-face plastic visors covered with blood. And that then they had instinctively run their cycles up the grassy knoll and, with guns drawn, raced behind the picket fence – there to be turned back by men who flashed Secret Service credentials. After Woods had been fired for challenging the official 'one lone nut' theory, the Secret Service had had to admit that there had been *no* Secret

Service agents in Daley Plaza that day, either before, during, or after the murder, except, of course, those actually riding in the caravan. The Warren Commission had castigated the Service for this state of affairs, but that was of no help then to Paul Woods, whose career had been smashed.

'Mr. Garrison, I'm Paul Woods.'

'Be with you in a minute. Gentlemen, these next shots are of individuals who were taken into custody immediately after the shooting by the Dallas police – and later released. Mark, would you take over for a few minutes?'

They walked into the deserted outer office. The entire municipal complex was empty on Easter Sunday, so Woods and Garrison were able to talk quietly as the rainclouds drifted lower and lower. Garrison moved slowly, favoring a pained back. He bent stiffly to pick up a manila folder. 'A group of law students going over the evidence. Part of my team of "irregulars", Mr. Woods.'

'Can you get any of that dynamite into court?'

'It shook you, didn't it?' Woods's eyes filled with tears as he turned his head away. Garrison's voice fell on him, Godlike. 'They shot him down in the streets. Since then, everyone's been silenced who's tried to cry out – but, as George Orwell wrote, "There was truth and there was untruth, and if you clung to the truth, even against the whole world – you were not mad." '

The dense moisture-filled air and light seemed to enclose them. Paul Woods felt as if he were being led by some noble presence in a recurring dream. A towering presence leading him into some inescapable boundary situation, and he felt his pity and terror passing over into a sense of fate. The tall man looked at him questioningly out of penetrating eyes underscored by dark circles.

'Mr. Garrison, let me come right to the point. I believe there are guns between Bobby Kennedy and the White House. You read my letter?'

'What have you got in the way of hard evidence?'

'Not much – a wire tap, a tip from an FBI agent.'

They had stepped slowly to the window. The storm would break now at any moment. Garrison's features were a mask of pain and resignation. Paul felt his own facial muscles begin, involuntarily, to mimic the older man's tragic cast; his left eyelid began to twitch as he felt himself falling forever into the 'limit situation' – he remembered Sartre's phrase – that he knew had claimed Jim Garrison half a decade ago. Garrison's voice was almost elegiac: 'It's a lonely battle . . .'

'I don't even know where to start.'

'Start at the top, Mr. Woods. The "Secret Government": war industry; out-of-control elements of the Intelligence Establishment; crime unions . . .'

'The "Secret Government"?'

'Intelligence – that's where you ought to start. Intelligence can take mob torpedos, political mental cases, exiled Cubans – the denizens of the gutter – and weave the whole crew into a seamless web of conspiracy. Then they'll plan it, pay for it, staff it, and after the job's done break it down into its original pieces again – and each piece is a revetment, a cover . . . Take this – for what it's worth.' He handed Paul the folder and walked away stiffly, more in pain than pride.

As Woods turned to go out into the gathered storm-clouds, the first terrific crack of tropical thunder drowned out the Easter bells.

April 15 *Los Angeles, California*

Helen Dukmejian, Ph.D., M.D., reread her carbon copy of Viv Easton's latest appeal for funds and facilities.

UNIVERSITY OF CALIFORNIA
DEPARTMENT OF MENTAL HYGIENE

VIOLENCE RESEARCH INSTITUTE
Center for the Health Sciences
Los Angeles, California 90024

April 13, 1968

CONFIDENTIAL
M.C. Bowman, M.D.
Director of Health
Office of Health Planning
State of California
714 'P' Street
Sacramento, California 95814

Dear Mike:

I am in possession of confidential information to the effect that the Army is prepared to turn over Nike missile bases to state and local agencies for non-military purposes. They may look with special favor on health-related applications.

Such a Nike missile base is located in the Santa Monica Mountains, within a half-hour's drive of the Violence Research Institute. It is accessible but relatively remote. The site is securely fenced, and includes various buildings and improvements making it suitable for prompt occupancy.

If this site were made available to the Institute as a research facility, perhaps initially as an adjunct to the new Center for Prevention of Violence, we could put it to very good use. Comparative studies could be carried out there, in an isolated but convenient location, of experimental or model programs for the alteration of undesirable behavior.

Such programs might include control of drug or alcohol abuse, modification of chronic antisocial or impulsive aggressiveness, etc. The site could also accommodate conferences or retreats for instruction of selected groups of mental-health-related professionals and of others (e.g., law enforcement personnel, parole officers, special educators) for whom both demonstration and participation would be effective modes of instruction.

My understanding is that a direct request by the Governor, or another appropriate officer of the State, to the Secretary of Defense (or, of course, the President), would be most likely to produce prompt results. Needless to say, I stand available to participate in any way that might be helpful.

Sincerely yours,
VIV

Thomas Vivian Easton
M.D.
Medical Director

cc:
Earl Kurst, M.D.
  Secretary, Health and Welfare Agency
John C. Older, Ph.D.
  Chancellor, UCLA
Marshall M. Sherman, M.D.
  Dean, School of Medicine, UCLA
Helen Dukmejian, Ph.D., M.D.
    VRI

Helen Dukmejian was disturbed that not only the revolutionaries on campus but some of her own most talented postgraduate tutorials were passionately opposed to the scientific experimentation, of which she was an integral part, now taking place at VRI. Students in general wanted the program, housed in the big gray slate building built by the WPA in the '30s, off campus, and because the work was classified the radicals and minority students were having a propaganda field day.

She checked her heavy stainless-steel watch and prepared to go down to the reception office to meet – she scanned her appointment calendar – a Mr. William A. Must, Jr. The letter from the man in San Diego, who had been signing himself 'Uncle Victor' on his letters to her for the past fifteen years, had made it clear that she should devote the entire afternoon to a very influential public-relations consultant named Must. She tried to analyze the floating anxiety that had begun in the pit of her stomach, caused by the sight of that name, M-U-S-T. Her association to the tension was that the name suggested an order, even coercion – Must-*must*; I *must* not disregard 'Uncle Victor's' request, I *must* meet this person who is pretending to be a public-relations man. What had the last one's cover been? She remembered: Department of Public Roads. After failing in his attempt to take her to bed, he had told her that his mission was to recruit her for the agency's Office of Medical Services. 'Never,' she had replied, rather melodramatically. She had held 'lack of objectivity' against the CIA – nothing else that she knew of then.

She sighed. Her field was not Freudian depth

psychology or psychoanalysis; she was a behaviorist, and her unease was simply explained, she decided. Mr. Must was a stranger, strange *stimulus*, and her response to unknown stimulus was, predictably, fear. Predictable because she had been born in 1938, one of those children caught between the tidal waves of fascism and communism, for whom every knock on the door announced the secret police, one of those children of the twentieth century who by the age of ten had been dragged across half the collapsing nations of old Europe. 'It is all quite normal,' she said out loud, with her slight Continental accent but impeccable British-learned diction. She smoothed the white laboratory smock over her flat belly, and on the stroke of one precisely walked out of her small office cubicle to meet the stranger. A classically molded woman with big very dark brown eyes and the large features much admired by southern Europeans. The boyish cut of her dark hair only emphasized the slim, graceful neck and the sensuous swelling of her high breasts.

Helen Dukmejian desired, above all else, to be uninvolved. Science was a prophylaxis or a membrane separating her from the politics and propaganda of everyday life in all its banality and evil. She had been a child during the European disaster when 'each one sold one' just to stay alive; when no one who survived was innocent. Her plan was to manage her life the way she executed the experiments in her laboratory. Her goal and her god was 'predictability'.

From a frightened, gawky refugee child, Helen was, at thirty, a strikingly handsome and clinically brilliant behavorial scientist. She was friendly enough with her colleagues but jealously protective of her private life. The truth was that her private life consisted of herself and her memories. She liked being alone. Alone, she could neither betray nor be betrayed. Betrayal – this was the radical fear that had eaten away her childhood like acid.

The study of the psychology of violence was, to her, a means toward understanding and controlling the thousand-year-old beast that Europe had become by 1940. A beast that lived in the nightmares of an entire generation of both victims and executioners, that might stir from its short slumber again, without warning. Only science, she told herself, can save the human race from mass homicide or suicide. She had seen the world poisoned by ideology and propaganda, and now she craved cold, objective facts the way some young women crave love or babies.

She took long strides but did not hurry. Passing colleagues were used to her not speaking. The large red-and-white sign shouting SHELTER and the fat white arrow pointing down stood out from the dull yellow walls in the fluorescent light, and for some reason it caught her eye now. She hesitated. Every classroom, every corridor in the entire University system, in the entire *country*, had these atomic-attack signs. Why did she react to the fear stimulus today? She tried to analyze: the unknown. Who is this man Must? He is probably a technical analyst who I am to help work up a psychological profile – like last time. There is very little chance that he will be Clandestine Service. What could they want with me?

She saw him as he entered the lobby. He stood under one of the spotlights hanging from the acoustical ceiling that dimly lit the public room, so that heavy shadows ran down his big white face. An old black man dressed in white was snoozing on a modern but well-worn orange sofa under a poorly executed painting of the city of Paris. It was quiet in the ugly beige-colored room.

Behind the burly stranger was a bold-faced slogan, on a plaque, adapted from Albert Schweitzer.

HERE,
AT WHATEVER HOUR YOU COME,
YOU WILL FIND LIGHT AND HELP
AND HUMAN KINDNESS

Underneath, a smaller legend recounted that the idea for the Violence Research Institute had been born on November 22, 1963, when 'a lonely and pathetic psychopath, Lee Harvey Oswald, blindly and without motive assassinated the young President of the United States, John Fitzgerald Kennedy.' On that day, the plaque stated, Dr. Thomas V. Easton first conceived of a center for research into random violence so that 'mankind might avoid a repetition of such senseless bloodshed.' Helen had read these inscriptions countless times; now she gazed only at her visitor.

Something about the reflections from the man's dark glasses jolted a subliminal flash across her memory – the nightmare image that had brought her awake screaming night after night when as an adolescent she had finally found security in America: an older man, her father certainly, strapped to a chair while another man, wearing dark glasses, questioned him in a low voice. The lips of the interrogator and the prisoner moving, but the sense of the dialogue stifled by the incessant reports from a firing squad's guns in a courtyard below – *crack*, *crack*, *crack*, like sharp slaps across a face.

She had the advantage of him as he stood there exchanging the sunglasses for clear lenses. She saw the pale blue-gray eyes focus on her and travel quickly up and down the length of her body. Somehow this look was different from the stares she was accustomed to noticing being directed at her tall, superb figure: There was nothing sexual in the man's appraisal of her, just the shrewd look a buyer might turn on a statue reduced in price.

'Dr. Dukmejian?'

'Mr. Must?'

'I bring greetings from your uncle.'

They walked along A floor. Something about the heavy-set man's cologne was familiar. A woman who appeared drugged, accompanied by a male nurse, passed them on the way to the rehabilitation area. Must flicked the sign in front of the area with his eyes, which in the harsh fluorescent light now looked to Helen to be gunmetal gray. The sign read ART IS A THERAPEUTIC MEDIUM. She slowed down, but he was clearly not interested in the small sculpture exhibit inside, nor in the tiny patients' library next door, which was empty and locked. Greetings from her 'uncle' – could this strange man possibly *be* her 'uncle'? Years before, when she had tried to picture the unknown 'uncle', her father's face had come to her. But she understood all that now.

The sign next to the elevator read VISITORS UNDER 14 NOT PERMITTED ABOVE B FLOOR. The man ignored her halfhearted attempts at small talk. On the C level he quickened the pace as they passed an auditorium where several students sat watching a revolutionary Latin American film. When they reached C West the sign said FOR ADMISSION TO WARD VISITORS RING BELL. She looked up at him. He rubbed his neck and cocked his head slightly, expectantly.

She led him at once toward the experimental wing of the Institute, hoping that a tour of the labs would satisfy her obligation. As they passed an all-white audiovisual room, Must broke the silence.

'Well, why don't we sit down in there and get acquainted. This new, ah – "technopsychology", is it? It's all Greek to me.'

Was it her imagination that he had placed an emphasis on the word 'Greek'? The image of the interrogation and the *crack* of the firing squad flashed through her. He was looking at her again, pleasantly enough, but she had no hope at all now that this 'PR' man was anything but an intelligence operative of some sort. Did he know her father, could he tell her if he was still alive? Could she perhaps see him again – and did she want to if she could? When off balance, Helen Dukmejian always acted decisively in order to regain equilibrium, so now she plugged in the automatic slide projector. As the tray began to turn, clicking from photograph to photograph, she began the familiar teaching lecture in strong, poised tones. 'This is what we call behavior modification. We're looking at the START plan – Special Treatment and Rehabilitative –'

'You've done government work before, haven't you, Doctor?' His husky voice cut in softly under her little lecture. Fine, she thought, let us come to the point.

'A bit.'

'When was that?'

'1965. I was finishing up my doctorate at the University of Chicago. I'm sure you're quite conversant with my *curriculum vitae*, Mr. Must, in your capacity as a public-relations specialist for . . . for whom did you say you were working now?' She saw the pale blue eyes widen slightly; she was good, *very* good, and she knew that he knew that now.

'I, ah, am on contract for several large philanthropic foundations, just now . . .'

'I see.'

She knew she had underestimated this large, neat-looking man when he hit her with his soft phlegmatic voice. 'Yes. Your father is presently, ah, working for us, or rather *with* us, in Greece.'

He had wiped the premature smile off her face. She turned away to unplug the slide console, fighting for time, forcing her will to block out the nightmare flash from her childhood. As she kneeled she knew the small pale eyes were roving at will over the planes and angles of her body. From one knee she looked up into his heavy, chiseled face.

'I have had no news of my father in almost three years.'

He let her kneel there for a second, then smiled.

'Yes, a great, ah, freedom fighter since the early days of the thirties.' So her father was alive! Or was this another lie? His timing: This man is a consummate sadist, she thought. She throbbed with humiliation at the way he referred to her father, but at the same time something about the thickset, muscular torso sitting on the white stool triggered a masochistic mechanism in her. A yearning almost to crawl to him, to writhe at his feet in a frenzy of self-abasement, to present her bare flesh to him for striking with his flat, square, manicured hands, to cry out, finally, 'Father, Father!' In a split second Helen had this regressive spasm under control. This is the sickness, she analyzed as she kneeled before him, the *folie à deux*. His illusion is that he is God, and mine is that I am shit. Rising slowly, she rejected the psychoanalytic concept, which she had never believed in, of the death wish. She was tall, five foot nine, and he let her stand over him. She, thinking, it is not absolute *power* that corrupts absolutely, but the *illusion* of absolute power . . .

'Mr. Must, or whatever it is – I would like not to play games, yes? I would like for you to tell me what assignment your "foundation" has for me. But do not be surprised if I refuse. I was assured that I had discharged any and all obligations incurred for services extended to my father during the war.' Could this man be bluffed? His eyes were on her full breasts now as she stood in front of him. She did not shrink, but stood even straighter.

'Please,' he said, 'don't I get the full VIP tour? I am really here to learn from *you*, Doctor. And everyone seems to be at lunch or attending the, ah, Victory for the Vietcong rally going on now, I believe, in the, ah, "free speech" area. So I can have my own, ah, private tour. I take it you will not be joining the demonstration? No. As a behavioral psychologist you, of course, are beyond such, ah, infantile paroxysms and hijinks of these student, ah, credit-card commandos. How do you see it, Doctor? Do they just all want to kill their fathers? Not you, surely. The Oedipus, ah, complex is, I believe, your charming term for this phenomenon of goldfish swallowing and –'

'This way.' She walked ahead; suddenly his diction had become as precise and ironic as a British artistocrat's.

When he spoke to her again, it was in his normal, flat accent. They had reached a corridor where a small official sign stated AUTHORIZED PERSONNEL ONLY.

'I'm afraid I'm a bit of an old hand. Exactly what is it you do here?' Her heart skipped a beat. They way he pronounced the words 'old hand' – his entire immaculate and murderous persona told her unequivocally now that this man was a black or clandestine operative. All right then, she told herself, we know where we are and who we are, Mr. 'PR' Man.

'If you'd been paying attention during the film you'd –'

'I know. Behavior modification – pain and pleasure – but how do you go about actually programming a man for a particular job?'

Something warned her to steer clear of whatever Must was getting at. 'There is no such thing as a Manchurian Candidate, if that's what you're looking for, Mr. Must.' She inserted a blue plastic clearance pass in the machine and unlocked a door to a long room divided into small cubicles.

Must partially blocked her way as she turned from the door. She could hear him jiggling change in his pocket as he questioned her softly, almost sympathetically. 'Doctor, what is your understanding, based upon what you're telling me, of the Copenhagen case? Do you remember the details? A man named Nielsen, I believe, was sentenced to life imprisonment for having hypnotized another man into committing one or two robberies and *two* murders.'

'No, that –'

'I mean, as I understand it, this Nielsen got his man to

act simply by saying or showing him the symbol "X". And also convinced him that he was a political hero.' The corners of Must's mouth lifted. His face is not unpleasant, she thought, and the man speaks cogently; he certainly is no thug. She allowed herself to hope again that the man's mission was really more or less innocent.

'I don't agree with the press reports of that case, Mr. Must. The man – Hardrup was his name – was *not* a Manchurian Candidate. Forget about the "X"; the point is that the hypnotist, Nielsen, was always *with* his subject, always in the background reinforcing the suggestions. And the triggering mechanism, the "X", is irrelevant; it was the constant "political hero" suggestions that were motivating Mr. Hardrup at the deepest level, and justifying his otherwise antisocial acts.'

He nodded slowly, as if following very closely. Then, gracefully, he stepped aside and allowed her to lead him into the Experimental Section.

At the first cubicle, a tense, white-faced child sat talking in a rushed, incomprehensible manner to a computer. Soft musical sounds were emitted intermittently from the machine. As they watched, a white-coated attendant carried the child out of a rear door. At once the back of the computer slid open and a midget walked out, blew his nose, waved to Helen, lit a cigarette, and exited through the rear door.

Must turned slowly and removed his glasses, half comically, but Helen knew that he was off balance for the first time since they had met. 'The girl is what we call "autistic". Children like this seem to relate better to, or actually *trust* more in, a computer than a psychologist.'

The next cubicle was empty; in the one after, a psychologist sat opposite a small boy. The man and boy stared at each other suspiciously. 'What you are seeing here, Mr. Must, is the successful result of decades of scientific experimentation. These are real breakthroughs in behavior modification.'

'Sort of a psychological moon-shot into, ah, *inner* space?'

Suddenly the psychologist spoke to the boy, who never wavered in his stare. The man's voice was cold and mechanical, emphasizing the first word heavily.

'*Where*'s the ball?'

After a moment the child, still staring straight ahead, pointed listlessly to a ball on the floor. With a stiff gesture the psychologist popped a gumdrop from his pocket into the boy's mouth, saying '*Thaaat's* a good boy' in the same stereotyped tone.

'*Where's* the book?' A flicker in the little boy's eyes showed that he understood the question, but was not going to respond. The man pressed a red button, delivering a painful shock to the child's legs through his wired chair.

'*Where's* the book?'

As they turned toward the next cubicle Helen noticed Must smile as the boy pointed toward the book. As if to make a friendly remark, Must bent down to whisper to his guide, 'Looks like the old carrot-and-stick technique to me. This project's funded for *how* many million dollars?'

Now they passed four smaller units in a row and Must saw: a middle-aged woman sobbing without letup; a young woman laughing hysterically; a black man, shackled, screaming vile imprecations; a man being shown erotic photographs by a slide projector as he played with his exposed and wired genitals, then receiving electric shocks powerful enough to slam him against the back of his over-sized iron chair.

'These adults are being hit with kilowatts, designed to correct abnormal behavior ... For sex problems we combine aversion therapy with a new drug called cyproterane acetate.'

'Chemical castration?' His face was as deadpan as hers.

She continued coldly, 'We use the penile plethysmograph – a device that measures the volume of the penis and hence the amount of erection. Then we put the patient into group therapy with male and female co-therapists.'

Next was a rather larger unit with mats on the floor on which sat and lay six boys and girls between five and eight years old. Must would have thought them asleep but for their open eyes.

'We dose the problem children with drugs that make them more manageable, and thus less likely to challenge –'

'– the status quo. Indeed. We call it, ah, "pacification".

Tell me, what do your bleeding-heart liberal colleagues say about all this?'

She felt a charge of hostility. This man seemed to create a profound ambivalence in her, and she was aware that she was vacillating widely in her responses to this orderly and potent *provocateur*.

'Million-dollar grants have an amazingly therapeutic effect on the wounded liberal conscience . . . Mr. Must, any scientific work may seem sensational out of context. I can only speak for my own motives.' There was no way to tell this man what science meant to her.

Must's nasty laugh was cut short when Helen opened a locked door. The cubicle was a bare space with a cotton rug on the floor. A full-grown female police dog with an electrode implanted in her exposed skull was vacuuming the rug with an electric vacuum cleaner. The dog stood on its hind legs, the cleaner strapped to her body. Must cursed under his breath. Helen thought for a moment that the big man might attack the attendant who sat against the far wall taking notes. When the attendant flicked a switch the dog stopped; when he flicked it again the dog reared up on her hind legs and commenced her crazy staggering again. Must was white-faced with anger. The typical sadist's sentimentality for animals, Helen mused. She imitated Must's earlier mocking tone now, turning the knife, trying to rip apart the man's megalomania.

'Beyond the solution to the, ah, servant problem, this work is really more sophisticated than it appears to the layman. The Rand Corporation, in point of fact, has been experimenting with the training of apes for use in land wars and –'

'This is really sickening, Doctor – may we move on, please?'

Must paused to drink from the wall fountain before following Helen across the corridor into a small monitoring room where they could watch the next room on closed-circuit television. Helen gestured him to sit, and the ashtray told him that smoking was permitted in this room. Helen turned up the sound on the set.

'*You stinking hunk of shit!*'

Must's head snapped toward the screen. A psychologist dressed in khakis was excoriating four other men dressed in blue denim work clothes – two black, two Mexican-American. Helen turned down the sound of the shrill tirade.

'These subjects are rebellious convicts. A drug called Anectine has been used to induce sensations of extreme terror, suffocation, and death.' Helen could see from the cheerful expression on Must's face that, as these were only human subjects, he was once again playing the role of her fascinated student. 'During the outbursts, you see, the authority figure screams at the victim, warning him to reform or face further treatment.

'Now, do you notice the prisoner with an electric transponder implanted in his wrist?' Must moved closer to the screen as she pointed out a fifth prisoner, a white man, whom he had not noticed. 'A small computer in the master bank records his every movement.'

'Complete control? This is what I came to see, Doctor!'

'This is a combination of biology and electronics – "bionics", for short.'

'What's happening?'

'Basically, it has to do with the decision-making process in the brain. The next step will be "bionetics" – the same process but minus any electronic instruments.'

'You mean monitor people and control them without any implants?'

'Exactly. We call it "biofeedback telestimulation," and we're very close to a breakthrough.'

Suddenly he was smiling again. Her association was of a big, strong Dutch Uncle. 'Would this help me stop smoking?'

She could not help smiling back at this new human face that he had put on. She let him draw her out. He seemed to be hanging on her words.

'Well, there is a man named Delgado at Yale who uses an equally homely analogy. He says that the brains of human beings can be regulated at a distance as easily as the doors of a garage can now be opened or closed merely by pushing a button.'

'Can be *now*?' His eyes stroked her; he leaned toward her slightly.

'Five years. Delgado eliminates the problem of distance. He simply puts everything *inside* the patient. A stimoceiver to ignite the message from the computer, a dialytrode for chemical feedback, and the computer as well! Then no radio link would be necessary – all the electronics would be inside the body. A closed circuit – biofeedback.'

'Remarkable. That *would* be a Manchurian Candidate?'

'*That* would be a Manchurian Candidate.' As she laughed she saw the blue eyes turn cold again. He stood looking down at her.

'Very James Bond. Of course, it's not developed far enough to help with our, ah, present problem? But then, the old methods still work well enough . . .'

Helen bit her tongue. He had manoeuvered her back to square one, played on her intellectual and scientific vanity, where she was far more vulnerable than to any physical blandishments from a man like Must, whose ambience of physical and psychic sadism stimulated in her only that fleeting humiliating tinge of masochism that she despised.

She had had no food since early morning, and the war of nerves with Must had drained her. Must, sensing her temporary feeling of defeat, spoke quite softly. 'Let me give you a good lunch – I'm afraid I'm a poor student. You've saved the best for last?' She looked at him, not understanding. 'You haven't shown me your own special experimental kingdom! Ah, "Suggestion and Auto-Suggestion: Some Super-Ego Vicissitudes" was the title of your remarkable doctoral thesis, I believe.' Her shoulders slumped. Men like this simply had to exploit and pervert every human encounter. They wore you down and out. Automatically, she led the way to her testing area.

Through the one-way glass they watched her best subject, a graduate student, climb a set of geometric bars. Each time he reached the top bar, her assistant awakened the subject and asked him what he was doing up there. And each time the subject gave a different reason for his absurd position: 'I was running from a snake'; 'I wanted to catch a butterfly'; 'I heard a call for help.'

Must and Helen walked slowly toward the campus exit of the building. 'Why?' Must asked softly.

'You see, his eyes are open, and he *will* do things that would inhibit him in waking life, and he always, in every case, will supply a reason for his behavior.'

'Why?'

'It seems human beings do things on compulsion from either inner or outer command, and *then* they invent a rationalization for their acts. And under really deep hypnosis amnesia is a common phenomenon.'

'Hmm ... What you're saying is, it would be possible to, ah, *program* in a cover-up from the, ah, beginning!'

She flinched at the professional tone of the word 'cover-up'.

They were outside in the old brick patio, sun-drenched, with high, ivy-covered walls. Must took off his coat and folded it neatly on a rusty lawn-type iron settee. 'You must love it here in California. What a life. What would you like to eat?' She ignored the new friendly tone.

'If you don't mind, I really have a lot of work to do. Could you possibly tell me why you came?' A loudspeaker became active somewhere beyond the enclosed courtyard, and a sweet, clear voice opened the 'Bring the Boys Home – Negotiate Now' rally.

How many roads must a man walk down
before you call him a man ...

Must put his dark glasses back on. Helen closed her eyes. The haunting song, the warm sun, the ivy and red brick of the enclosed courtyard – for a moment she was able to wrap herself in the sensuous stimuli, to cancel out the exhaustion and sense of remembered nightmare that this man, Must, had provoked in her.

Yes, and how many years can a mountain exist
before it is washed to the sea ...

'I'll give you a raincheck, then. We'll have dinner. What do you say to Thursday? That'll give you a chance to look over the dossier I've brought for you.' She could see herself reflected in his sunglasses.

Yes, and how many times must a man look up
before he can see the sky ...

The song had ended.

'Did you come here to ask me to do another psychological profile?'

'That's it. I have the file in the car, we can –'

'I was told in 1965 that I would not be –'

'Yes, I know, but when you hear more about this case you'll see that it all makes sense.' They had to lift their voices now to compete with the blistering attack on the Asian war that was echoing off the buildings adjacent to the Free Speech Park.

Must's thick jaw set with suppressed rage at the rhetoricalinterruption. 'Let's talk as we walk, shall we? Let me put you in the picture . . .'

She dug her fists into her lab-smock pockets; with every word, idiom, euphemism, double meaning, he was compromising her, drawing her into some intrigue, disrupting the uneventful daydream that her life at the University had become.

'. . . Our man is a young Palestinian Arab refugee – with a twist. The family is Christian – outcasts among their own people. Interesting? Rejected by the father. Lives now with his mother and four brothers, I think it's right near here, in Pasadena. Let's see, what else? . . . Oh, he was an aspiring jockey until injured in a fall from a horse. Interests are Rosicrucianism and the occult in general. Sex, of course – basically heterosexual but, ah, very insecure, I think. Altogether a bright fellow . . . generous to a fault.' They had reached the VRI parking lot. Students had begun to materialize, criss-crossing the campus on their way to class. The rally was over, and the tower bells were ringing for the one o'clock sessions.

'This is it.' Must indicated his rented Chevrolet by kicking the tire.

'Why me?' she asked without looking at him.

'I thought that would be obvious. We need a complete psychological workup on an Arab; you're a clinical psychologist with a second degree in Cultural Anthropology, you've lived and studied in the, ah, Levant, as we used to call the Mid-East –'

She cut him off, the pseudo Ivy League routine he had slipped into again grated on her nerves. 'Yes. All right. The semester ends this week; I can give you a few days. But that is –'

'Champion!' He unlocked the car to hand her the dossier from his attaché case. 'I'll pick you up for an early dinner on –'

'I prefer to meet you some place.'

'Whatever you say. Where? ... Do you know the Beach House, near Malibu? You do. Used to be first-rate. Six o'clock?'

She was already walking away into the bright early afternoon and the peal of the bells. Realizing that she was no longer hungry, Helen headed at an angle back toward the VRI, thinking, I will eat dinner, give him some academic boilerplate about Arabs, and find out if my father is alive or dead. And that will be that. The migraine made her feel as if the top of her head were going to explode.

Must watched the receding figure, the superb carriage descending from the bare, regal neck. The arrowlike thrust of the poised spine flowing into the crease and volume of the subtly swelling hips and buttocks, then abstracted down the long supple legs under the plain white laboratory overdress, striding, now, away from him. Must's face was like a blunt hatchet as he followed her, from behind the dark glasses, into the distance. The bells ceased.

That little Arab, Must thought, still standing there with the door open, will sell his *soul* to get between those legs!

April 16 *Washington, D.C.*

Judith Shankland, Paul Woods, and Gil Hernandez sat in the screening room of the Brown and Doar Advertising Agency watching a rough cut of a one-minute Kennedy TV campaign spot. She stroked Paul's hand in the dark, feeling very close to him after a long late-night confidence from him about New Orleans and Thurman, the FBI man, working back into some of his fears. There was an intimacy between them this morning beyond anything she had ever experienced in any previous relationship. She realized what a powerful effect the sharing of a personal problem can have. Realized that for the first time in her life she herself did not feel like a bundle of secrets.

The conclusion of the campaign ad was a fast sequence of scenes showing RFK and Senator George McGovern listening to the story of suffering of the Sioux Indians at Pine Ridge, South Dokota; RFK walking through the East Los Angeles *barrio*; RFK attending church services in the Hough District ghetto of Cleveland; RFK kneeling with Cesar Chavez in a central California grape strikers' prayer vigil. 'Beautiful,' exclaimed Gil Hernandez as the spot went to white.

'Out of sight.' Paul Woods was equally impressed with the images of formal compassion in the short film. They both peered at the young woman.

'Well . . . I . . . well . . .'

'Come on, lady, what is it?'

'Christ's sake, Judy, spit it out.'

'Well, I think he should be – uh – seen with some – uh – white people, too.'

A moment of complete silence; then the dim screening room erupted with the sounds of affectionate laughter from the three young Kennedy aides.

They had reason to be happy. An advance copy of *Newsweek* magazine's new delegate count showed 473 Democrats uncommitted, 478 supporting favorite sons, 541 for Humphrey, 272 leaning toward McCarthy – and 858 going for RFK!

April 18 *Los Angeles*

They had the old restaurant almost to themselves. Must had chosen a window table overlooking the rocks and crashing waves below. Helen entered exactly at 6 p.m., as the sun burned its way down the horizon over Point Doom.

Must lavished a look of applause on Helen's open plum-colored silk-jersey top and short skirt. He almost bowed with delight at the sight of her skirt swishing in its miniature veronica seven inches above her knees, playing the bull to the sword of her long molded legs. She wore a soft salmon tie looped loosely around her throat, and a single gold chain with one oblong charm lay across the exposed olive flesh of her upper breast. Must made much of the difference between her hospital whites and this clinging ensemble. He was proud, he said, to be with her, and she reminded him of his daughter or his dead wife, he didn't know which.

This man simply has a job to do, she thought; I was just hungry and irritable, had a migraine, the other day. Give him a chance, she thought; so he is clandestine – well, so was my father in World War II . . .

Assuring her that he was on an expense account, Must insisted on much good wine and urged a delicious crab-and-lobster specialty of the house on her over very weak protests. Helen could not help enjoying the food and wine, and even William A. Must, Jr., she had to admit as she ate with gusto, seemed considerate and rather charming in a fatherly way.

He did not press her at all concerning the profile until their Irish coffee had arrived, and then he drew her out with small sounds, expressions, and gestures of appreciation for her obvious mastery of her subject. He appeared to be fascinated with her analysis, and as she expatiated at length Helen found herself hoping that her after-dinner disquisition would satisfy Must's demands on her. If so, her plan was to simply ask him for news of her father and refuse any offer of payment from Must's 'Company'.

'Tell me your opinion of Mr. . . . ah . . . let's just call him "Mr. Nobody" for now, shall we? Would he be a good investment for my Company?' Then he called her 'Helen' for the first time since they had met, and shifted his heavy shoulders to block the rays of the descending sun from her eyes. His pale eyes now actually smiled into her dark, radiant, almond-shaped ones, encouraging her to speak freely. She brought the plain folder and her notes up from the shoulder bag next to her on the seat and put on her glasses. The bar was starting to fill up. The sun was a red ball hanging as if by a thread in the middle distance.

'Well, to begin with, whoever made this preliminary "vet" of Mr. – of your subject's biography knows nothing about the Middle East. Of course, I have no idea what your Company's interest in him is, and I don't *want* to know,' she added parenthetically. Must nodded understandingly and lit a fresh Marlboro. He thought, Talk on, talker.

'For instance, let's see . . . Here: "rejection and beatings by father." Now, as you know, my expertise is the Algerian and North African Arab cultures, but the child-rearing customs in such widely divergent regions as Lebanon, Upper Egypt, and, in your subject's case, Palestine all disclose the same basic pattern. Before we get into that, I have to point out that there is really no such things as "the Arab mind" except for purposes of discussions like this, but there *are* striking cultural parallels.' He smiled as she paused to let the waitress set down their fresh coffees. She had to admit that he looked distinguished in a dark blue Palm Beach linen suit and a conservatively striped 'old school' tie of some sort. In the pause the waves below boomed up to her like the sound of a tragic Greek chorus. He waited patiently for her to begin again as if the mundane lecture and book quotes were all a revelation to him; guessing, correctly, at her intellectual narcissism.

'The Arabs have an ancient legend that illustrates their cultural complexity: When God created the world, He also created, it is said, ten character types: faith, honor, courage, rebellion, pride, hypocrisy, riches, poverty, humility, and misery. Faith said: "I shall go to Yemen"; "I shall accompany you," said Honor. Courage said, "I shall go to Syria"; "I shall go with you," said Rebellion. "I shall go to Iraq," said Pride; "I shall accompany you," said Humility. Poverty said, "I shall go into the Desert"; "I shall go with you," said Misery.

'So – now, child-rearing. The *mores* of the culture *demand* that the father act the role of the severe, stern authoritarian while the mother is, by contrast, loving and compassionate. What's more, a study of Lebanese mothers, for instance, showed –' She shuffled through her notes for the quote while Must smoked attentively. 'They, the mothers, were "more likely to approve of the harsh disciplinary actions of a severe father than those of a non-severe father."' Through the brine-covered picture window the sea was beginning to blur into the mist that seemed to have come up to meet the sun's final rays.

'Now, your man comes from Palestine.' She found another quote. 'The Palestinians have a proverb current among the *fellahin* that "character impressed by the mother's milk cannot be altered by anything but death." This kind of saying reveals the importance of the Arab attitude toward early child rearing. Now, do you really want me to go into this kind of detail?' She smiled.

Must chuckled and shook his head slowly. 'You are quite extraordinary. Take your time, and *eventually* we can skip past the nursing stage.'

'Which in the case of a boy lasts two or three years.'

'Just for the boys?' Must pursed his lips humorously.

'Oh, yes. Girls only get the breast for one or two years. As for the boy, both the actual treatment accorded to him and the expectations he will develop are fundamentally different. While still being breast-fed, there is the tendency on the part of the mother to pamper him more than she would a girl child. By the time the boy is weaned he has learned to walk, run, play, and control his elimination. What is more important, he has learned to talk, and so can and does ask verbally for the mother's breast whenever he wants it. And since the principles followed by the mother include both pampering the boy and demand-feeding him, he actually gets the breast whenever he asks for it.' Outside, the ocean had been swallowed by the night. She pushed her notes over under the red reflection of the candle.

'Mm.' Must blew his nose and glanced surreptitiously into the contents of his handkerchief. No question about it, he seemed uch more human to her now.

'This verbalization of the one major childhood desire, the mother's breast, is followed, in most cases at least, by instant gratification. And, what is psychologically equally important, the emphatic verbal formulation of the wish carries in itself, almost automatically, the guarantee of its fulfillment without the need for any additional action on the part of the child. This experience, repeated several times a day for a number of months, cannot fail to leave a lasting impression on the psyche of the boy child.'

'I'd like to hear more about that.' She was certain that Must was not merely feigning interest.

'Yes? Well, the prolonged period of lactation also impresses into the mind of the boy child a special image or archetype of the male-female relationship. For a period of up to three years, the mother was unfailingly at his beck and call. Her breast, his greatest source of pleasure and gratification, was his for the asking. This experience cannot fail to become a contributing factor in the general mold to which the boy will eventually expect his relationship to all women to conform.'

'Mm.'

She opened a small volume and found the page she needed. Must shifted his heavy haunches on the leather seat of the booth. His flat eyes were fixed on the gold charm that lay on her breast. He screened out the chatter of the dinner crowd beginning to fill nearby tables.

'Here. "The male" . . . no . . . "this comforting and soothing of the baby boy often takes the form of handling his genitals. Mother, grandmother, other female relatives and visitors, as well as his older siblings, will play with the penis of the boy, not only to soothe him, but also simply to make him smile. Among the fellahin of Upper Egypt, the mother may attempt to prepare her son gradually for the circumcision operation by caressing his organ and playfully endeavoring to separate the foreskin from the glans. While doing this, she would hum words to the effect that what she is doing will help to make him to become a man amongst men." Since circumcision is usually performed any time before the boy attains maturity, this motherly caressing of the boy's penis may well go on to an age from which the boy retains distinct memories throughout his adult life.' She folded her notes, sipped coffee.

Must applauded her with his eyes, began a sarcastic attack on the 'idiot who wrote up this dossier,' and reassured Helen that she was putting everything in perspective brilliantly. He looked at his watch. 'Last question.' He grinned. 'In the dossier, our idiot analyst comments on Mr. Nobody's, ah, temperamental instability. What about that?'

Helen drew a deep breath. Her coffee was now cold, and Must's ashtray was overflowing with cigarette stubs.

'The statement is meaningless. Generalizing again, but it is rather difficult to distinguish between the Arab concepts of bravery and courage.'

'Mm?'

'Their reactions may appear unstable to ethnocentric bigots like your analyst.'

Must showed his teeth in agreement. 'Mm.'

'Circumcision, for instance. Occasionally this occurs as a direct preliminary to marriage, with the bride looking on. The most painful form is the operation performed among some tribes in Saudi Arabia, where the skin of the entire male organ is removed, as well as the skin of its environs on the belly and the inner thigh. While this is being done the youth must show unflinching courage, standing upright, shouting "with a mighty joy" and brandishing a long dagger! Throughout the operation his bride sits before him, beating a drum and trilling the traditional shrill, sustained cry of joy.'

Must bit his tongue, secretly against the pain of the hateful words. He had always despised all teachers.

'The courage which is expected of the Arab youth is primarily a matter of *outward* appearance. One is almost inclined to say that the Arab boy child is socialized to be able to *act* courageously, to display a *show* of fortitude, without any consideration of his true feelings. He believes in himself and is not aware of the internal weakness that may be driving him into such bombastic behavior. Where his internal weakness does become manifest, at least to the psychologically aware observer, is when any allegation that he might be afraid causes a most vehement reaction. Also, it has been pointed out that it is *because* of this externality of his courage that the Arab has a passion for performing fantastic *beaux gestes* that appeal to the imagination, and on many occasions performs feats that are not commensurate with his abilities, but the momentary intensity of his feeling empowers him to attain extraordinary achievements.'

Now Must was following her as closely as a hunter, leaning in. 'So he *would* rise to the occasion if motivated. Would even, ah, kill if he had to.'

She kept her response didactic, uninvolved.

'*Muruwwa!* Manliness. That is the key to your man. Last lecture: I studied the Kabyles, Berber tribes in Algeria. They traditionally had political and warlike leagues that used to pursue their hostilities in the form of a strictly regulated game, an ordered competition. Whatever our opinion of the manliness evinced in this brand of conflict, one thing is certain: It is more humane conduct than the kill and overkill patterns developed by the Western world in its recent armed conflicts. And I say this because everything I've said tonight is an oversimplification and, what's more important, I have given you the straight party line of bourgeois Western anthropology. *Everything* I've said could be turned around – depending on who the profile was for.'

'No, no, fine, perfect.' Must stuck up ten fingers of

gratitude. 'But will he follow through? Will he achieve his *kismet*?'

Helen's eyes widened, and Must quickly explained with a smile, 'I was in Cairo for a week in fifty-two, spent the whole time playing poker at the Royal Automobile Club, picked up a few words.' She felt the tinge of anxiety for the first time since she had entered the restaurant.

'That's what it comes down to, Mr. Must. A "few words": *Karam*, *ird*, *hadith*, and *Sharaf* – honor, tradition, "face", potency.'

'Our man is a Christian Arab, does that –'

'Makes him *twice* an outcast. Dr. Habash, the most radical of the insurgents, is a Greek Orthodox, correct? The Christian minority, out of fear of the Moslem majority, gravitates toward Marxism and class war rather than religious war, so . . .' She searched his eyes behind the rimless glasses for a sign of amusement or boredom – surely she was treading on his territory now. Or was she? Could he be just a bureaucrat for Clandestine, perfectly harmless?

She handed him a University library book. 'This is by a Swiss Arabist named Hans Tutsh. I've marked a passage for you. You can drop the book in the mail after –' But Must had turned to the page. She saw his flat eyes light up as he scanned, moving the book under the candle.

She looked out to find that the ocean had melted into the darkness. Only the smashing of waves on rocks signified the primal power just below them. Must's heavy head was reflected in the wet window. He was rereading certain passages. Would he let her go? She would not even ask him details about her father if he would let her go now. She cleared the table of books and notes while he read silently from her book.

> . . . While these seizures last, Arab temperament goes on a rampage and hostility can easily become irrational. Once they pass, sincere contrition follows, accompanied by bafflement and a total lack of comprehension of what one has done and how one could have done it.
>
> . . . the personalization of problems goes so far in the Arab countries that even material, technical difficulties

accompanying the adoption of elements of Western civilization are considered as resulting from human malevolence and felt to be a *humiliation.* Where the Arab encounters an obstacle he imagines that an enemy is hidden. Proud peoples with a weak 'ego structure' tend to interpret difficulties on their life path as personal humiliations and get entangled in *endless lawsuits* or throw themselves into the arms of *extremist political movements. A defeat in elections*, a risk that every politician must face in a democracy, appears to be such a humiliation that an Arab can thereby be induced without further ceremony to take up arms against the victor and the legal government, or to ally himself with those who promise him success the next time. . . .

'That's very good,' he said, handing her back the book, 'very, very good . . . Nightcap? No. Me, too.' She pushed the dossier over to him as if to say 'That's it.'

She wondered why he paid the bill in cash instead of by credit card, like most men on an expense account, but all she wanted now was to ask about her father and then get home to her West Los Angeles apartment to resume her encapsulated academic life.

In the parking lot a cool sea breeze played about them. Helen was buttoning her Irish sweater, cream-colored against her olive skin, when Must said the words she had been dreading: 'Just one or two more matters to discuss, Helen, my car is over here.' She turned on him as if to protect herself physically. Her whole erect body proclaimed *No!*

'About your *father.* We'll take my car.' His voice was flat but still neutral. 'I have an urgent message from your father for you. We can drive back for your car later. We can talk privately in my car. I have something I want to show you.'

She followed him wordlessly to the Chevrolet, not speaking until he had pulled out onto the Pacific Coast Highway leading back toward Los Angeles.

'What about my father?'

Must responded in a slow monotone, carving every word. Helen stared unseeing to her right, toward the black sea.

'Your father is in very great danger. How long since you've seen him?'

'Twenty years. I was ten.'

'In Greece?'

'In Greece.'

'And since then your only contact has been through the man who signs his letters to you "Uncle Victor." ' She did not bother to answer him. Her body burned with shame as if he were stripping her naked. 'And all the money for your schooling and living expenses came from "Uncle Victor", but in all these years you have never *seen* "Uncle Victor", have you?'

Silence. Was her father alive or dead? Yes or no? The lights of Santa Monica shone ahead. The shuttered beach-side stands would soon be opening up for the summer crowds, she thought, as the car sped evenly along at 60 m.p.h.

'Have you ever heard of an organization from World War II called the Ustaci? Or the HRB? No? The Ustaci was, and is, a militantly anticommunist – some people say fascist – terrorist organization from the Yugoslavian province of Croatia. The founders of the group were Dr. Ante Pavelic and his assistant, a man named Andrija Artukovic.' He paused, knowing that she would ask 'What has this got to do with my father?'

She knew, too, that he would ignore anything she might say until he had told her everything he wanted her to know.

'The main headquarters of the Ustaci are in Germany and Argentina, but there are branches in Australia, Canada – and the United States. Now, the United States began to work with Ustaci after the war, when Communism replaced Nazism as enemy number one. These boys play very, very rough, and several Western intelligence agencies were embarrassed because, unfortunately, many of the Ustaci freedom-fighter leaders are still wanted in various countries for war crimes against humanity.

'The government of Yugoslavia claims that, ah, certain people are responsible for the liquidation of seven hundred fifty thousand Serbs and twenty thousand Jews. Now, so far the U.S. has stalled and covered for these men because we consider them anticommunist patriots and because one of them, Doctor Hubert Strughold, is a very prominent aerospace research specialist for the U.S. Air Force. Some of these, ah, wanted men have even had U.S. agents guarding their homes, and certain Congressmen have been able to shield them from deportation, but now two outstanding young Department of Immigration officers are quitting and threatening to go public – because they believe that the U.S. Immigration Service is protecting the same persons it says it is investigating. And whole files of evidence against Ustaci members in the U.S. are, ah, missing, and that looks so bad. Now these young men are threatening to go public. So . . . we are going to have to find other means to protect our freedom fighters . . .'

Instead of turning back along the ocean highway to get her car, Must gunned through the tunnel and onto the Santa Monica freeway. Helen still stared out into dark ace, waiting for the blow to fall.

'Yes. There was the little matter of three hundred thousand Jews and other political prisoners exterminated at a Ustaci camp, one of twenty-one in Yugoslavia, called Jasenovac, south of Zagreb. It seems that Yugoslavia, among others, wants to question Dr. Pavelic and his wartime Minister of the Interior, Andrija Artukovic, about this . . . whole affair. But Pavelic received asylum from Franco and is working out of Spain, while Artukovic was last heard of in Huntington Beach, California.' He let that register, driving silently for several minutes.

'Artukovic has some powerful protectors in this country, so he's been able to evade extradition all these years. But – and this is where you and your father come in – he has agents all over the world – Ustaci has plenty of money from somewhere – and if they are captured then they will be prosecuted for war crimes.'

They were on the way now to the Harbor freeway and the interchange near downtown Los Angeles. Must stubbed out his cigarette and opened his window slightly. He was just toying with her, and he knew that she knew it. This could all be a lie, she knew; all that was left of her father, perhaps, was the twenty-year-old photograph of torture yellowing in her memory. She felt for the moment like opening the car door and throwing herself out on the freeway. If her father were dead she would still have to play along part way with this man Must, who had been sent to her by her secret 'Uncle Victor.' Or was he, Must, 'Uncle Victor' – as she had half suspected all along? She bit her lip to keep back a whimper. And he, with the sensitivity of the sadist, rasped his voice into her pain. When he finally said it, she almost felt relief, thinking, maybe now the nightmare will die.

'Your father is one of Artukovic's agents. And Andrija Artukovic is none other than your dear and generous "Uncle Victor". Sometimes referred to as the "Himmler of Croatia." '

She would not give him the satisfaction of breaking down. He waited. They were driving faster now, headed for the interchange that would let them onto the Pasadena freeway. She was aware of each freeway sign, the lights of the city, the slow, hypnotic whizzing of passing cars. Her sense of abandonment was complete; she realized now that she wished that her father were dead, once and for all. Wished that she herself had died as a child in a refugee camp, never heard of America, never received money from 'Uncle Victor', never become a scientist. She wanted to scream at him: He's *dead*, isn't he? But, of course, Must couldn't leave it at that, neat and final.

'You see, your father may have been *forced* to co-operate during and after World War II with Ustaci; at any rate, money and security for you and your education was part of his deal with them.' Now, he thought, she will break, but the only sound was the whizzing of the light 9 p.m. traffic. They had reached the interchange, so he rushed the last bit in, finally. 'Now, your father also worked with, ah, us – the Free World, you know – so the only way his life can be saved – oh, I did mention that he had been apprehended in Sweden, didn't I? The only way your father can miss a firing squad is for the government of the United States of America to represent to the Yugoslav government that Ladislav Dukmejian has been a double agent all these years, working for the Central Intelligence Agency, for instance, as part of the invisible war against terrorism. That just might do the trick.

'Am I losing you?' His tone was warming up, as if to indicate that a relationship of trust, communication, and mutual advantage had now developed between them. Each play of his cast out a new net for her to fall into. She felt cold, permanently cold. His husky voice could not warm her. He was speeding now, changing lanes. She fantasied the car crashing in flames – anything to stifle his terrible, persistent voice.

'See, Artukovic is old, seventy-four, living in hiding in a guarded compound on the ocean. His mind wanders a bit, too . . . In other words we may have to give up Artukovic in order to save other agents – like your father. You see, Artukovic was the big cheese, he even shocked the Nazis. So we give them Artukovic and, say, Bishop Trifa from . . . Don't worry, "Uncle Victor" is only a code name, someone else will remain in contact with you.

'Ah, but, you know, we have to make a firm offer. Artukovic in return for safe passage for your father and x number of others, so forth and so on . . . Now I must tell you, Doctor, there are some people, on our side, who do not entirely trust your father, in fact who never trust *any* double agent – and your father has, ah, seen it all. So we – you and I – have to provide some bona fides for him. You follow? You and I . . .'

This section of freeway was old, narrow, built many years before the boom. Pasadena is a dying, old, ugly city, she thought.

He turned off at the second Pasadena exit. The only question in Helen's mind now was, what were *they* – whoever *they* were – going to ask of her in return for saving or for pretending to save her father's life? Her father, whom she only remembered in dreams as the man in the chair. Who was the other man, in the nightmare, in dark glasses, torturing him? The Ustaci, the Communists, the CIA? What was the difference, they were all victims and executioners both, at the same moment. What role had William A. Must, Jr., come all this way to hand her – was she slated to be a victim or an executioner? He angled the car off at the Orange Street exit. At the stop sign she finally asked, 'What proof do I have that –'

'He's alive.' Must cut her off. 'This is a luxury furnished building. I think you'll like it. Brand new.' The street was lined with palms. Old mansions slated to die loomed in the shadows of the weak street lamps. The block was broken up by the shadowy bulks of partially completed structures that would soon be the chrome and glass avatars of the original seekers of the new frontier, from a generation now dead.

The elevator let them out on the third floor. There were only two doors that she could see. Must unlocked 3A.

He ushered her on a fast tour of the one-bedroom flat, so new that there was plaster dust in the corners. She noted, dully, the naugahyde and plastic and an alienation as complete as that which Helen felt now, seated across from Must at the small glass dinette table. Must's face was like a gray-and-white rock, his voice terse and final.

'Dr. Dukmejian, within twenty-four hours I will have a contract to present to you. A legal instrument spelling out our understanding.' The cynicism of the man was stunning. He has just informed me that he will sell out 'Uncle Victor', and me, and everybody else, she mumbled under her breath. Must watched her lips moving like a crazy person and dropped his steely voice a notch.

'First: in exchange for your services, I am empowered by my principals – of course, you understand that you do not need to know *their* names – by my principals to guarantee your father's safe conduct to the U.S.A., complete with legal papers of all kinds, and subsequently he will be granted citizenship status.

'Second: Upon completion of your assignment, you will receive the sum of ten thousand dollars in laundered bills, deposited in a bank of your choosing anywhere in the world – all ongoing expenses will be reimbursed, of course, on a week-to-week basis. Finally, your assignment will *not* involve you in any *overt* illegal act.

'Now, your assignment: You will function as my agent – reporting only to me. I will be your "case officer". *I* will "own" you until completion of Operation Terror, which is an antiterrorism operation.'

The sharp, heavy face hung in the air, disembodied, before her unfocused eyes. When had she had this feeling of being a spectator at the unwinding of some inexorable scenario before? She remembered: In a courtyard behind a temporary shelter for displaced children; she had stood paralyzed as a dirty gray cat advanced on an unsuspecting bird as she watched, mesmerized, unable to lift a hand or utter an outcry, bound hand and foot by the invisible cords of her masochism – or sadism, she would never know which.

She struggled with all her strength, while Must studied her blank, immobile face, to keep from hallucinating that she *was*, again, that dying bird.

'I will put you in the picture, as far as I can.' The lips of the rocklike countenance began to move again.

'A worldwide wave of terrorism, rooted in the Palestinian insurgent movement, has been predicted by U.S. intelligence. In a joint effort, an attempt is being made to penetrate and disrupt this conspiracy before it becomes operational. Are you with me? Our job is to infiltrate a fanatic – but *our* fanatic, one that we can control – into the conspiracy. That is where you come in. All strictly legal . . . counterintelligence.' He smiled mechanically and kept talking.

'You are, as soon as possible, to arrange to meet our candidate – "Mr. Nobody" – to bring him to this apartment, which will function as a safe house, and to do *to* him or *for* him whatever you have to do in order to turn him into a revolutionary fanatic, a kamikaze, and to do it without his knowing who we are or what our eventual plans are.' He tapped the table top lightly with a thick finger.

She had bitten her lip until she could taste the blood, until from somewhere she found the will to focus her eyes on the presence across from her. 'Who are "we"?'

'Counterterrorism. I've given you the story.'

'The story?' Her voice was dead. 'The story? Or the cover story?'

'Many lives are involved, so of course we will have to be satisfied that the man can perform for us when the time comes. So you will, ah, modify his behavior, using your own techniques, until we feel he is ready to perform the *beau geste*, the, ah, limit situation or heroic, ah, suicidal act that you lectured me about so brilliantly this evening. You will condition him to assassinate a high political figure, a symbolic figure. When he is prepared to commit that act, your assignment is over.'

'A high political –'

'Mm. For instance, King Faisal, Richard Nixon or Robert Kennedy. I think that, ah, Kennedy might be the best symbolic selection, all things considered, don't you? Or Mr. Humphrey or Mr. Rockefeller – they will both be in the race next week with their "politics of joy". Well . . . Let's try Mr. Kennedy for the time being.' Inside her a door slammed shut.

She stumbled to the bathroom somehow, and vomited convulsively until she was empty. She was on her knees on the tile floor with her forehead pressed against the cool rim of the toilet bowl when she heard him talking to her again in the rich, flat voice, from the side of the bathub, where his heavy body crouched.

'We have complete faith in you, Doctor. It's true that your previous government assignments have been merely abstract exercises in analysis, as compared to this present, ah, action profile we've assigned you, but your experimental work in behavior modification uniquely equips you, we feel, for a challenging assignment of this magnitude. Actually, of course, you've been working for the government all along. Your "pure science" comes under our heading of "psychological warfare." '

She raised her head. His voice had taken on a crueler edge.

'You must know that your work at the, ah, Violence Center is plugged in to similar projects operating out of prison medical facilities around the country, but mainly right here in California, as well as a number of, ah, detoxification units housed in municipal hospitals on the East Coast.

'You remember last year what your supervisor at VRI said in his Washington speech, don't you? Paraphrasing . . . mm . . . "The real lesson of the current urban violence is the need to pinpoint and *treat* those people with low violence thresholds before they can commit violence," et cetera. Why do you think he's getting the kind of government subsidy that allows him to pay *you* a big fat salary? Don't be naive.' She stared at him like a zombie, saw his face seem to swell, heard his voice modulate into a warmer timbre.

'All right, forget the money, forget your father, what about your country? Aren't you a guest of this country? You have it made here – don't you owe a little something? These Arabs talk about Palestine being "a small drop in the great Arab ocean." "Arab ocean" – what the hell is that kind of talk but Hitlerian pan-nationalistic poison? Sheer racism, fanaticism. You see, this is a fight against both communism and fascism! Are you in or out?'

She had never seen anything like this man. He was feeding her 'play material', stringing her along, playing on every key, from blackmail to bribery to guilt and patriotism. And she knew that he knew that she knew that he was lying without letup, but that despite his utter bad faith that she would use his lies to finally rationalize what she had no choice but to do anyway – use the lies like any other behavior-modification subject.

So now he threw her reasons like bread pellets to a rat in the laboratory. Knowing that she would do what she was frightened not to do, that the reason beneath the reasons was just that: raw, suppurating fear. In the silence, then, she stared at his heavy rich cordovan brogans.

She was beaten, and no longer cared that he saw that she was beaten. Tears filled her dark eyes. She tried to part her sticky lips to whisper 'No.' The deceptively mild, pale eyes of the man on the edge of the bathtub were like two cornflowers that had been driven into a rock by the wind.

'Yes.' Now his tone was rasping again. 'Your clean, pure, scientific games are the perfume the Department of Defense sprinkles over the stench of the *real* world where the battle against evil takes place. Where do you think your funds have been coming from since the outbreak of world terrorism? You and your "Uncle Victor" are just two more soldiers equipped with different kinds of guns, employed by the Pentagon . . . Wash your face, I'll take you back to your car.'

The ghastly gallows humor of it all, she thought. Must is using exactly the same rhetoric as the radicals trying to close down the Violence Center. I am a bird, she fantasized, to this great cat – No. She almost laughed aloud. I am an executioner.

Must, misunderstanding the meaning of the glottal shock of suppressed hysteria from her vocal cords, thought she was going to protest again. He drew an envelope from his inside jacket pocket, 'Here's enough money to get you started, and you have the dossier,' he said, standing.

'No, I –' She started to speak hoarsely as she rose on both knees.

'Listen, you.' His voice bounced off the bathroom walls. 'There is no discussion! My principals will not hesitate to expose you, your "Uncle Victor", *and* your father, the whole filthy lot of you, and deliver you all to a Communist war-crimes tribunal! You *will* do it! You will do anything and everything we *order* you to do.' His voice had risen to a resonating shriek. Must's sensual rock of a face was tumescent now with power. 'If I order you to strip and get into this bathtub now while I urinate on you, *you will do it!*'

Yes, she thought, I will. Not for my father's sake but because I am nothing but a stinking corpse already; this madman is signing a contract with a zombie, a dead woman, and he doesn't know it, or that he is dead, too; that this is a contract between two corpses. From the depths of her nihilism she rose on her knees and licked her lips. 'If that's what turns you on,' she mouthed in a husky voice, 'include a codicil to that effect in our contract.'

Then she stood, washed her face, took the door key and the money from Must, and followed him out to the elevator.

'After this,' he told her as they descended, 'our demands on you are over. You can walk away and never look back.'

Neither of them said a word on the drive back to Malibu. She crossed the empty parking lot in the cold fog. She never felt the chill or turned on her car heater, never remembered that she had left her favorite Irish sweater on the front seat of Must's car.

April 19 Pasadena, California

Helen Dukmejian had decided not to kill herself.

Within days she had efficiently, even imaginatively, begun to accomplish her secret agenda. Cover stories for the Violence Center and her few professional friends were easily concocted, and her code routine for contacting Must every other day was already second nature. I am, she congratulated herself – with that nihilistic self-loathing irony that had been born in her as she kneeled in the bathroom that night and that would never leave her again until the day she died – a functioning, highly effective, ambulatory schizophrenic. 'Saladin,' she told Must, was to be the code name for 'Mr. Nobody.' His laugh had sounded like the report of a silencer. Then he had handed her a contract from the Domestic Operations Division to sign: '... critical to National Security ... unauthorized disclosure ... subject to a ten-thousand-dollar fine or ten years imprisonment or both ...'

The sterile apartment had been transformed into a den of delight. Rugs, hangings, ornaments from the Mid-East were everywhere. She had literally set the stage as carefully and cunningly as any inspired designer would for a Broadway play. She had chosen the lighting and music, the dishes, the books, the perfume, the food, the clothes – every prop required for the comedy, as she had begun to call what she was about to do.

She lay in wait for him in the Pasadena Public Library. Helen had removed her glasses, and wore an expensive long-haired wig the same color as her own short hair. Her cotton mini-skirt and clinging white batiste blouse made her a pattern of provocation.

As she saw him come out of the stacks, from the occult section, she pretended to be engrossed in one of the pile of books spread before her, occasionally looking up to make a note. From the corner of her eye she saw his legs stop as he became aware of her. She sighed as she read, so he would see her unencumbered breasts rise and fall, and shifted her position slightly so that the short skirt climbed up an inch higher. Then she leaned back in her chair, pretending to read a note, so that he could see into the shadows where her legs disappeared under the mini-skirt. She was naked under the dress, but she doubted he could actually make out the thick black bush of pubic hair. As if lost in thought, she began to stroke the inside of her thigh just above the skirtline.

Now she saw the Levi's move as he sat down at the reading table next to hers. She knew he had had to sit for fear the librarian or someone would notice the bulge in his blue jeans.

I hope he didn't come. She was making mental notes as if the young Palestinian emigré were one of her laboratory animals. What had Must told her that night? You need never look back She was fully aware that she had begun to play out the comedy with the cool lucidity and audacity of a classic psychopathic personality.

She took up another book, a duplicate copy of one she had reason to believe he would have withdrawn, from the stacks – *The Life of Madame Blavatsky* – and turned further in her chair so that he would have to remark on the coincidence of the identical books.

'Hey –no kidding.'

She looked up, feigning surprise. 'What?'

'Our books, see? They're the same . . .'

'Oh – yes.' She lowered her head again.

'Er . . . You interested in the occult, miss?' His accent was still quite heavy. She had to be very careful; she knew that the American stereotype of picking up a girl was totally alien to Arabic mores, that the taboos drawn tightly around the meeting of a man and a woman in the Arab world could send him running away in defense against his own aroused sexuality. She had to shift away from the threatening physical level before he panicked. Now she was the cat and he was the bird, and she made her moves as if from instinct.

'Shhh,' she whispered, indicating the librarian at her desk. 'Yes, I'm doing some research in parapsychology.' His huge black eyes brightened as he stood to come over to her table. She made the move easy for him by spreading the books for him to judge as she whispered, 'Are you in this field?' His large, liquid eyes narrowed slightly; then, seeing that the woman seemed sincere, he smiled at the flattering question.

He was lean, very short, she noted, wearing a white shirt, threadbare but clean, sleeves rolled up to his elbows, blue jeans, loafers. His hair was rich and full, long-headed – the typical Arabic phenotype. Lean schizothymic physique, handsome in a tense, driven way. Never had she felt so 'objective'.

He fingered her books. 'Sure, I know. Mysticism, ESP, the supernatural . . .'

She turned her book around to him, pointing out a section. 'Maybe you can explain this paragraph?' Her whispering and flattery made him literally glow with a temporary potency. Not knowing what to say, he began to read.

> The work of the race spirits is readily observable in the people it governs. The lower in the scale of evolution the people, the more they show a certain racial likeness. That is due to the work of the race spirit.

She bent close as he read, seeming to follow along with him, so that he could smell her.

> One national spirit is responsible for the swarthy complexion common to Italians, for instance, while another causes the Scandinavians to be blond. . . .

As he finished she nodded gratefully. Smiling, he whispered, 'Are you Italian?'

'No, my father was Armenian. What are you?'

'Palestinian.'

'I've been to Palestine.'

'You have! When?'

'*Shhh!* . . . I'll tell you later. Listen to this – I don't understand it. "Our occult philosophy teaches us that there are three kinds of 'doubles'. First, man has his 'double' or shadow around which the physical body of the fetus – the future man – is built. The imagination of the mother, or an accident which affects the child, will affect only the astral body." '

Her husky-voiced soliloquy together with the closeness of her body had him, she sensed, in a genital fugue, almost hypnotized.

'That's heavy, miss. I think . . .'

'My name is Elaine Bemar.'

'My name is –'

'*Shhhh!* . . .' she whispered softly, like a gentle night wind in summer.

April 21 *Pasadena*

Their first weekend together.

Her plan for stealing his soul was elementary. First, food. As 'Elaine Bemar', Helen made certain that their first few discussions of parapsychology took place over good restaurant food. 'No, order *that*. I have a research grant, remember, it's all expense account.'

Next, money. If the man she would call 'Saladin' could

devote the majority of his time to her and the experiments she would soon be telling him about, then she would request $500 from her institute for him as well as immediate expenses. Thus it was that 'Saladin' was able to buy $150 worth of new clothes at the Pasadena May Company store. With the clothes Helen was able to manipulate him into taking her to more expensive restaurants.

Building a cage of pleasure around him, she thought, before locking him away forever in a prison of pain.

So while he drove her newly rented convertible proudly, squiring her about in his new-found affluence, Helen cunningly forced him to rely on her totally for any actual cash. So that while the car and the clothes seemed to produce an almost manic pride of identity in his lonely, passionate nature, in reality, his dependence on the woman was, in this clandestine fashion, becoming more and more profound.

Their activities were all carefully organized by Helen around the simulated work of the research psychologist and her new apprentice. In the midst of these discussions of ESP and hypnotic states, only occasionally would Helen use an Arabic word or reference in order to stimulate the traditional feeling, *hadith*. But she would often say 'we' when indicating the Arabic point of view about, for instance, death, heaven, the soul. And when she would contrast the psychological world-view of time and space as between East and West, she ranged the *kismet* of herself, 'Saladin', and the East against the 'heartless materialism and alienation' of the West.

This preliminary regime of work was her strategy of setting her victim up for the sexual onslaught. (Helen refused, in her planning, to use any but the most brutal terminology to describe to herself the thing that she was preparing to do.)

They had the bridle path in South Pasadena to themselves for most of the early Sunday afternoon. She let him instruct her, all the while expressing admiration for his mastery. Today would begin the sexual downfall of the *ird* of this youth who now displayed a really touching eagerness to help, teach, protect, to function as a man to the womanly helplessness that she feigned so expertly.

She sat as cunning as a sphinx on the old gray gelding he had thoughtfully chosen for her. The day was smog-free, in the upper seventies. The smell and weight of the horses seemed to inspire the intense youth: His eyes shone, his skin glistened, he talked with a new animation as he circled her, guiding her, having to touch her hands and hips as she called out girlishly for his help.

About a mile out from the barn she begged for a rest. He helped her dismount, lifting her down by the thighs; she could feel his wiry fingers through her tight blue jeans. They stood patting their horses while he told her about his riding experiences and how he had injured his leg. She reached down to touch his lower thigh as if in the grip of a sudden sympathetic impulse: 'Does it still pain you?' He blushed when her horse defecated, but the rich odor, mingled by the hot sun with that of the horses' sweat, helped provide just the ambience of sensuality that she was striving to create.

Letting her horse free to browse, she led him to talk about the temperament of the big brown stallion that he had chosen. As he expounded on the equestrian arts, she began to touch and stroke the stallion's flanks. 'Tell me about the breeding farm where you worked.' Soon the stallion's thick-veined organ was jutting out, so heavy that it curved downward at an angle. In the hot noon glare 'Saladin' continued to chatter, pretending not to notice the horse's tumescence, but Helen could see that the crotch of her companion's worn jeans was bulging with his own erection,

That evening she treated him to a candlelit dinner in a small French restaurant ('Some night I am going to cook for you. Something special.') He could not keep his eyes from devouring her naked breasts, offered up to him through the gossamer folds of her East Indian blouse. Her make-up-free skin was flawless in the soft light, her eyes as liquid as his.

Their conversation ranged far beyond parapsychology this evening, into their strangely similar philosophies of life and love. Helen played on his impressions with deadly skill, always steering the subject matter away from the personal back into large, safe categories of general philosophical agreement. She touched him, taking his hand to read his palm, gaily toying with his hopes and fears, amazing him.

'Wow! Jesus, you know you really have a gift, Elaine, you're really *reading* me, you know!' So happy and enthralled, so vulnerable and alone.

I should kill myself while there is still time, she screamed silently to herself as she held out her slim, cold, tanned hand for him to read.

April 23　　　　*Pasadena*

On April 23, Helen, speaking in a monotone, summed up her methods and progress to Must as 'Food, money, sex.' He required a meeting with her, a 'treff', to use his term of art, every two days until she could report that the subject was ready. She felt, correctly, the short leash he was keeping her on. They walked slowly, unseeing, through a Picasso display at the Pasadena Art Institute. 'I can't guarantee a thing, you know.'

'No, but I can,' he half whispered, standing with his back to a reduced print of *Guernica*.

Helen stared over his head at the screaming striations of the mad, burning horses, seeing the story of 'Saladin' and herself embodied in the suffering of the terrified, dying nightmare horses.

'Why him?' The question was directed over Must's head. He gazed down at her full, arched neck, throat upturned as she stared at the Picasso above his heavy, short-cropped hair.

'Doctor, what if somebody asked me why *you* in particular? I've given you all the reasons you need to know. You know we can't use a professional to, ah, infiltrate a revolutionary organization – or any project of that magnitude.'

She thought, He's not even bothering to keep the cover stories straight any more. She could feel a trickle of perspiration running down her side. Her eyes sank slowly to his opaque dark glasses; she could picture the dead blue eyes sitting there behind the tinted lenses. She was sorry the moment that she answered him.

'Laboratory modification is one thing, but actual field control –'

'Controlling him won't be enough, Doctor. You've got

to give him *politics*: suicidal revolutionary politics – Black Panthers, Al Fatah – and get him into the sack.' He rammed it down her throat so that she now knew she was under surveillance, too.

He let her stand there powerlessly; then, with that uncanny killing instinct, he symbolically wiped her face in her own humiliation, just as he had threatened to actually do that first night in the bathroom.

'You'll be using a combination of what – pleasure and pain? Remember to minister to his politics, Doctor, and don't hesitate to innovate or, ah, improvise.'

He walked away without looking back, leaving her with a pitiful attempt at a dignified rejoinder on her lips: 'The scientific method is *not* incompatible with ingenuity . . .'

She looked up through her tears at the *Guernica*, at the awful and terrific horses of death and the twentieth century, praying, let him be kind enough to kill me soon, let him not be too cruel to kill me too. Almost saying the words out loud as she had every night until her mother's disappearance in 1947: 'God bless Poppy and –'

Her knees began to shake. The colors in the painting were beginning to glow and undulate, plastic and slimy, as if the paints were blood and body fluids. Her knees shook, because she recognized this kind of sensory delusion as an early warning of schizoid break, exacerbated by stress.

The museum guard trotted heavily toward the statuesque young woman sagging against the far wall.

April 25 *Claremont, California*

The House of Fun had stayed empty since closing in 1947, when the name had been 'The Soldiers' Club'. A dusty, cavernous old place where yellow-tasseled red silk scarves, 16 x 20, had proclaimed TO MOTHER, TO SWEETHEART, or any other relationship short of incest that could be sold for $1.50 to the dog-faced American soldiers of that period when they wandered into the club on payday to have a Coke and peanut-butter crackers and to write home to 'Sweetheart'.

Now the new management was catering to the students of the four-plus campuses of the Claremont College complex. Amateur talent and professional artists Thursday through Sunday. THIS WEEK ONLY – DR KNOW

– HYPNOTISM – NO COVER. 'Take him there,' Must told her.

Student waiters in red-striped shirts, white aprons, white saddle shoes, and straw boaters rustled pitchers of beer and large pizzas to the small opening-night crowd that had come to view Dr. Know. 'Let's celebrate,' Helen said, signaling for more beer. He ate his cheese pizza hungrily. This was the first night they had gone out together outside of Pasadena. He could feel her sending him some special exciting message. On the dance floor for the slow numbers only, Helen held herself against him lightly. In her woven sandals she was just slightly taller than he, so simply by arching her pelvis slightly she could brush subtly against his loins.

When Dr. Know demanded volunteers and foils for his 'amazing hypnotic powers,' she coaxed him, like a proud mother, to go up on the makeshift stage. The performer – a cadaverous-looking German who would be dead within the year by his own hand, according to the coroner – moved mechanically toward the finale of his first act.

While three Pitzer College students were ordered to simulate a game of hide-and-seek, the hypnotist stretched the Palestinian between two chairs. Helen, straining to see, concluded that the students were only pretending to be hypnotized, but that 'Saladin' was unmistakably under. Her subject shivered and trembled as the pasty-faced magician sat primly on his outstretched body.

Slowly the audience grew still, including the students faking their trances, waiting for the slim body to collapse. Minutes went by while the German continued to perch on the rigid form. Helen flinched at the sharp sound of one person applauding heavily. She snapped her head around to see William A. Must, Jr., standing at the beer and wine bar, stimulating the audience to general applause by the slow slapping together of his meaty hands. The hypnotist flashed a yellow-toothed death's-head smile and snapped his elongated nicotine-stained fingers in 'Saladin's' face, and the student orchestra struck up an unsteady climax cadenza. The risen sleeper picked his way through the tables, obviously pleased by the smiles and calls of appreciation and a second round of scattered hand clapping.

As they danced, Helen related the details of his triumph to him. Surreptitiously she searched the big, poorly lit hall for Must, but he was gone.

She had not replenished 'Saladin's' expense money, so now she slipped him bills under the table so that he could pay the check, and felt him stiffen slightly with embarrassed resentment. In the parking lot she said, 'You're higher than I am. Let me drive.' The warm air blew their hair about as she headed the convertible onto the San Bernardino Freeway. He seemed happy and relaxed; the evening had been the high point of their relationship, as she had intended. To blot out of her imagination what she had to do to him now, Helen switched on the radio. A newscast of a Robert Kennedy campaign speech filled the air with the familiar accents. She quickly adjusted the dial to a music station.

Near the Pomona city limits she turned the car off the freeway and headed for the neon sign that announced a vacancy at the Farm Hand Motel and Courts. She saw him watching her out of the corners of his big, shy eyes, trying to find appropriate words to say to her.

Inside the brightly lit motel office she covertly handed him more money to pay for their room. He seemed confused, his euphoria from the nightclub evaporating by the second; after an awkward pause, Helen signed the register, 'Mr. and Mrs. C. Rodriquez', and gave the prematurely bald nightman a reassuring smile.

Helen turned down the double bed inside the anonymous, impersonal unit. 'Saladin' had failed to close the bathroom door completely – he appeared to be drunk and somewhat disoriented – and she could hear him urinating. She sensed his fright at this first overtly intimate confrontation. He did not come out at once after flushing the toilet. From where she had positioned herself, she could see him standing motionless, looking at his face in the bathroom mirror. She watched as he made a clumsy attempt to imitate the German hypnotist by passing his hand in front of his face in the gratuitous gesture favored by third-rate practitioners. This pathetic little pantomime struck her as so poignant that she was forced to turn away.

As he emerged, she entered the bathroom wordlessly

and closed the door; they had not really spoken since she had parked the car. Inside, she methodically disrobed, hanging her dress over the shower frame. She washed, inserted her diaphragm, opened the door, and walked naked into the sleeping area.

He lay, sharp-shouldered, on the turned-down bed, with his back toward her, curled up in the fetal position. She paused to study his regular breathing. He was asleep, or pretending. Then, purposefully, feeling nothing but an inner coldness, she walked around to his side of the bed and snapped on the night-table light. His eyes opened and focused on the rich black hair that began where her legs came together and curled up in profusion to cover her mound of Venus. This dark forest was less than a foot from his face. She watched his eyes climb slowly up to the slight arc of her belly, past her navel, on to the full, rosy-pointed breasts, to rest, finally, on her expressionless face. She noted clinically that his huge eyes were filled not with desire but with a combination of hurt and fear.

Before he could move to turn out the light, she lay down beside him, blocking any escape. She continued to look at him with a friendly but detached gaze. After a minute she lifted one of his rigid hands and placed it on her breast. In her mind's eye she could see the patient at the Violence Center, strapped to the chair, being shown erotic pictures while at the same time receiving painful electric shocks.

Having placed his hand on her, she now lay feigning total passivity, staring at the ceiling. His fingers twitched involuntarily. Helen produced a high-pitched giggle as if he had tickled her, and turned on her side, away from him. She heard him slam his fist into the headboard. Again she pictured the patient in the experiment, slammed back by an electric jolt.

She turned back to reach up and pull him down beside her. Now, at last, she turned off the cruel bed lamp. He was sweating profusely, mumbling brokenly. 'Hell with it. Too drunk.' She stroked and kissed his bruised hand, covered them both with the cotton bedspread, and eased his head down to her breast. She could feel the hot tears that were running down the side of his nose as they fell onto her nipple. She cradled and rocked the thin, tense shoulders, and when at last she trusted herself to speak, the pity in her voice was as true as any she had ever felt. 'Poor little wanderer ... little wanderer ... poor little wanderer ...'

April 26 *Los Angeles*

Helen was aware at once of Must's sadistic irony by his choice of their meeting place: a diseased, ancient movie palace stuck in the rotting core of downtown L.A., featuring X-rated films. She stared without interest at the screen. The film, *Pornjoy*, was actually rather well done, a soft-core comedy about a male prostitute. So innocuous was the lighthearted effort that the theater was almost empty. She sat in the wine-fumed, semen-smelling old emporium, waiting for her case officer. Though the air was stale and heavy, she shivered at the thought of Must's brutal symmetrical face and blocky body. Feeling cold and thinking of Must, she thought, I hope the poet tells the truth that Divine Justice weighs the sins of the cold-blooded and of the warm-hearted on different scales. Someone snored loudly down front.

Must eased in softly beside her. They were alone in the back row. A few more lost men wandered in to escape the noon-hour heat and daily smog alert. Must dropped a key into her hand: 'For a locker at the Greyhound Station. The film and slides and other items you wanted, and some more money.'

Before he could rise to leave, she whispered, 'He is very restless. Meet me here again in two days and I will let you know if I think I can go on. No threats, please.' Somewhere in the hollow gloom some man hacked and spat into the darkness as the movie's antihero collapsed from overexertion.

'No sweat, Doctor. Just keep thinking of number one. Complete your contract or we have a little talk with your superior at the think-tank.' Must's consciously vulgar, gangster-movie diction and his breathy whispering began to undermine her cold armor. A fire engine wailed in the hot street outside.

'No threats. Stop terrorism – serve humanity ... protect your position ... save your father ... earn your money.' His slow whispering had dropped in volume, the obscene shopping list of her destruction on his dry pale lips competing with the harmless double meanings on the soundtrack of the pseudo pornography on the screen. Then, abruptly, he clasped her hand where it lay in her lap, as if they were adolescent lovers at a midnight show. She could smell the mint on his breath as he bent close, his hand light and cool on hers. 'It won't be long now, Helen. Trust us. We know what we're doing,' the voice husky, soothing. She closed her eyes but he kept on, seductive, pitiless.

The modifier modified. Her powers of reasoning, even of irony, continued to function, though his prehensile hand was like a deadly tarantula on her and the low, resonant glottal shocks of his voice were waves washing her will away.

'You know your Greek. Be wise. Remember Plato? "Behold men, as it were, in an underground cavelike dwelling, having its entrance open toward the light, which extends through the whole cave. Within it, persons who from childhood on have had chains on their legs and their necks; so they can look forward only, but not turn their heads around because of the chains, their light coming from a fire that burns above, far off and behind them." '

No whisper had ever seemed so obscene to her. It was as if he were programming her with the ancient poem.

' "And between the fire and those in chains is a road above, alongside which one may see a little wall built, just as the stages of magicians are built before the people in whose presence they show their tricks. . . . Think you that such as those who live in the cave would have seen anything else of themselves, or of one another, except the shadows that fall from the fire on the opposite side of the cave? And if the prison had an echo on its opposite side, when any person present were to speak, think you they would imagine anything else addressed to them except by the shadow before them? Such persons would deem truth to be nothing else but the shadows of exhibitions." ' His mint breath was in her nostrils.

Behind her fluttering eyelids the painted images of childhood danced, colors changing as the words played into her ear and sank down into her nervous system.

Outside, the sirens, the Friday traffic, and the smog were pressing down on the city like a plague.

The Palestinian had informed Helen at breakfast that morning that if they were not going to begin their work then he would have to start looking for another job, so she understood that tonight was the night, and so informed Must. Later, when she telephoned his house, she had told him that her assignment and his employment had been terminated. 'But don't be too depressed. I have something even better for us! You be here at eight sharp – *don't* eat first. I'll tell you all about it . . . No, I don't want to talk about it over the phone. But it's *good*. All right? All right. Good-bye.'

His eyes opened when he saw the baskets of flat discs of Palestinian *pita* bread. He laughed like a child when Helen tied the napkin around his neck, her fingers lingering for a a moment on the high, tense shoulders. She was literally hitting him where he lived with the food: *kubbe, foule, humus, shish kebab*. Beans and bread and lamb and sauce. His mouth was watering, his nose twitching; the ethnic aroma permeated the stage set of the trap. 'I've eaten. I am going to serve you.' The intensity and magnitude of her deception nauseated her, but she forced herself to drink wine. The fact that William A. Must might be monitoring this banal farce electronically did not inhibit her any more than an audience disturbs an accomplished actress.

Tonight the lights were low, as was the Arabic folk music Helen played on the handsome antique gramophone that had been chosen in order to reduce the alienation of the expensively furnished apartment. This was his first visit to 'her' apartment – purposely delayed, for once she brought him in, she knew, he would never leave a free person.

He gazed around at the Arabic objects and hangings, the shadows of the long room pierced by the rays of the full spring moon shining through the sliding-glass balcony door. After he had stuffed himself, she bathed his hands, rinsing them slowly in the warm water as he listened and looked. 'Some more wine, now, and a – "cigarette". We will talk later, yes?' He patted his stomach and smiled sweetly. He is starving, she thought, for food, love, life. She had never seen eyes so peaceful.

Her olive skin seemed to glow by contrast to the black cloth of her modified kaftan; the long gown modeled her body yet provided the reassuring traditional stimulus that she felt he needed. He had arrived in his old clothes, too proud to wear the new outfit she had purchased for him, wanting to earn his own money.

They reclined on the large stuffed floor pillows encrusted with sewn-on mirrorlike brilliants, drinking wine out of oversized goblets and smoking good marijuana cigarettes. They lay back, content to listen to the traditional music and watch the full moon move across the star-filled sky. The wine was almost gone before she reached for his hand. 'Friend,' she said, 'do you drop acid?' She crossed to the bar and held up a cube of sugar.

'LSD?' he questioned uncertainly.

She held a cube in each hand. One was plain sugar with nothing added; the one intended for her victim contained a powerful hypnotic phenothiazine drug laced with LSD-25.

'If you're afraid . . .'

'Let me see it!'

As Helen put the cube on his tongue she saw the little boy at the Violence Center, the doctor pushing the candy into his mouth, intoning '*Thaaat's* a good boy.'

By midnight he was staring at the moon, transfixed. Helen, behind him, turned the music up slightly, then began to unbutton his shirt. Crouching over and behind him, she began to massage his neck and shoulders. 'Listen . . . if we're going to be really close, we can't have any secrets . . .'

'Right.' The moon bathed his face and chest as her hands moved over his upper arms and neck.

'And I have secrets . . . But I want to tell them to someone . . .' Her hands kept him from turning back to face her. She massaged his temples, keeping his face upturned to the swimming moon.

'Tell me, Elaine.'

Her voice was a melodious croon rising and falling, merging with the repetitive melodic line of the Arabic music, the *naghamàt*. Her fingers brushed his skin like snowflakes.

'I know I can tell you, little friend . . . My father was Armenian. We lived there. The Turks came. They de stroyed our entire village. My people were massacred – men, women, little children. Can you understand?'

'I understand,' he murmured sweetly, his eyes moon-filled and unblinking. My poor lunatic, she thought, a spasm of self-loathing sending a shiver through her, but the hands never stopped moving on him.

'I knew you would. I . . . I don't think I could have told this to anyone but you . . . My mother . . . they raped her to death. My father and I stumbled from country to country, looking for a home. I was just a little girl, frightened to death, with no mother . . .' She bent lower, resting her head on his shoulder, her leg muscles cramping, whispering now in his right ear, beneath the ever-repeating *tiba* of the music. 'I . . . I don't know how to tell you . . .'

'I love you, Elaine . . . I love you . . . *Tell me.*' His voice was drawn down to the level of her resonant whisper. She paused, genuinely moved by his openness, waiting for another record to fall into place on the gramophone. Still touching him, then beginning again coeval with the solitary tones of the ancient folk music. As she delivered her speech in that disembodied musical whisper, she too stared into the pregnant mass of the moon. Breathing, sipping air like a consummate actress as she enmeshed him in the lies, afraid that if she stopped she might lose her powers of both reason and speech forever.

'At the end of the war we finally found a home in Palestine. A real home. For the first time, we were happy again. Then the Zionists came . . . My father died, fighting shoulder to shoulder with the freedom fighters. The people who had taken us in were slaughtered. We were driven out again. Even then I swore vengeance. Palestine had become my home – it is *still* my home.'

He was trembling with pity for her. She let him turn to face her at last, his eyes glowing as she whispered, 'Do you know what those Zionist criminals did to our people? *Our* people!' She could see the grief in his peaceful eyes blaze up in anger.

'I know – *I know!*'

She kneeled over him, gripping his thin arms. 'This is your story, too – *isn't it?* This is your secret? *This is what has made you sick?*' He was gasping air through his mouth. The music throbbed on in its timeless monologue. 'Fate, *kismet*, has brought us together to save our people. Do you understand what I'm telling you?'

'Yes,' he gasped pitifully.

She stood over him now, calling down to the trembling figure. 'To be a *real* man, you have to face your destiny. You can't hide behind mysticism and spirits. I am going to give you your chance to be a man, little one . . . Now I will tell you *my* secret. I am a Palestinian guerrilla fighter! I am acting under orders to help free our people. Do *you* dare to join us?' She pulled off her long fall. 'They shaved my head. I wear it this way as a symbol – look – so I can never forget!'

He was on his feet, reaching for her. Her body under the kaftan was open to him. His hips began to jerk automatically up against the heat from her thighs. She slipped smoothly to the record player to turn up the volume, with the other hand turning off the lamp that hung over it. The wash of moonlight was now the only illumination.

The voice of the Arab Folk singer, rising and falling, dominated the moon-filled room. She loosened the small frog fasteners on her gown, one at a time, from her throat to her navel, and stepped out of it, naked and dancing to the pounding pulse of the heavy rise and fall of the folk song.

She arched and rotated her pelvis, hips, belly. She unbuckled his worn leather belt, worked the zipper down over his swollen phallus. Then, dropping to her knees, still swaying to the pulse of the music, she untied and removed his shoes while he stood over her, staring wide-eyed and rapt into the face of the sinking moon.

She slipped his thin gabardine trousers and ragged undershorts down to his ankles. Her nails sank into his buttocks. He was immobile, trapped where he stood as if by chains, mesmerized, the sweat pouring down his brown, moon-glistening body. As the music pounded, not a muscle in his face registered as she enclosed his tumescent phallus deep within her mouth. Only the Adam's apple of his exposed throat rose convulsively as she slid her tongue and lips, wet and slow, back and forth over his proud and pulsing flesh. The moon ran down his body like melted butter.

Before he could come in her mouth, she drew him down beside her into the shadows of the huge, glittering pillows. He gasped as if he were dying. She took his hand and put it between her moist thighs, moving his fingers in and around slowly while she talked to him. 'Saladin ... Saladin ... yes ... you are like a *Saladin*. Do you remember Saladin?'

'Saladin ... yes ... defeated the Kings of Europe who invaded our homeland ...'

'Saladin was of low birth, but he became King of Egypt ... Oh, wait, Saladin, wait ... From Armenia he came to become our King ... to defeat the invaders of our homeland ...'

She could not hold him off much longer. She cupped her breasts, passing them around the outside of his lips, then letting him bite and suck the enlarged nipples, talking to him, rhythmically, insistently.

'I see the strength in you, little one. You must release that strength and become another Saladin ... Yes, now, you mount me. Here – slowly, slowly ... Yes, ride me, the way you ride your stallion ... slowly, slowly. You will not fall and hurt yourself in the fog again. I will hold you.'

Her long legs locked around his lower back with such force that a low cry was forced out of his open mouth. He arched up and back into the moon beam, her voice rising with him, over the music: 'That's it. Ride me. Ride me, Saladin! Ride me, Saladin! ... Swear you will help our people, that you will never betray us. Saladin, the mighty ... Saladin, the defender ... Saladin, the invincible ... Saladin, beloved of God and his people ... Release it – release it. *Saladin!*'

He lost consciousness, crying out one final strangulated '*Yes!*' as he fell from his arched stallion height sideways into the pillows. He never heard her moaning up at the moon like a mad animal.

April 28 *Long Island, New York*

Paul Woods did not look like a mourner, striding through the maze of gravestones, monuments, and mausoleums of the vast crazy-quilt of the Long Island cemetery. Woods wore a beige rain hat and coat against the fine warm drizzle that had been coming down since early morning.

The supple, muscular figure paused next to a hulking family vault (THOMAS O. WINFIELD FAMILY) and checked his watch.

'Over here.' Bill Thurman stepped around from the side of the Washburn monument. In his dingy, cheap raincoat, beneath which Woods could identify a ten-year-old suit and tie, Thurman looked every inch the fifteen-year FBI veteran that he was. 'Top dressers,' as Hoover always called his G-men.

'Got something.' Woods shook hands, speaking abruptly, without preamble. They walked slowly along the deserted rows of grave markers, which stretched as far as the eye could see.

'So do I,' mumbled Thurman. 'Oswald –'

'Lee Harvey Oswald?'

'Yeah. He was an informant for the Bureau. Two-hundred-a-month punk. Number S-172.'

'No shit.'

'Yeah. That and a dime'll get you –'

'Look, Thurman, I'll take anything you get . . . I went to see Garrison.'

'What did you get?' Thurman muttered, disappearing for a moment behind the Halz monument, Angel of Death regnant.

'Garrison talks kind of funny, but he gave me something. It might be a dead end.' Thurman studied the sky for more rain. Woods looked down at the passing grave markers, talking low. 'Maybe a safe house or a listening post. Not the big boys, but something. You'll have to do a bag job and plant a bug.' He handed the FBI man the Garrison folder.

CD 631

Attachment A

Out Message No. 74673, dated 10 October 1963 and filed at 0800 hours, to Department of State, Federal Bureau of Investigation, Department of the Navy.

Subject: Lee Henry OSWALD

1. On 1 October 1963 a reliable and sensitive source in Mexico reported that an American male, who identified himself as Lee OSWALD, contacted the Soviet Embassy in Mexico City inquiring whether the Embassy had received any news concerning a telegram which had been sent to Washington. The American was described as approximately 35 years old, with an athletic build, about six feet tall, with a receding hairline. . . .

CENTRAL INTELLIGENCE AGENCY
WASHINGTON, D.C. 20505
24 MAR 1964

Commission No. 631

MEMORANDUM FOR: Mr. J. Lee Rankin

SUBJECT: CIA Dissemination of Information on Lee Harvey OSWALD, dated 10 October 1963

1. Reference is made to paragraph three of your letter, dated 16 March 1964. You requested that the Commission be furnished a copy of the dissemination on Lee Harvey OSWALD made to several Government agencies by CIA on 10 October 1963.

2. An exact copy of this dissemination (Out Message No. 74673) by teletype, is attached. It was transmitted to the Department of State, Federal Bureau of Investigation and Department of the Navy. A copy was concurrently made available by hand to the Immigration and Naturalization Service.

3. Please note that OSWALD's middle name was erroneously given as 'Henry' in the subject line and in paragraph two of the dissemination. (The same error occurs in the message to the Navy discussed in paragraph four, below.) The maiden surname of Mrs. OSWALD was mistakenly listed as 'PUSAKOVA'.

4. On 23 October (the correct date), a teletyped message (Out No. 77978) was sent to the Department of the Navy referring to Out No. 74673, and requesting that the Navy furnish CIA as soon as possible two copies of the most recent photograph of OSWALD that was available, for use in checking the identity of the Lee OSWALD in Mexico City. These photographs had not been supplied to this Agency by 22 November 1963. Our conclusion that the photograph did not refer to OSWALD was based on press photos generally available on 23 November 1963.

Here is 'mystery man' (Commission Exhibit 237, Warren Report) and perjury 'disinformation' from CIA.

Thurman looked closely at the man in the photo.

Then follows documents from same source (classified, suppressed) leaked to me that prove that someone else (the man in the photo) was posing as LEE HARVEY OSWALD.

'Mystery Man' or second Oswald may have used the name MIST or MUST during this period.

Thurman squinted at the rest of the unorthodox report – a tangle of CIA bureaucratic double-talk and paranoiac security classifications – and continued to read. Woods stared off into the army of tombstones. The drizzle was slacking off.

The grim-faced FBI operative muttered a curse as he scanned the last page. A gust of wind seemed to drive the misty drizzle down the collar of his worn raincoat.

'The guy you're looking for is this Mist or Must? And you've got an address for him? Government building?' Thurman closed the manila folder.

'A hotel in Washington,' Woods answered, taking back the folder, 'maybe the boys behind that super bug you found in Michigan – the day we first met.'

'Who?'

'The suite is one of four, rented by a corporation. People from out of town come in and out all year.'

The businesslike rendition came to an end. They stopped.

'That it?' Thurman scanned the horizon. Woods stood in profile looking at him.

'That's it. How soon can you move on it?'

'These things take time.'

Woods kicked at the soft thin grass of the path. 'I haven't got any time!'

The sharp, pinched face of the smaller man collapsed slightly, and he chuckled dryly. 'Tell it to all *these* good folks,' Thurman said, removing a hand from his raincoat pocket to gesture at the stones with the names of the dead, starting with the small half-covered marble slabs almost under their feet that hemmed them in as they stood in the spring drizzle. Woods followed the gesture, his eyes roaming out over the labyrinthine and unending graveyard.

'The dead?' He paused and breathed deeply. 'My mother used to have an old saying – "Pray for the dead, but fight like hell for the living." ' He bent down and placed a pebble on an overgrown headstone at his feet. 'Get me some more on Oswald. Documents.'

Thurman gave Paul one of those Richard Widmark rat smiles. Then they shook hands and went their separate ways, each disappearing into the forest of marble.

April 28 *Los Angeles*

'Saladin's' feet dragged as he followed Helen down the night-lit corridors of the Violence Center.

She had not left his side for twenty-four hours, maintaining his drugged state with a flow of strong marijuana. She had talked to him about his new obligations to the liberation struggle; then, when he closed his eyes to sleep, through her technical ingenuity brought him to sexual climax again and again, always simulating her own orgasm and expressing astonishment at his sexual powers. Then back to talking to him, always stressing that when he was 'ready' he would be permitted to meet face to face with the underground leadership of Al Fatah based in Canada. She swore to him that they would go north together for the meeting, and from there directly to the Holy Land, where he would be greeted as a hero. All this while avoiding any specific description of what his actual heroic feats in the United States would be, just that 'We must train, ideologically and militarily, beginning tomorrow night. We have only a few days.'

The clock on the corridor wall read exactly 1 a.m. as she unlocked the door and led him into a stark white soundproofed audiovisual room, equipped with only two white chairs. The bare white wall of the ten-by-ten unit served as a screen for the projector enclosed in glass high up on the rear wall. Helen was attired for work in a blue-jeans slack suit, glasses, and no fall over the short boylike haircut. The room's only illumination was a covered twenty-five-watt red bulb next to the door, near the floor. Her subject sat passively in the dim red light, waiting.

She flicked the start button for the preprogrammed projector. The preliminary montage of horses racing in slow motion began. Within thirty seconds Rorschach patterns started to interrupt subliminally. 'Saladin,' she spoke softly in his ear.

All of the film pieces that Must had given her had been spliced according to her directions; the film was without sound. The hypnotic slow-motion horses gave way now to other images. The logic of the program that Helen had planned for him was extremely simple: suffering overcome by violence. First the camera's documentary eye roved through the desolation of mass squalor and suffering that is the Palestinian refugee camps: babies and young children, staring, with flies crawling over their faces; old people unable to walk; adolescents rotting with boredom and alienation. While the screen flickered with the story of the deracinated and dispossessed Palestinians, Helen continued to speak softly, interjecting Arabic words and idioms.

'After a few steps in the darkness, you will find comrades gathered around the fire . . . The shadows of violence have fallen on our brothers and sisters . . . our mothers and sweethearts . . . The murderers of our people are at large . . . They prowl among us like the creatures of the night.'

As the scenes shifted to newsreel footage of world starvation, he began to shiver slightly, a sure sign to Helen that he was completely under her suggestion. Now the blasted landscape of Indochina rose up before him. Starving dogs, beggars, and everywhere children in the streets of Saigon; the countryside of Vietnam, Cambodia, Laos, awash with uprooted populations; hideous napalm victims; despoiled forests and vegetation. He was sweating now as the doomsday machine unraveled its increments of torture. She loosened and slipped his shirt over his shoulders and off.

Slowly the iron logic of the film's dialectic established the author and origin of this systematic sadism and torture of the poor: the West. Old, yellowed frames of the British whipping black rebels in Kenyan concentration camps, Belgian and Portuguese beheadings and atrocities across Africa, and then, again, sequences of the Palestinian humiliation. Everywhere the pale, deadly North Americans: Latin America, the Mid-East, Asia – shocking pictures, terrible pictures of castration and disemboweling of alleged Vietcong. Vietnamese mothers and infants being burned alive while American GIs laughed.

She let herself become narcotized by the propaganda. Propaganda, she was well aware, because the desperation of the Palestinian masses was not equated on film with the Jewish holocaust of World War II and the surviving remnant that had settled Israel. And among the cruel tableaux of the super-rich rolling in a riot of abundance she had instructed Must not to include any footage of Arab sheiks on the Riviera throwing a million pounds away at roulette while at home the *fellahin* ate camel dung and sold their children into slavery. It was as if she had sucked the blood out of the world since 1950 to inject it now into the trembling Palestinian's nervous system.

He was panting, twitching with increasing agitation as the montage of terror and pity spun on. The second half of the twentieth century flowed inexorably, remorselessly, on a beam of light into his huge, black, staring eyes.

The cruelty reached its zenith, and just as Helen feared that he could stand no more, the god from the machine appeared: *Revolution!* Fidel, Che, Mao, Ho, Al Fatah, the Black Panthers – Algeria, China, North Korea, Egypt – scenes of revolutionary violence and victory. Helen gripped his shoulders as he responded to the new stimuli of victory, her voice rising:

'And friends *have* gathered by the fire. Men of tomorrow; men of vision and strength; the lions of the East; the lions of the people. To you *only* do they dare to speak. Turn and turn about, in these shadows from whence a new dawn will come . . . Make no mistake about it – by your mad fury, by your bitterness and spleen, by the permanent tensing of your powerful muscles, which are afraid to relax, you have become a *man*. We are living at the moment when the match is put to the fuse . . . it is the moment of the boomerang. It is the third phase of violence. *It comes back on them – it strikes them!* The "liberals" are *stupefied*.'

As she spoke the screen began to reflect footage of the richest people in the world: on yachts, in casinos, at palaces. The ruling elite of the tortured planet laughed, ate, drank, flirted, danced. She could feel his muscles tensing. Helen went to the whip now:

'They admit they were not "polite" enough to the "natives" ... they have to *answer* to our people. They must *die*. You are killing two birds with one stone. You are destroying our oppressor and yourself *at the same time* ...' She backed away from his chair, her voice lashing him – and herself as well – pulled a small pistol filled with blanks from her attaché case, and forced it into his trembling right hand.

Images of disgusting elitist excesses intercut evenly with images of the suffering Palestinians, and 'Saladin' was up and moving. The chair was overturned; he crouched and swayed as scenes of revolutionary counter-attack and rebellion flickered into the screen's dialectic. Then, dodging and running, he was firing the gun at the screen as she cursed, '*When they die, the slave in you dies at the same instant!*'

The film was pumping up target after selected target for him: generals, secret police, Zionists, plutocrats. Then, without warning, the smiling face of Robert Francis Kennedy filled the screen and froze there.

He hesitated, dropped his arm, turned in confusion toward Helen. 'I can't, I can't, I can't, I can't ...' He panted like an animal. Her bitter cry rode over his gasping: '*Saladin!* Child of death! Child of violence! They have sown the wind – *we will reap the whirlwind!*'

Standing frozen as if in tableau, she saw with horror that the static and smiling image of Robert Kennedy still coming from the projector was shining, playing on his naked torso. The shivering youth was dripping with sweat, and superimposed over his panting chest and haunted thin face was the full-color Kennedy image. The projector's beam blinded him, held him rooted there until with a pitiful cry of '*Can't*' he stumbled forward to collapse at her feet. She kneeled to touch the alternately burning and freezing shoulders.

'They were men at our expense – now make yourself a man at *theirs*. A *new* man – a superman! Think,

Saladin!' she shrieked at him. 'This man will be the leader of the Western world, the *symbol* of our torture, the *symbol* of Zionist power, *the symbol that must be smashed!*'

He clawed up her body in a paroxysm of torment, screaming in Arabic and English. He clenched the gun with both hands and whirled, firing blanks at the eternally smiling face on the screen. As he fired they both shrieked into the deafening *cracks* of the sound chamber the cubicle had become. Helen's screams were her first opportunity in days to ventilate the madness of her secret agenda and possession by evil; as he fired, she screamed like a madwoman.

He was spent. The pistol dropped at her feet; she sank to the floor with him, crouching over her creature. She held him across her lap in a grostesque Pietà, and spoke with the voice of a mother to her dying son:

'Violence is your therapy, Saladin. Violence can purge us, make us clean. Cure us, Saladin. The humiliation and impotence are nearly over, Saladin.'

She unbuttoned her blouse and held his head up to take her breast. She let him suck for a moment, then gently lifted his head to her eye level. On the screen the magical image continued to glow.

'You will kill when and where and *who* I say. Do you understand?'

'Yes.'

'What is the signal that only I can give you?'

'You will call me by my true name – Saladin.'

'And when you wake, what will you remember?'

'Nothing.'

'And if we should have to die?'

'We die together.'

'And if you are captured?'

'I will remember nothing until you come to me with the name – Saladin.'

An acrid smell of powder filled the room. She went to her shoulder bag, then helped him to right the chair and sit, before placing a blank diary and pen on his knees. He moaned when she said, 'I may die and you may live . . .' She opened the book and uncapped the ballpoint pen. 'You have to be able to go on without me, Saladin. Maybe they will kill me – the *liberals.*' She placed the pen in his right hand. 'RFK,' she whispered.

'RFK,' he repeated dryly and automatically.

'RFK must die . . .'

'RFK . . .'

'RFK must die. RFK must die.'

'RFK must die.'

'RFK must die. RFK must die. RFK must die . . .'

She guided his hand. They were chanting now. 'RFK must die . . . RFK must die . . .' The pen scrawled unsteadily across the white page. Their voices rose as if joined in a diabolical prayer to the god of death.

'RFK must die . . . RFK must die . . . RFK must die . . . RFK must die . . . *RFK must die!*'

May 7 *Indianapolis*

The small, crowded ballroom at RFK headquarters was being led in song by four young women wearing the symbolic Kennedy straw hats.

> This man is your man.
> This man is my man.
> From California
> To the New York Island
> From the redwood forest
> To the Gulf Stream waters . . .

At first Judith Shankland refused to believe Paul Woods when he informed her that the composer of the original 'This Land Is Your Land, This Land Is My Land,' the great folk singer Woodie Guthrie, had been blacklisted in the 1950s. 'Arlo Guthrie's father? I don't believe it.' Their debate was interrupted by the telecaster's voice over the PA.

> There is no question now. Senator Robert F. Kennedy has won his first primary here in the State of Indiana . . .

In mid-sentence Paul and Judith embraced and kissed as the crowd cheered the news. The Kennedy Girls ran to the middle of the room, followed by the television crews. Joined by a young man with a guitar, they began their satiric takeoff on 'The Wabash Cannonball' that so delighted the younger Kennedy staffers. Woods and Judith joined in, laughing as they saw several senior aides, including Henry Lord and John O. Lake, frown and turn away toward the bar. Soon the whole assembly was singing or humming along.

Oh listen to the speeches that baffle, beef and bore.
As he waffles through the woodlands, and slides along
the shore.
He's the politician who's touched by one and all.
He's the demon driver of the Ruthless Cannonball.

He came down to Logansport one sunny April day,
As he pulled on through the depot you could hear those
Hoosiers say,
He's the heir apparent, full of chutzpah, full of gall.
I'll bet he wants our helpin' hand on the Ruthless
Cannonball . . .

His Eastern states are dandy, so all the people say,
From Boston to Virginny, and New York by the way,
The blacks in Gary love him, the Poles will fill his
hall . . .

Paul and Judith shouted out the finale and collapsed in each other's arms.

There are no ethnic problems on the Ruthless
Cannonball.

It was after 3 a.m. when the Kennedy staff finally left the ballroom for their hotel. They spilled out into the quiet street, the Kennedy Girls still humming and animated. Paul and Judith had just turned to tell Henry Lord and John Lake that they were going to look for a coffee shop when Woods saw the car. The smile froze on his face. 'Wait here,' he breathed to Judith.

Woods walked rapidly, then ran toward the parked blue Mustang. Suddenly the automobile with an Oregon license plate spun out and roared past them, down the street and around a corner.

'Paul – Paul, wait!' Henry Lord, the senior aide, called

after him. Woods was racing; the powerful former All-American halfback shot past the silent knot of Kennedy aides. 'Paul, come back here!' He stopped, the diminishing roar of the invisible vehicle fading in the dark silence. The sound of their shoes on the sidewalk sounded unnaturally loud as they hurried up to him where he stood, his body riveted with conflicting impulses.

'Paul, you've got to stop this. You're making everyone nervous. The Senator's got enough to –'

'Look, Henry, that car has been on our tail for two weeks now. I've asked you –'

Woods's voice was low and contained, but it escalated sharply when one of the men in charge of security, John O. 'Red' Lake, interrupted.

'Look, Paul, we've traced down three suspicious vehicles for you – zero. Nothing. You tear apart phones in hotel rooms . . . We *have* a security force. If you want to protect the Senator, stay close to him. *We have a security force!*'

'We do? You guys aren't even armed! We don't even *have* any good ol' Secret Service boys. At least Jack Kennedy had some good ol' –'

'No,' snarled Lake, 'no good ol' SS boys and no pack of whores following them –'

'Why, you honky punk –'

Henry Lord was a distinguished-looking New England aristocrat, and there was no mistaking the authority in his voice as he stepped between Lake and Woods, whose voice had taken on a savage rising edge. Judith was gripping Paul's arm as Lord spoke.

'Oh, for Christ's *sake*, Paul, come off it! This conspiracy business is absolute rubbish! Stick to public relations. Stop playing gumshoe – and that's an order!'

They all watched Woods in the tense silence, the mood of victory turned sour and ominous. Lake, a big redhead, was flushed with fury. Paul shook Judith's hand off his arm and stalked away. She caught up with him. The others stood where he had left them, staring at the retreating figures. When they had turned the corner she ventured a question: 'Paul, do you really believe in . . . do you really think there's anything *to* this?'

He stopped and looked down at her. There appeared, then, an expression in his eyes that made her want to weep.

'Then what's the use?' she pleaded. 'I mean, if they're everywhere, then it's hopeless, then we're living in a madhouse and we might as well kill ourselves before "they" get us.' Her eyes were clouded over, and she stood as vulnerable as a child before him.

'No.' He rested his strong hands on her shoulders; she searched for his eyes in the darkness. He breathed deeply, calming down. 'Judith, I'm going to tell you something . . . I *know* how you feel. It's what I thought at first. "What can one individual, with no official power, do against a massive conspiracy that extends into every nook and cranny of the system?" ' She took one of his hands and touched the pink scar tissue that traced the old clete marks. 'But that's a false question. These crackpots call what they do "intelligence", but it's the opposite of real intelligence – it's just crackpot scenarios. The CIA calls its Clandestine Section "Plans", but they *don't* plan, they just organize violence to play God with nations and people – it's the opposite of planning.' She shook her head, trying to understand the rush of words. His voice was the only sound in the dark, deserted street.

'That's why they bungled in Cuba, in Vietnam – and in Dallas.'

'Dallas?'

'Yes. Left a trail a mile wide, but everybody with any power was either paralyzed with fear or . . . like those people back there that are supposed to protect Bobby were just now . . . like *you* are now . . .'

She kissed his hand softly. 'Go on, Paul, go on, love,' she said.

'These are not supermen, baby. These people are sick, twisted psychopaths. *But* they are ruthless and very violent, and they count on our passivity and fear, that's all. The media knows, everybody knows, but the Establishment believes that if the *people* knew there would be complete anarchy, they believe they know what's best for *us*. But the people *do* know, know it all, that's the pity. And a handful of gangsters, Ivy League or otherwise, in or out of the CIA, haven't got a chance against the genius of an aroused public.

'They can be stopped and caught because they are stupid and so arrogant that they leave clues around like turds –'

She laughed, her fear gone for the moment. 'The people?' They stood there hugging in the chill.

'Yes. It doesn't *matter* about how violent they are. Whether it's Cuba, or Vietnam or the good old U.S. and A. They always forget that people, ordinary *people*, can see through all the propaganda and dirty tricks when they get up the nerve to open their eyes and see these rotten sons of bitches for what they are. Let them conspire, people can *plan*; let them try to play God with their weird manipulation, *people* can imagine a human future. We can demythologize this super-spook scum. I believe that, I believe that Bobby believes it – no matter what the senior aides do or don't do – otherwise why in the hell would he have hired a nut like me?'

'Ordinary people, you say?'

'That's right, lady.'

'You didn't know you were a revolutionary, did you, Paul?'

May 10　　　　*Washington, D.C.*

Leroy Anderson's 'Sleighride' played on the Muzak as William Thurman, Jr., stood outside William Must's Watergate apartment door, listening. Next, Thurman stepped to the elevator and punched both the UP and DOWN buttons, then quickly tried three lockpicks in Must's door. The third instrument turned over the lock. Thurman, wearing skin-tight rubber gloves and coveralls, pushed his small toolkit through the open door. The entire operation had not taken more than fifteen seconds.

At the street level, the officer of the day sat in the security office reading *Argosy* magazine. Suddenly a light on a large panel began to flash. The middle-aged guard reacted quickly, opening his coded guest directory and reaching for the telephone simultaneously.

'Yes . . . Officer? I want to report a burglary in progress. Watergate Hotel. Suite 53D. No, I don't know how many . . . I'm night security . . . we've got an access-activation signal system here. My name is Richard Salvatore. Sure, I'll meet your men at the front door . . .'

One of the special agents who had picked him up at the D.C. jail made the obligatory crack – 'Give your soul to

God, Bill, because your ass belongs to the Director' – as they sat in the outer office waiting for Ralph 'Scotty' Scott, Thurman's superior, to arrive.

At 9 a.m. precisely, Scott walked through, gesturing for Thurman to follow him into the office. Scott sat, Thurman stood. Scott looked balefully at the wrinkled coveralls, so out of place in these immaculate offices of thin-tied men. From across the street the jackhammers pounded; the mammoth new J. Edgar Hoover FBI complex was rising.

'Now, I want you to tell me again.' He scowled. 'I could play the tape you gave Internal Affairs, but I wouldn't believe a machine.'

Thurman's voice sounded worn out from his ordeal. 'I told them. I got this call about a – conspiracy to kill a government official.'

Scott grimaced. 'And you don't know who the "official" is? Or who the apartment belongs to?' Thurman nodded hopelessly. "Incredible! And the tipster was an "anonymous informant"?'

'Uh huh.'

Scott touched his neat-gray hair with the rigid palm of his hand, then balled the hand into a fist. 'So you violate rules by the numbers, because of an anonymous phone call!'

'Christ, Ralph, the informant said they were planning a killing for today . . . I had to act on my own initiative.'

'Initiative my ass! Bill, we're going to check out everything you're saying.'

Scott's tone was low and pained as he stared at Thurman's slumped figure from behind the orderly desk, the family photographs, the miniature flag.

'You had a career going straight up in the Bureau, Bill. I don't mind telling you the Director had his eye on you. But I'm not going to tell him. I'm the godfather of your children, for Christ's sake. But I'll tell you one thing – you're going to the boondocks. You're going to sit through boring, endless, I mean *boring*, political meetings. You're going to rallies and marches – and your reports will be *ten times* as long as any of those marches. And maybe in ten *years* the Director will be dead, and if you haven't stolen any hubcaps we'll forget about this little escapade.'

Silence. Thurman stared at the green rug. The older man's face reddened.

'I'm sorry, Bill, but you'll have to leave for California immediately. Joann and the kids can follow later ... maybe when school's out ...'

'Jesus, Ralph, can't I –'

'That's it, Bill. San Berdoo, California ... Better take an oxygen mask.'

May 14 *Omaha, Nebraska*

Judith Shankland stood on the edge of the small street-corner gathering waiting patiently for the candidate. There were no jumpers or screamers here. A few people held ALL THE WAY WITH RFK signs. The weather was more like March than May.

She could hardly believe the polls that showed the Candidate claiming over 50 percent of the vote against both McCarthy and Humphrey. Nebraska was a farm state; only 2 percent of the population were black. And there had been many ugly signs: WE WANT A MAN NOT A NAME; DID 20,000 AMERICANS DIE FOR A COALITION IN VIETNAM?; WHO KILLED YOUR BROTHER?

She did not know that the angry farmers would vote along with the bluecollars for RFK – because they perceived the Kennedy brother as a rebel launching a kind of uprising against the monster of the Eastern Establishment that they so distrusted and hated. They had even laughed the day that a slip of paper blew off the Candidate's podium at an outdoor farm rally and he smiled infectiously, saying, 'Give me that back quickly, That's my farm program. I need it.' Somewhere a horn was tooting now, and the knot of people on the corner looked up hopefully.

She watched with frustration and concern as Paul Woods prowled around the periphery of the all-white spectators like a black panther.

May 14 *Pasadena*

'Saladin' stared at the pattern of sunbeams on the cream-colored ceiling. They were lying under a sheet on Helen's bed. The sound of bird song floated in on the warm breeze. Under the sheet, Helen's hand massaged his limp phallus.

The sun patterns on the ceiling rippled and flowed as the air rustled the curtains slightly. Her voice was light, too.

'Do you know that the Prophet had an empty tomb built in Mecca? It is still there.'

'You mean, besides his own?'

'Yes. He built it for Jesus. It is waiting for Jesus. He recognized Jesus as a prophet. A peer.'

'I didn't know that.'

'He would not recognize Buddha, because Buddha was born a prince. Mohammed and Jesus were commoners . . . they were willing to die for the people. If something goes wrong, *you* may have to die, Saladin.'

'I'm ready.'

'I know you are. I can tell.'

She could feel him rising under her long, supple fingers. The curtains rustled, and the ceiling was alive with strange, shifting shapes.

May 14 *Omaha*

Judith helped Paul feed a bag of peanuts to an arthritic brown squirrel. She had made him come with her to a park, to get away from the pressure of the campaign 'just for an hour.'

They had not made love in days, had hardly talked. He was drawn and taut; she felt completely powerless. 'Paul, what's happening to this country?' The question sounded stilted and pretentious to her, but his eyes were not judgmental. He kept tossing nuts to the squirrel as he talked.

'You study about the Gracci? Brothers in ancient Rome, supported by the, you know, the publicans, "the people." Well, they killed the Gracci brothers one by one.' The squirrel begged.

'The people killed them?' She felt good when he chuckled.

'No, lady, the *people* didn't kill them. The fat cats did it. You know – "they".' His face was somber again.

'Look, Paul, that squirrel's limping. Can't I help you? I know you're involved in some private plan to protect –'

'My one solid contact, and he's left town.'

'Who? The FBI man you said was helping you? I can't believe the FBI can't find one of their agents.'

'Oh, they know where he is, all right. They're just not saying.'

'What are you – we going to do?'

A fat boy of about six ran down from the low rise behind their bench. The squirrel staggered away to hide behind a tree. 'He ran away,' the boy said.

'Don't worry.' Paul smiled gently. "There'll be another one along soon.' He handed the boy the bag of peanuts with a look that said, These are for the squirrels.

'I love you very much,' she said to him as they climbed the grassy incline.

May 19 *Los Angeles*

'Mr. Heston? I'm sorry to call you on a Sunday. My name is Paul Woods. I'm calling you from the Robert F. Kennedy for President headquarters here in Los Angeles.' He slipped his blue-hosed foot out of his loafer and began to rub Judith's leg.

The campaign strategy of big crowds and primary blitzes seemed to be working, but California would be *it*, Paul kept reminding her. So they needed the movie stars who had not already joined the McCarthy campaign, the glamorous trappings of irresistible success. Judith told Paul that she despised the narcissism of the Beverly Hills world, and the studio executives whose big-money contributions they were courting: 'They're gangsters!'

'Yes, I believe Tiny Tim is supporting Senator McCarthy. Ah, ha, ha, that's very true . . . Well, here's our list so far, Mr. Heston:

'Lauren Bacall, Warren Beatty, Marlon Brando, Geraldine Brooks, Carol Channing, Bill Cosby, Tony Curtis, Bobby Darin, Bette Davis, Sammy Davis, Angie Dickinson, Patty Duke, Eddie Fisher, Henry Fonda, Aretha Franklin, Ben Gazzara, Mahalia Jackson, Jefferson Airplane, Gene Kelly, Alan King, Peter Lawford, Janet Leigh, Jack Lemmon, Alan Jay Lerner, Trini Lopez, Shirley MacLaine, Rod McKuen, Henry Mancini, Kim Novak, Jack Paar, Gregory Peck, Sidney Poitier, Andre Previn, Ned Rorem, Diana Ross and the Supremes, Dan Rowan and Dick Martin, Sonny and Cher, Maureen Stapleton, Rod Steiger, Barbra Streisand, Andy Williams, Shelley Winters.

'Yes, sir. I hope to hear from you . . . Bullshit!' slamming the receiver down and tossing the list into a drawer.

'Another ego trip?' Judith asked, setting down coffee. 'Can we get out of here for lunch?' Before he could answer, his extension buzzed again.

'All the way with RFK!'

'May I speak to Mr. Paul Woods?'

'Speaking.'

'Hello, brother. This is Osgood. I been leavin' messages for you. Look here, I don't want to talk over the phone, you know, but I got something very important to tell you. Meet me in an hour.'

'Wait a minute. *Who* is this?'

'Look here, your little old Bobby boy is a dead motherfucker if you don't stop some madmen that done put out a contract on him.' The hustler's rap ran on. 'Meet me at the zoo in an hour.' Woods started to ask how he would know him. 'You'll recognize me – I'll be the nigger in the red hat in front of the gorilla cage.'

Paul had held the receiver away from his ear so that Judith could hear Osgood's raucous fast talking. He touched her hair and ears with tenderness when she insisted on driving him to the assignation and surveying the area against entrapment. 'I'm not paranoid,' she said, 'I just can't afford to lose you after having invested so much.' He kissed the crooked smile.

Woods saw the man in the red wool golf cap as soon as he turned into the path leading to the apes. He took in the apparition of the lanky, kinetic figure talking and gesticulating with animation toward the huge silver-haired male gorilla just fifteen yards away on the other side of the moat; the great ape was moodily chewing bubble gum, and actually blowing a big pink bubble from time to time. The gorilla stared flatly at them, the little eyes focused and concentrated, not reflecting like the big cats', but sparkling with ratiocination. As if the ape had tipped him a wink, Osgood whirled to greet Woods.

'My man!' Woods ignored the palms-up 'gimme five' hand. 'Come on, brother, what it is?' Osgood purred, keeping the down-slanted open palm outstretched. Woods put a $100 bill in it. 'Right on,' Osgood burbuled, and without taking a breath launched into his street saga.

'You know Big Vito Donocchi from New Orleans, don't you? Okay. Now I'm gonna tell you, that's my contact. I was workin' undercover for the LAPD in New Orleans.'

Osgood watched Woods's eyes as he talked, waiting for comprehension to register.

'Okay, now, the Mafia and the CIA work tight together, right? Okay. So now there's –'

'What the hell are you talking about?'

'You're not listening, brother. Now there's this house nigger – calls himself "Gibson" – contacted me in New Orleans, tells me there's a Muslim contract out on Bobby K. and do I want a piece of it – a ten-grand piece, you see? Now this "Gibson" ain't no Muslim. I had some of my people follow the cat, and guess where he goes.'

'Big Vito?'

'Right on! Then, after that, he leaves Vito and goes into the International Pavilion! You dig that?'

'No . . .'

'Man, you're too much. The New Orleans International —'

'Oh, the Pavilion. Yeah, CIA.'

'*Now* you see where I'm coming from. So I played along with this punk, "Gibson", then I crossed him so beautiful it was pathetic, and now I'm givin' it all up to you.'

'But you don't have any contact or leads right *now*, right *here* in –'

'California? That's what I'm trying to lay *on* you, man. They told me the hit was gonna be *this* month, in L.A. or San Diego. They got *beaucoup* Dagos and hit men ready to go in San Diego, at a country club – La Castro, something like that . . .'

'No date? No exact place? Where's this "Gibson"?'

'He's long gone. That's it, brother. I'm clearin' out of the country. Word's out on the street they got a contract on me too! But it'll be a cold day in hell 'fore they catch up with ol' Osgood!'

Osgood fingered Woods's jacket pocket for a cigarette. Woods had an expression on his face that told the man that he had given at least $100 dollars' worth of satisfaction. The two black men leaned on the chain-link security fence, shoulder to shoulder, smoking. Osgood spoke reflectively, tired now from his performance.

'Gonna tell you one thing, sure: They ain't gonna set up no dumb Texas dude for a trigger man this time.'

They smoked quietly as the afternoon passed on and the seven-hundred-pound anthropoid looked squarely into their eyes. Osgood sucked on the glowing cigarette butt. 'Who does that big bull gorilla remind you of?' The ape had ceased his gum chewing for the moment, as if he too had heard Osgood's question.

'Can't say.'

'Study the lips . . . thin, ain't they?' He shot Woods a brotherly glance. 'Just like a white man?' He held out his palm for slapping.

Judith had never seen Paul so angry. He stood with his back literally against the wall of Henry Lord's Biltmore Hotel suite facing Lord, John O. Lake, and two junior aides.

'. . . And I say we haven't any security worth a damn down there. San Diego is Minute Man country, for Christ's sake. How many death threats have we received so far?' His voice was still low.

Lake's eyes dropped from the level of Woods's burning stare. He and Lord, Judith could see, were going to try to take diversionary action.

'Let's see . . . The Senator has two speeches scheduled for San Diego, and we . . .'

'Paul may have a point . . . The country's largely Republican anyway, and –'

Then, Judith told him later, he blew his stack. 'You mean the shit hit the fan,' he replied.

'Jesus Christ! Is that all you bastards think about – *votes*? The man could be *murdered*, and you're counting the ballots already!'

Lord and Lake looked more whitefaced than ever in the blast of Paul Woods's black rage. Their personal masculine mythology demanded that they make some rejoinder.

'Take it easy, Paul. You're not responsible for the Senator's security.'

'We really can't cancel out on San Diego, anyway, because –'

Woods did not look at Lake as he brushed past them, with Judith following. 'They're not going to do anything, are they?' He gave her no answer, just touched the elevator button with his finger like a man tripping an explosive device or who is tired unto the death.

'Without hard evidence, what *can* they do?' she asked.

He turned his head slowly toward her, looking at her the way he had looked at them. 'Hey.' She tried to appear casual. 'I'm on *your* side.' He nodded almost imperceptibly. Judith shivered. She thought, I am going to lose him; I cannot much longer compete with ghosts or the dead, especially if their name is Kennedy.

May 20 *Los Angeles*

The three black men with handkerchiefs on their heads relaxed on the greasy mattress under the overhang of the shuttered gas station. They drank their wine and greeted one and all, black and white, as if they were hosts in hell instead of just fixtures of the south-central Los Angeles ghetto street scene. Their backs were propped against the wall of the three story 'hotel'. 'All right,' they called, grinning like God's spies, to the stream of people heading past them towards the Southern California Headquarters of the Black Panther Party, two store fronts past the 'hotel', next to the pool hall, at Forty-second and Central Avenue.

The early-evening awakening of the street was dominated by a recorded voice singing out from the loudspeaker over the Panther office front door.

> You tell me that the sun belongs
> To you and should surround you.
> But, when I turn to look
> I see they've snatched
> The sun from all around you.
> Why you hardly seem
> To want what's yours
> You hardly seem to care.
> If you love the sun,
> It's where you've come from

Then you had better dare
To seize the time
The time is now
Oh, seize the time
And you know how.

Elaine Brown, the singer, a gorgeous light-brown young woman, was standing in front of the office bantering with two welfare mothers who were attending the regular Monday evening neighborhood organizing meeting. The royalties from Ms. Brown's record albums went to the Party. She was one more of the lucid and audacious generation of the Panther, ready, in the words of their leader Huey P. Newton, to commit 'revolutionary suicide' – that is, to live and die for 'the people.' This evening she would introduce Bobby Seale, the Chairman of the Party, from Oakland, California, Central Headquarters, the party's spokesman while Huey P. Newton was imprisoned, locked up in solitary confinement.

From where Helen and 'Saladin' had parked, on Forty-first Place, a half block away from the Panthers, they could hear the stabbing lyrics and soaring melody.

You worry about liberty
Because you've been denied.
Well, I think that you're mistaken
Or then, you must have lied.
'Cause you do not act like those who care
You've never even fought
For the liberty you claim to lack
Or have you never thought
To seize the time
The time is now
Oh, seize the time
And you know how.

Helen fastened down the convertible top. Trying to encompass the Palestinian's attack of nerves, she gripped his hand. The palm was wet. They watched the friendly street people as they greeted each other, the men slapping hands: 'Hello, brother,' 'Good evening, Sister Elaine.' The storefront office pictured a 32 × 40 poster of leader Huey P. Newton holding a shotgun in one hand and a law book in the other: the flesh and blood dialectic – combined with the photographs of the Panther survival programs of food, health care, education – which signified to a growing number of America's wretched of the earth the way toward freedom. 'For our people,' Helen said finally, and opened the door for him. Dim street lamps went on, the traffic flow thickened; the Panthers called, the street answered.

Inside, 'Saladin' found a rear seat and studied the poster-covered walls. China, Cuba, North Korea, liberated Africa, Al Fatah, the insurgent 'Third World' glared down at him. There were other images, too: Sojourner Truth and Frederick Douglass, Malcolm X and Nat 'the Prophet' Turner, the damned and heroic figures from four hundred years of black rebellion.

The song had ended, and now Elaine Brown, in person, was introducing Chairman Bobby to the expectant assemblage of some forty people, including the three wine-drinking ambassadors from the corner shed.

'All power to the People!'

'*All power to the People!*' the audience sang back, like a revolutionary church. The Panther leader was a lean, vibrant man; the empathy between speakers and crowd was complete. This, they fervently believed, was the start of the renaissance locked in the unconscious of the dumb, the damned and powerless giant that the audacity of the Panthers had stirred so profoundly.

'This here is a big meeting for Dodge City. That's what I call L.A. – Dodge City . . .'

The Panther guards stared at the Arab type as he fished a pencil and notepad out of his blue-jeans pocket.

'We're gonna talk about these racist pig police in Dodge City tonight. But first, I want to run down the ten-point program for all of us. These ten points come from the genius of Huey P. Newton. Point number one: Huey said . . .'

The guards leaned down, whispering politely. 'Can I ask why you are making notes there, brother?' 'Saladin' stared front, stonily. 'What is your name, please?' In front, the Chairman was enunciating demands as old as the Neolithic age: '. . . and we want land, bread, peace . . .'

The crowd was cheering, unaware of the guards escorting the young man to the door after he had refused to let himself be patted down. The Panthers could not take the chance.

Shaking with anger, he slammed the car door and glared at Helen as she pulled out into the ghetto traffic. 'To hell with it!'

'Saladin.'

'Bullshit, miss!' The use of a formal term of address was always a clear sign of his deep anger. 'When do we stop playing these children's games? When am I supposed to meet the leadership? Training, training, that's all I do is training!'

Her heart thudded as they approached the freeway. Now, her mind raced, end it *now*. Tell Must and let him do his worst. *Let* him kill me, let him kill – The dim remembrance of her father screaming silently in his torture room made her bite her lip just as she was on the verge of blurting, 'Then get out of the car now!'

What she told him, in fact, was 'You made a commitment to the liberation movement. Not for money or honor – though you will have that. If you're not a man, if you want to run away now, just say the word and I will tell them.' He seemed to sink into the corner of the seat like a defeated child as the car sped toward Pasadena.

May 20 *Pomona, California*

'Remember, this is just a dry run,' Helen told him as they left their convertible in the lot and walked toward Bobbie's Restaurant, with Helen in the lead. He followed with a jacket over his arm.

Inside was the usual seething mass of press and people. TV lights raked the upstairs lounge, flashbulbs popped, the tousled boyish figure in the light gray suit smiled tiredly as he repeated the most repeated campaign call: 'Give me your hand!'

FBI Special Agent William Thurman, Jr., working undercover while the RFK campaign was in Riverside County, stood at the bar watching the noon-hour pandemonium, when his roving gaze fastened on a woman at the edge of the room. She was in a tailored black suit; she looked like the actress Sophia Loren to Thurman. Same long legs but smaller tits, he ruminated, drinking in the face and form, then frowned as a slight young man whom he took to be a Chicano sidled up to the expensively dressed beauty, whom Thurman had begun to imagine in a sexual context. The acrobatic fantasy was spoiled by the cheap punk who was making a play for her. Thurman's eyes widened to see the woman whisper in the Chicano's ear and straighten the coat the kid carried over his arm.

The mob was stomping down the stairs behind the electronic media on their way to the parking lot. Thurman turned toward the bar so that Paul Woods could not see him. In the mirror he saw Woods deep in conversation with Leroy Aarons of the Washington *Post*; neither man saw him as they trailed the noisy crowd down the stairs. Thurman watched the reflection of Sophia Loren and the Chicano following her, walking stiffly with the coat over his arm as if ... Thurman passed them on the stairs, pretending to trip and grabbing the punk. He was not carrying a gun under the coat, Thurman was certain of that now. He apologized for his clumsiness, smiling his buck teeth toward the woman.

'Are you with the press?' Thurman had a press credential sticking out of his handkerchief pocket. 'Western News Service,' the card said. It tickled Thurman's curious sense of humor to use a press card from a long-time Los Angeles Police Department intelligence front. Since the days of Chief Parker in the '50s the FBI and the LAPD had been mortal foes, and Thurman identified with the old guard at least on this score.

'No.' She smiled. 'I'm a speechwriter. Excuse me. I have to catch the campaign bus.' She descended quickly. Thurman tried to place her accent as he looked into the glazed black eyes of the companion she was now pretending not to know and asked, 'Who are you?' Thurman looked straight into the tense brown face. Thurman stepped down one step to get closer to the abstracted young man. He saw the blank eyes focus into a sudden coldness. The voice was sibilant and sharp: 'What is it to you, *sir?*' Two steps at a time, like a sleeper awakened, he bounded lithely down the stairs. At the foot he caromed off the restaurant's manager, glared at him, and hurried out.

Thurman stood alone at the head of the stairs debating whether or not to follow the unlikely couple. Typical. Since the transfer to San Bernardino, nothing made any sense to him any more.

May 29 *Los Angeles*

Judith watched Paul out of the corner of her eye. A half dozen Kennedy aides, who had stayed on in California to work on the June 4 primary, were sprawled around a campaign-communications hotel suite.

> Political pundits are speculating today on what effects the Oregon primary results will have on next month's voting here in California. On his return to Los Angeles from Oregon, today, the Senator had this to say . . .

No one spoke. The newscast cut to a press conference at Los Angeles International Airport.

> . . . if I lose in California, I will drop out of the race . . .

Paul Woods snapped off the set. Judith felt like a traitor for admiring the successful, ironic McCarthy campaign that had just triumphed in Oregon. She knew that her former co-workers with Eugene McCarthy would be wild with joy at this, the first defeat in the history of the 'Kennedy machine,' as she had used to call it. How depressing, these punishing, endless internecine battles are, she thought, while all the time Americans and Asians die in the illegal endless war and the real machine – Nixon's – chews deeper and deeper into the 'middle American' majority. Would it ever end? Were she and Paul just two more casualties of the two endless wars? Then they all had to smile at the grace and poise of their Candidate as he talked into the cameras:

> As Abe Lincoln said about the man who was carried out of town on a rail, 'Except for the honor of the thing, I would like to have passed it up.' . . . If I died in Oregon, I hope Los Angeles is Resurrection City.

Their smiles faded. Resurrection City and Doctor King were unannealed wounds. Paul looked over at Judith, and she forced herself to smile.

May 29 *Buena Park, California*

Following Must's instructions, Helen turned off the Riverside Freeway onto Beach Boulevard and headed north toward Knotts Berry Farm and Ghost Town. She had suggested the Japanese Village or Movieland Wax Museum as alternative meeting places, but her case officer had insisted on this sprawling re-creation of the American frontier.

The boulevard leading to the compound was crowded with motels and franchise food units. Her sense of depression and alienation deepened as she parked in front of a cluster of simulated nineteenth-century buildings that looked like the stereotyped sets of the old B cowboy movies that she watched at night while trying to fall asleep. She walked through the Ghost Town slowly. Must's instructions were that she meet him in front of the assay office in Fiesta Village at 4.45 p.m. exactly. She paid two dollars to the teenager at the gate to the exhibits – a price within the budget of the white working and retired people who could not afford the inflated cost of nearby Disneyland. Following the souvenir map, she boarded the Denver and Rio Grande railroad car, killing time.

As the *Calico Express* started to wind its way into the Ghost Town, a fat young man with a bandana over his face leaped through the door brandishing a six-shooter. 'Put your hands up.' His bored voice and bogus desperado demeanor seemed to amuse Helen's fellow passengers, especially some of the children.

The fat youth noticed Helen in her form-fitting blue-jeans suit and was inspired to snarl at the passengers, 'I'll blow your head off,' convulsing twin girls sitting across from Helen. Then he leveled his six-gun at Helen's breasts and blew his foul breath in her face. 'If you don't put your hands up, lady, I'll blow a hole in your nose that'll turn you into a doughnut!' Some of the passengers applauded as the train ground to a halt. Helen let the others exit first.

She walked slowly past the Hunter's Paradise Shooting

Gallery and the Calico Saloon. Through the saloon's swinging doors she studied a large mural over the bar, *Saturday Night in Old Calico* – 1888. The mottled canvas pictured an old western street being consumed in an orgy of murder and debauchery. Next to a fake mountain leaned the General Merchandise Store; drained, she entered and sat down by the vintage potbellied stove. On- and off-duty law-enforcement and service men shopped cheerfully at the hat and souvenir counters. She had never seen so many stetson and cowboy hats: Panhandle, Ranchero, Bison, Lariat, Stampede, Bunkhouse, a half dozen more. She swung back to the glowing stove that burned winter and summer: Lone Star #10, Evansville, Indiana, was the brand name staring at her. Her eyes twitched with fatigue. She rose and left to avoid the glances of the men.

She paid no attention to the wax male figures of gun makers, poker players, Chinese laborers, grinning nigger shoeshine boys, or to the real children panning for 'real gold,' with the help of white-bearded actors posing as prospectors. She stepped like a sleepwalker through the poisonous nostalgia of the multi-million-dollar tourist trap.

She stopped to check her watch in front of the Calico printshop. (Why is everything named Calico? she wondered dully, not knowing that Calico Mountain, California, had been, in the 1800s, a 'glory hole' stuffed with eighty million dollars' worth of gold, or that the mustachioed men who had climbed into the mountain's hole after gold would have spat on this latter-day imitation of the last frontier as a piss-poor copy of Mother Nature's handiwork, their America, which the poet had called 'the gift outright.') 4.40. She glanced at the old newspaper poster in the window.

AUTHENTIC HISTORY . . . FASCINATING OLD ADS

Tombstone Epitaph.

THURSDAY MORNING OCTOBER 27, 1881

Statement of Wyatt Earp

I was tired of being threatened by Ike Clanton and his gang. I believed from what they had said to others and to me, and from their movements, that they intended to assassinate me the first chance they had, and I thought if I had to fight for my life against them, I had better make

Billy "the Kid" CLAIBORNE

You were asked on your cross-examination if you were not sometimes called "the Kid." Please explain how you came to be called by that name? A. I

Tombstone Corral,

Fremont St., bet. Second an Thir

(Opposite Ham Light's old place.)

Isaac Clanton

later, Wyatt Earp came up, but did not say anything. Morgan Earp told me if I was not "heeled" then, when I came back on the street to be "heeled." I walked off, and asked Morgan Earp not to shoot me in the back. I did not see Morgan Earp nor

YESTERDAY'S TRAGEDY

at the OK CORRAL

Three Men Hurled Into Eternity in the Duration of a Moment.

Stormy as were the early days of Tombstone, nothing ever occurred equal to the event of yesterday.

Tom McLowry fell first, but raised and fired again before he died. Bill Clanton fell next, and raised to fire again when Mr. Fly took his revolver from him. Frank McLowry ran a few rods and fell. Morgan Earp was shot through and fell. Doc Holliday was hit in the left hip, but kept on firing. Virgil Earp was hit in the third or fourth fire in the leg, which staggered him, but he kept up his effective

G. F. SPANGENBERG,

PIONEER GUNSMITH Locksmith

The only Complete Gun and Locksmithing Shop in Arizona

FRENCH RESTAURANT,

Helen stared into space, thinking: Men and guns, men and guns, this is the most violent culture in the history of the world. Thinking like an anthropologist until she remembered what she, a woman, was doing to another human being; thinking of her 'Saladin' until the image of Robert Kennedy, splitting his face with an enormous grin, replaced 'Saladin.' What about me? she thought, and what I am doing? *Boom.* The long brown-and-gray building and a semicircle of families caught her eye just as the very loud blank shots rang her ear drums. It was 4.45. Now she knew why Must had chosen this place and time.

Two shrill, jerky actors. The 'marshal' fired at the 'villain' on the roof, who fired back. The sound was deafening. The reports triggered the echolalia of her nightmare: shots, the torture room, the man wearing dark glasses, the sound of the firing squad. *Boom.* The actor playing the marshal was now firing a double-barreled shotgun up at the roof, the acrid powder from the blank cartridges drifted across the rapt crowd.

'Very amusing.' Must stood at her shoulder as they watched the conclusion of the hollow spectacle. *Boom, boom.* The actor on the roof fell to a lower balcony. The crowd could hear him hit the mattress.

The marshal clomped up the building's exterior stairs and turned to the crowd below: 'What do you want me to do with him?' '*Shoot him!*' they yelled back. A burly father yelled 'Kill him!' and slugged his silent male son between the shoulderblades. 'Kill him,' sang out the son and looked up for approval. *Boom.*

Was the marshal a returned Special Forces veteran from Vietnam? Why was he looking down directly at her? She turned to face Must, anxious to get the interview over. His dark glasses, like those in her nightmare, stared back at her.

He led her to a rear table of the Gold Trail Saloon. The walls were plastered with savage yellow handbills identifying wanted fugitives, long since betrayed and dead. Must waved the waitress away. Helen lifted the diary out of her shoulder bag and pushed it across the table to him. Must studied the frantic, compulsive sample from the text:

$$ F May 20, 9:25 AM

R.F.K. must die—RFK must die—assassinated by
Child of death—please accept this——
this this this this this—KILL THE MAN
Saladin the Great—your name is
Child of death—death death death death death
Kennedy must fall, the man must fall
must fall—no no no
Saladin S pay to the order of $$$$$
RFK must die—die die die die die Saladin S

'It's hard to read. Needs editing. I'll keep this.' He looked up. A western country-music band had started up outside in the street. The music was sweet false folk.

'He is ready,' she lied, 'my work is finished.' The band would not quit.

'You have a serious problem, Doctor?'

'No, why?'

'*You* contacted *me*.'

'Well . . . I assumed you would notify me that the operation was canceled – after the Oregon defeat.'

'Not at all. We expect him to win here. The minority vote, you know. As far as our estimates are concerned, the only thing between him and the Presidency is . . . us.'

Try one more time, she thought. 'What you're doing may be scientifically possible, of course – but politically? After all, Los Angeles isn't Dallas or –'

'Dallas, Saigon, Athens, Los Angeles. There's no real difference, believe me.'

'But you don't have the same public passivity as existed in 1963. The protests, and . . .'

She could see her face distorted in the reflection from Must's glasses. The band had stopped or drifted away. With his cold smile and soft rasping tone, Must put her in mind of a killer priest. 'Your baby-sitting chores are almost over.' His thin lips turned up under the sunglasses. 'A man you don't know yet will be your control for San Francisco. He'll contact you later tonight by phone. Special Forces type, very good. Use the medical code.' He gauged her shallow breathing and clenched fingers. Her lips formed the words 'San Francisco?'

'You're only responsible for the scientific aspects, Doctor. We'll take care of the logistical and political problems.' She tried to focus her eyes on his slash of a mouth, because his face was making her dizzy.

'But how long can you continue this kind of thing?'

'As long as we have to. Everything in your dossier suggests you are a survivor, Doctor. Why this sudden –'

'Your dossiers are composed by theoretical idiots. Where do you plan to –'

'San Francisco is the first choice. May thirty-first.'

'That's two days! Why didn't you contact me before?'

'I would have, tomorrow. Too much thinking time can

be bad for the, ah, organized mind.' His full face seemed to be changing shapes before her eyes. 'Don't panic, it's just another dry run.'

Her head hung, beaten. Must debated ordering her a cool drink, but only for a moment. Her fingers trembled as she tried to light a cigarette and failed, her hands twitching on the table at last like dying birds. He bent close to her. I am having a schizoid episode, she lectured herself as the lights in the room seemed to go dark and Must's voice grated through her skin.

'If this seems crude, just remember that *our* laboratory is the nation itself. These Kennedys are fanatics. Their appeal is to the anarchists and the rioters. Outside your antiseptic laboratory is a nation edging toward chaos! The decent people have an obligation to stop this army of criminals, and it's Utopian to think they can be pacified one by one with your "psychotechnology."' She had given up trying to keep track of his cover stories. She fought to control her thoughts. 'This is the first stage of a new civil war, and you and I are just *taking orders*. Our civilization demands –'

She cut him off, finally, in a shaking voice. 'I'm a "deportable." I have no choice, do I?' *Boom!* The actors across the square began firing their guns again; again there was the sound of applause and the laughter of children. She tried to focus her eyes, to ask the questions that would fill in the holes in Must's insane 'dry run' games.

'Nobody does. That is to say, we all have the *one* basic choice: to live or die; the past or the future; pleasure or pain. You follow me?'

'Mr. Must, I leave you with a Greek word – *hubris*.'

'Reaching too high for power? But that is precisely what *they* have done. And "fate," the gods, must bring *him down!*' He touched her hand lightly. 'You know, don't you, Doctor, that *we* are on the side of the gods?' He squeezed a small envelope into her hand.

Must left her sitting there after putting down a two-dollar tip, though they had not even had a glass of water. 'Try the chicken dinner over at the restaurant.' He smiled. 'It's first class.' Looking pleased with the entire transaction, he picked up the diary and manoeuvred his thick, erect body through the swinging doors and out into the gunshot-echoing street.

She walked automatically, looking for the way out of the Ghost Town, finally having to ask for directions at the Freedom Hall. People were busy buying up patriotic propaganda; she had to wait for a clerk to help her. In large letters on one wall was a quote:

> LABOR WAS PRIOR TO CAPITAL, BUT PROPERTY IS THE FRUIT OF LABOR . . . THAT SOME SHOULD BE RICH SHOWS THAT OTHERS MAY BECOME RICH . . .
>
> A. LINCOLN

'Turn right at the Butterfield Stage Coach,' the tired-looking clerk told Helen. Near the gate, a plaque informed the guests that the John Wayne Theater would soon begin construction. She sat vacant-eyed in her car. Through the window of the enlarged Chicken Dinner Restaurant she thought she saw William A. Must, Jr., and another man, fat and possibly an Arab, teasing a young waitress. She imagined that she could see them licking their lips over their chicken dinners, hot buttered buns, berry jam. She sniffed the envelope Must had left her. Heroin.

She opened the door and vomited.

May 31 *San Francisco, California*

The Kennedy California campaign had risen from the ashes of Oregon to tumultuous motorcades through the black and brown strongholds, the near hysteria of the crowds forcing the Los Angeles and San Francisco police to retreat angrily from the scene. The big blonde running alongside the open car was yelling, 'Piss on Oregon, piss on Oregon!'

The candidate was far ahead of McCarthy in the underclass but the 'goddamned liberals are killing us,' Paul Woods told Judith Shankland. Woods sided with those aides who believed that a major effort for the Jewish and liberal vote was a waste of time. McCarthy would carry the 'real' liberals and Humphrey the Jewish and suburban backlash majorities, he argued.

The noon rally in San Francisco's Chinatown was triumphant. Firecrackers popping, ocean wind blowing, bright sun, sixty-five degrees. This, insisted Woods to Judith, was the winning strategy, these were *the people*. The streets roared as RFK passed down Washington and Sacramento. Signs in Chinese sang his praises. Woods regaled Judith with the story of Richard Nixon's debacle on these same streets in 1960 when Dick Tuck, the Democratic prankster, had commissioned derogatory signs in Chinese WHAT ABOUT THE HUGHES TOOL LOAN? and Nixon had pointed to them proudly.

Talking and laughing loudly over the Chinese firecrackers and high-school bands as they walked behind the motorcade through the throng down Grant Street, Paul and Judith never noticed Must's man, James Jerrold, in the telephone booth that had been set up as a temporary command headquarters. From the booth, Jerrold was in contact with the doctor and her 'patient' through a miniaturized walkie-talkie, 'fargo' system. With the receiver in his hand and his lips moving, Jerrold appeared to be an ordinary citizen using a public telephone.

Helen's fargo receiver was strapped under her beige sari. The light brown cord running under the wig to her ear was virtually invisible against her olive skin. Her long hairpiece and costume made her look like another of the vital young females in a city famous for its beautiful women. The attenuated electronic sound of Jerrold's voice resumed again inside her ear: 'When he heads for the car, start your firecrackers. Are you reading me?' Who was he talking to? She did not have any firecrackers. Below the level of the crush of bodies she gripped her 'patient's' hand, thin as a child's.

The crowd began to surge, the candidate was calling to them, 'We can do better . . .' 'Saladin' was light and brittle. She could not push him forward fast enough; the riptide of the crowd was sweeping him irrelevantly away from the Man.

'Doctor! Get your patient in position. Get your patient moving.' The candidate's car was beginning to move slowly. A volley of firecrackers, the *crack!* jerking the nightmare image of her father and the firing squad before her eyes. Trying to reach her 'patient,' who was looking past her, his eyes disoriented, she swam through the sea of flesh toward him as he spun and tossed in the mass.

Crack! and Helen's mind flashing – My God, someone else really has shot him – before the fargo started up in her ear again.

'He's getting away from you. Abort! *Abort! Repeat – operation aborted!*'

As they drove across the Golden Gate Bridge, he continued to shiver. No question that he was, is, under, but he cannot do it alone and I cannot control him to the end, and I will not, Helen thought as she watched him begin to unwind slightly. He leaned against the window, his sad, peaceful eyes drawn to the glistening bay below. For a moment she perceived the irradiated water from his point of view: She knew that he wanted to hide, disappear in the enfolding sea. She knew this because there was an ache in her spine pulling her down to the depths with him.

To keep from sinking she made her mind focus on a logical problem: Who was the man on the walkie-talkie that she had talked to only once, on the telephone at Must's direction? Who had thrown the bunch of Chinese firecrackers into the Candidate's car? How could she set off firecrackers and control the Palestinian at the same time? Why had she been told that this was 'just a test' when there were real bullets in his gun? And 'Saladin,' who was no marksman, had not spent more than six hours on a pistol range firing his secondhand .22 – was this to be the murder gun? Who else had been on the walkie-talkie; why had it suddenly gone dead?

Was there a covert logic to Must's game? She and 'Saladin' were constantly being exposed by Must – to what end? *In vivo* – she knit her brow – a 'transaction *in vivo*,' to use the psychological term, placing a subject in a life situation as a rehearsal for an otherwise traumatic event. He never will have to fire that pistol, she thought, just look and act like he could or has, and talk like a fanatic and go to the gas chamber. Or was Must sincere about building 'Saladin' into a legend and then spiriting him out of the country and into the Al Fatah as their agent?

The circular logic of Must's manipulations brought her full circle. She saw that she was simply a conduit between the two men – burly, swollen Must and her frail, wide-eyed

'Saladin.' Somehow Must was killing the Arab youth, and possibly Kennedy, *through her*. This she actually felt now for the first time. Must was using her body, had somehow invaded, infested her body – or she had let him! She gagged. Must was moving in and through her like a dybbuk, the ancient Hebrew concept of the possession, by a ghost, of a maiden's body. That palpable. As if Must's rich, rasping bass voice might come pouring out of her if she opened her mouth.

Now the sea was a dark magnet drawing her to drive the car right off the bridge. She grasped the wheel tighter and arched her aching spine and drove into the gathering fog.

JUNE, 1968

June 1　　　*Downey, California*

William A. Must, Jr., scowled as he approached the big hollow van and storage building. The deserted warehouse sat in one corner of a weed-covered lot. An off-duty policeman standing in the open door took the price of admission, ten dollars, from Must. Inside, where the dogs fought to the death, it was eerily quiet.

Must pushed his dark glasses up on his forehead, trying to adjust to the dim interior, looking for the fat Arab. He peered into the group of some thirty-five men who were busy getting their bets down for the next fight. A black man was cleaning the pit, an old carpet topped with a pink-flecked tarpaulin and enclosed by blood-spattered plywood walls, three feet high and fifteen feet square. Must knew that he had to find the fat man before the fight, which could last as long as three hours, or he would be forced to witness this slashing, choking, chewing filth.

He moved toward the betting circle, where upward of fifty thousand dollars was changing hands. Several times a year these men came from all over the West Coast to fight and bet their dogs. Each owner down on his knees in the dirt talking, whispering into his dog's ear. The dogs, themselves, making no sound, as silent as symbols, fighting while they bled, fighting with their flesh hanging in ribbons – one, two, three hours, the men in the watching circle uttering short, low empathic sounds as the handlers in the pit talked low to the animals: 'Come on Red Lady, atta girl.' When it was over, Must knew, the owner of the winner would have to kill his own animal as well.

Must nodded his head slowly to a skinny yellow-haired man who passed carrying a case of beer. 'John,' he said softly. Must had to force himself to visit these bi-monthly slaughters because here were pimps, narcotics dealers, money changers, off-duty cops, and members of the National Rifle Association looking for action – because wherever men like these gathered, Must had to have access to that place and these men.

A man with a huge pendulous belly, bare from the waist up, nodded to Must. Like many there, the man was tattooed: two naked women spinning a spider web, a fiery serpent with a human torso, and on one meaty shoulder a finely wrought pattern of two fighting dogs, fangs bared. Must was spared talking to the man, Fugler, because a lanky cop in a red sleeveless tee-shirt, with dogs tattooed on his shoulder also, came up to pick a bone with Fugler. Must turned, looking for the fat Arab. Behind him the two men talked dogs with gusto, with Fugler drowning out the cop.

'Now, you don't want to throw a kitten in there with the puppy right away for it to kill; it'll just go crazy for more. What you want to do is get yourself one of those cats and put it in an onion bag and string it up on a rope from the top of the garage. Use a spring – you know, like a front-door-screen spring – and hang that cat up there so its paws are out through the onion bag. You want to get yourself some clippers and clip the claws off.

'Then you let the puppy at it. The cat'll bob up and down, and the dog'll go after it. Pretty soon the dog gets tired and sweaty and you pull it off and drag it back to the corner and hold it against the wall. It'll be hell to hold, but you hold it and then turn it around and – *hyaaaah!* – you let it go back at it.

'If the cat gets pretty mauled up in the bag, just take it down and keep it till the next day, and then throw it in and let the dog kill it.'

'Bill!' The fat Arab moved toward him as he emerged from a portable toilet at the far end of the warehouse, zipping up the fly of his expensive Dax slacks.

'Bill, you want to get a bet down? Huh, no? *You* don't bet? You're not serious? Bill, it's the system – "dog eat dog"! Man's best friend!' He ha-hoed garlic into Must's face. 'You should see this bitch work the stifle, you know, the throat . . .' The fat Arab pushed his pudgy fingers into his goiter of a throat. 'She works the ears, the legs – she's beautiful, Bill. A Staffordshire terrier, beautiful, ribs like a washboard, lean, mean. George Pasternkowsky's dog, from Vegas, he feeds her red meat, exercises her on a treadmill, she's sweated down to thirty-five, thirty-six pounds . . .'

The fat man babbled the American idioms in a British accent. Must tried to close his nose to the reek of old sweat and gore. The fat man knew that Must did not come to these gatherings for the fights, despised the men and their dogs, but as the fat man was a sadist he could not refrain from trying to torment everyone, including his American control, William A. Must, whom he had genuinely respected and reared since Cairo, 1952, when Must had put him under contract to the Company. Now his black, almond-shaped eyes were shining and his lips were red and wet; his curved nostrils flared as he inhaled the warehouse stench with gusto.

'Follow me – a beautiful bar and snack table with –'

'No,' said Must, 'thank you. I am very short on time.' He saw a man and a dog walking toward the pit and felt his bowels begin to turn. 'Let's go over here.'

'I won seventy-five hundred dollars the last fight.' The Arab chattered happily. Then, businesslike, to Must: 'You're looking well, Bill.'

'I haven't time for any more frills. I want you to take over the final programming. I just don't trust all this think-tank stuff.'

'Can we trust this subject completely?'

'Hell, no! I just told you. That's why I want him baby-sat by your people the rest of the way. And get him to a pistol range – make sure he's noticed. I need window dressing – a range, guns, bullets . . . you know what to do.'

'What about the cunt?'

'She's a problem – but brilliant. We've been running her father for years. But you're my insurance policy.'

'And afterwards?'

'The subject will be eliminated on the spot. As for the woman, ah . . . well, we'll see . . .'

The Arab's eyes lit up as a low, guttural group-sound announced the start of the death struggle. 'Call me every day till Monday, then, starting Tuesday, call me every hour,' Must instructed, slipping the sunglasses down over his eyes.

He turned and walked out fast, holding his breath to block out the smell of the fresh blood.

June 1 Los Angeles

Judith Shankland sat on Woods's lap in the crowded control booth to watch the Kennedy-McCarthy debate. The candidates were arguing over misleading campaign advertising. She felt frustrated. Somehow the root issues were never discussed. The public had been lied to and infantalized for two decades of hot and cold war and, if Paul was correct, bullets not ballots now dictated the fate of the nation. Her attention came back to the two men. The ironic poet frm Minnesota was talking:

'... I said this is one of the things we ought to talk about, is the process by which decisions were made with reference to this war, because one of our problems has been to find out who decides and who is responsible, and on what kind of evidence did we have this kind of escalation?'

'It also said that I intervened in the Dominican Republic.'

'That's right.'

'Now how did they get that?'

'Well, I think what they did, I had –'

'I wasn't even in the government at the time.'

'Well, you weren't out very long.'

'I wasn't involved in the Dominican Republic, I wasn't even in the government, and I criticize that.'

This bitter end of the campaign – would it replace her glowing memories of March and April? They had hit Wisconsin running full tilt, veterans of New Hampshire. Platoons of students sleeping in dormitories and churches. She had been a part of McCarthy's army, ringing 1,250,000 doorbells across the home state of the other, dead Senator McCarthy, the ogre who had been challenged first, back in the '50s, by the young Gene McCarthy.

The last time she had seen him in person was in March. She had gone back for one last hurrah before joining Paul Woods and the Kennedy campaign. McCarthy, caught up in a tremendous demonstration at the Madison Memorial Coliseum, had quoted Whitman.

Judith knew that never again would politics – or America – mean to her what they had that cold, clear spring day in Wisconsin. She tried to tune out the tired, petty absurdities of the candidates in the studio, tried to remember Wisconsin and hope.

June 1 *Pasadena*

Helen stood in the bathroom preparing the heroin injection, still afraid to begin using it. She could hear the political debate from the television set. She walked into the dark room as Kennedy was saying 'I do think we have some commitments around the globe. I think we have a commitment to Israel, for instance, that has to be kept.'

Israel. The word penetrated the narcotic armor of denial and 'masochistic paralysis' – her term – that she had to don every day now. She looked at 'Saladin' for a long moment. His eyes were closed. She sat down and stared at the bright screen, hypnotic in the darkened room.

'But what I don't think is that we can be policemen of the world, and go all over the rest of the globe and settle every internal dispute with American soldiers or American arms . . .'

June 1 *Los Angeles*

William A. Must and James Jerrold – like a shark trailed by a pilot fish – walked softly around the unlit, empty Ambassador Hotel Embassy Ball Room, Must whispering back to Jerrold and the younger man jotting down logistical details: dimensions, locks, doors, exits, power, floor plan.

In the dull light of the empty ballroom, where RFK would hold his victory celebration, Must's pale eyes looked to Jerrold as if they were made out of smoke.

Must played the beam from a miniature flashlight over his rough sketch of the floor plan. His thick finger indicated to Jerrold that all roads led to the Colonial Room, where the world press would be waiting for Kennedy on victory night. He tapped the 'outside stairway to courtyard'; Jerrold nodded, understanding that that would be his route. To Must, Jerrold's eyes looked as yellow as a cat's in the gloom.

'Who's in the other ballroom?' Jerrold whispered.

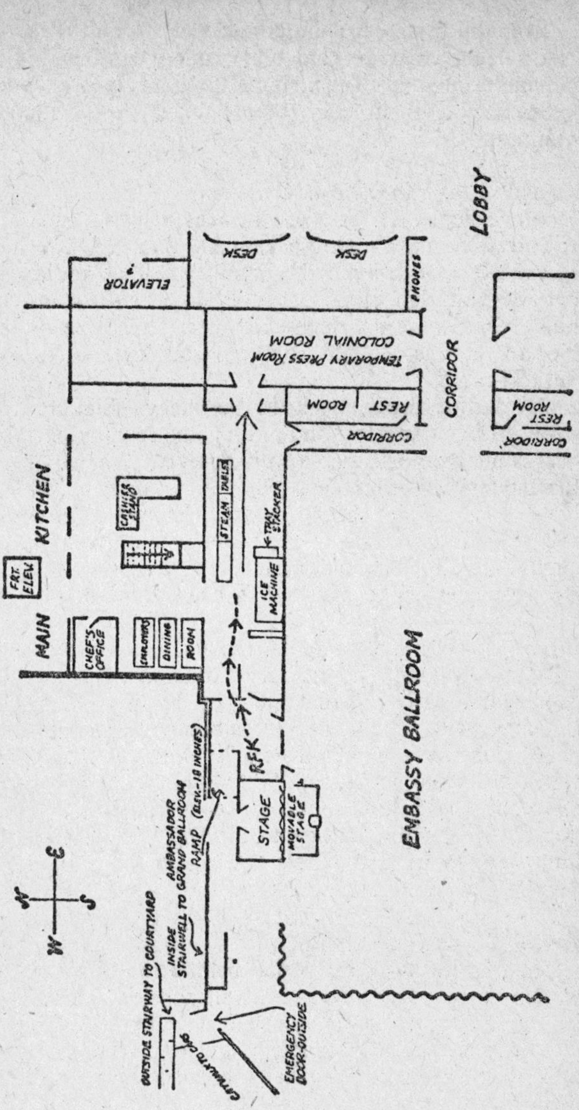
MAIN KITCHEN
FRT. ELEV.
CHEF'S OFFICE
EMPLOYEES DINING ROOM
STEAM TABLE
TRAY STACKER
ICE MACHINE
RFK
STAGE
MOVABLE STAGE
EMBASSY BALLROOM
AMBASSADOR RAMP TO GRAND BALLROOM (ELEV.-18 INCHES)
INSIDE STAIRWELL
OUTSIDE STAIRWAY TO COURTYARD
EMERGENCY DOOR-OUTSIDE
ELEVATOR
DESK
DESK
PHONES
TEMPORARY PRESS ROOM
COLONIAL ROOM
REST ROOM
CORRIDOR
CORRIDOR
REST ROOM
CORRIDOR
LOBBY
N
S
E
W

'Republicans,' Must mouthed, and showed a corner of teeth. He sniffed. Jerrold had passed wind in his clandestine excitement. Must shone the light up into Jerrold's eyes, turning them gray, then back down on the crude diagram.

June 2 San Diego, California

Judith called Paul Woods, who was in Los Angeles with the advance unit. 'I *have* asked,' she shouted into the pay phone when he demanded to know why the Candidate had canceled his San Diego speech. 'Have you *actually seen* him?' Paul's voice frightened her. 'Yes. He is alive. Good-bye.' She debated whether to quit right then or wait until Tuesday.

As Judith drove back in the heavy Sunday traffic toward Los Angeles, images of the campaign played across her memory, as if it *were* all over. 'Tragedy is a tool for the living to gain wisdom, not a guide by which to live,' she had heard Kennedy say in Indiana. I believe that, she thought as she drove through the overdeveloped southern California countryside, but Paul doesn't, yet. She had not understood Kennedy's accusation that Lyndon Johnson had appealed to the nation's 'darker impulses' – But now I do, she thought, and her long, sensitive face looked less youthful than it had just ten weeks before.

She smiled slightly, remembering. The medical students had asked who was to pay for 'a better life for the poor' – 'You!' shot back Robert Kennedy. And all the cuff links torn from his shirts, and Ethel and the dog in the convertible with him, and the open black faces shouting, 'Make way for the President . . .' And that led her to see Paul Woods in her mind's eye again, and to feel the weight of his burden in her heart.

June 2 Los Angeles

Helen and the fat Arab stood behind the one-way glass watching the young Palestinian sit shivering in the white communications room, where he had been undone that night in May by the terrible film images.

The fat man reeked of a heavy expensive cologne. He kept managing to rub his leg or paunch against her. Helen had been called without warning, and her nerves were raw again.

She could smell a liqueur on his breath as he confided to her, 'Here is what I want to do, Doctor: First, I pour water on the floor, then we fasten a wire to the second toe of the left foot and a spring-clip electrode to the nipple of the left breast.' His voice was heavy with a kind of sibilant suductiveness; his black eyes glittered with excitement.

The Arab spoke with a British accent, she noted, and as he described the torture to her he lightly touched the nipple of her left breast. She flinched abruptly. 'Yes, the nipple of the left breast.' He closed his fat, powerful thumb and forefinger on her nipple like the spring of a trap. She swayed from the pain. Holding the nipple, he pulled her close to him, talking steadily and softly to her. 'Then after half an hour we shift the electrode from the left breast to the left ear.' He released her.

How can I kill him? she screamed silently. She wondered if this was the man she had glimpsed with Must at Knotts Berry Farm. It was clearly not the man who had been her control in San Francisco. She knew now that she was merely a bit player in this nightmare drama.

'Then we place the clip on the base of his penis . . .' She gave him a look that made it clear that she no longer cared what happened to her. Her hand was in her shoulder bag; there was no way for him to know whether she had a gun pointed at him or not.

'No,' she said, 'you can't even talk to him unless control –'

He jerked the bag toward him, pawing for the pistol. If I had brought a gun, she thought, I would kill you and then him and then – The fat man had her by the wrist. She did not struggle.

'I said *I* will take over from here on. The honeymoon is over. You get busy on his diary. Control wants a lot more politics –'

'But Control *has* the –'

'Shut up. Politics, revolutionary slogans – that sort of thing. Doctor, you have misjudged his "DDD." '

She tried to plead with him now. 'I have not misjudged his Debility-Dependency-Dread syndrome! He is obviously going into panic and suicidal –'

'Let's go, I will make him eat his own excrement!' He hit the door into the communications room open with his belly.

She bent down over the boy. His teeth were chattering now. The Arab's perfume seemed to disturb him, so that she had to speak to him in a tense tone of command.

'Saladin – I am telling you again, I am giving you over to a revolutionary brother. You must trust him absolutely. He is in charge now.'

The fat man pushed her aside with a thrust of his hip. She was trembling now too. The Arab took off his Shantung-silk sport coat, handed it imperiously to Helen to hold, reached down, and ripped 'Saladin's' thin shirt off his back. She slid along the wall to reach the door as he screamed at the youth in Arabic, the sound bouncing crazily off the walls.

'Stand up! You are nothing! Your father was nothing! You are a queer! Your father was a woman!'

As she closed the door she heard the broken sobbing: 'I can't, I can't . . . I can't . . .'

'You can't? *Now you will eat your own excrement!*' the fat man screamed in Arabic. Half falling against the outside of the door, she shook uncontrollably.

June 3 Los Angeles

The mariachi band and dancers led the RFK caravan into the Old Town Plaza of *La Reina de Los Angeles.* Olvera Street and the market were pouring out to greet the man who had kneeled in the fields with the grape strikers.

California legislative leader Jesse Unruh was trying to open a path through the throng in the red-brick-paved square, but the press was too much for him, so an athletic aide lifted the bundle of nervous energy that was Robert Kennedy onto a cement rise in the middle of the Plaza.

Woods and Judith scanned the periphery of the crowd for the arrival of Cesar Chavez, expected momentarily to make a statement of support for RFK for the television cameras. Woods's fingers were squeezing the blood out of her hand.

'Paul – take it easy, please!'

'I'll take it easy when we leave California.' He held on to her as if he knew that part of her wanted to run away.

'That's only thirty-six hours,' she shouted, and he smiled and nodded. He gave her a grateful look, speaking intensely.

'I think we're going to make it. Bobby may reorganize security for the last day. Yesterday, while we were in Bakersfield, he took off on his own to look for a woman that had called the FBI on November 21st, 1963, to tip them to an assassination plot she knew something about, concerning his brother . . .'

'Then you *are* getting through to him!' She kissed him lightly. 'Want me to get you a taco?'

She left him smiling. Neither of them was at all aware of the thickset man wearing dark glasses, watching them from the canopied Mexican restaurant terrace as he sipped a Dos Equis beer.

Dos Equis = Double XX = double cross. The play of words made Must laugh to himself.

June 3　　　　*Los Angeles*

The Beverly Hills matron on lunch-hour duty at the Wilshire Boulevard Miracle Mile Kennedy campaign headquarters looked up as the three men entered. She mistook them for Mexican-Americans. 'Saladin' walked slowly between the two men – who had not left his side for the last twenty-four hours – as if he were a prisoner. The fat Arab's agents both were taller than the Palestinian; both wore authentic-looking mustaches and appeared to be in their mid-thirties. They stood silently, waiting to make certain that 'Saladin' would be seen and remembered. But they did not trust the little Palestinian to go in alone.

The woman called over to a male volunteer. 'Will you see if you can put those people to work? We never let anybody stand around and talk. Everyone works.'

'Would you like to help us elect Senator Kennedy President?'

'I'm sorry. We're waiting for a friend.'

As he walked back to his desk, the Kennedy volunteer heard one of the men address the other two in a Palestinian dialect. He knew it was a Palestinian dialect because he himself spoke a halfdozen Arabic dialects, learned during his Mid-Eastern tour of duty for Standard Oil.

When the volunteer looked back he could see that two of the men were pushing the third, smaller youth out the door. He tapped a pencil against his teeth, then made a notation of what the tallest man had said in Arabic, and a rough English translation: 'We will get him tomorrow.'

June 3 *Corona, California*

'Saladin's' baby-sitters parked the dirty '63 Plymouth station wagon in front of the Lock Stock 'N Barrel gun store. The two older Arabs, with their patsy between them, approached the clerk standing behind the counter.

'What can I do for you?'

'Saladin's' answer was barely audible: 'Two boxes of .22 caliber.'

'Do you know these mini-mags? They have about twenty-five percent greater muzzle velocity than the .22s. They're effective for a mile and a quarter. Only ten cents more for a box of fifty . . .'

'Okay. Two boxes.'

One of the Arabs interrupted in a heavy accent. 'I take two boxes of Super X long rifle .22s.'

The clerk took the money, unable to understand the language they spoke in loud voices as they left. It appeared to him that the small one was arguing about something with the other two.

The fat Arab watched from his Mercedes as his agents pushed the Palestinian kid into the front seat of the station wagon. Before the wagon could pull out into traffic, 'Saladin' had leaped out of the car and was standing on the curb yelling, 'No, I'm not going to! I can't!' The fat man reached for the Luger in his glove compartment.

The two agents were out on the street now, trying to wrestle their prisoner back into the car. The fat Arab cursed furiously as he heard one of his men scream at the kid in English, 'Get your ass in the car! We have to get him tonight!' What did that moron mean, 'tonight?', the fat man raged.

'I don't want to. I'm afraid!' All three turned at the long blare of the Mercede's horn directly behind them. They seemed to freeze in their postures of struggle as they recognized the glaring countenance of the fat man in the expensive car. The horn ceased. Without another word or gesture, the three men reentered the station wagon.

With the Mercedes trailing, they headed for the Corona Police Department Gun Range as scheduled.

June 3   *Pomona*
FBI Special Agent Thurman swayed at the urinal. After washing, he stared into the dirty mirror, mocking the countenance of the aging Boy Scout he saw there: 'Yes, sir, Mr. Hoover, sir. Kiss my rosy ass, sir . . .' He felt like vomiting.

As he headed back to the bar, a local news special in loud progress assaulted his numb senses.

> It was three days ago in San Francisco's Chinatown that Senator Kennedy's campaign began rolling into high gear . . .

The sound of firecrackers penetrated the alcoholic haze. Thurman tried to focus his eyes: They sounded like pistol shots. The bartender set up another bourbon and water for him as he sank heavily onto the bar stool. Then, suddenly, Thurman was functioning: The TV camera videotape was focused in tight on a section of the crowd, featuring a striking long-haired woman and a thin, dark-complected youth. He remembered.

He grabbed the drink and pushed away from the bar, looking for the pay phone. Thurman fumbled through his small address book, then dialed O.

'Person-to-person call, please. Mr. Paul Woods – W-O-O-D-S, just like it sounds . . .'

JUNE 4–5, 1968

June 4 *12:15 a.m.* *San Diego*

Must would not sleep until it was over.

John W. Bottoms's old alarm clock read ten minutes after midnight when he was interrupted in his biweekly masturbation ritual by Must's soft knock at the rooming-house door. The technicolor image – of a beautiful black film star sucking his fantasied fabulous sex organ – faded from his imagining as he rose to answer the door, his erection falling fast.

Bottoms cracked the door; his heart thumped when he saw the big shot 'Mr. Edwards,' the name he knew Must by, standing there waiting. Must always enjoyed little visits with wretched true believers like John W. Bottoms. Why, a short-order cook, a nonentity like Bottoms, Must had lectured Jerrold, would gladly commit suicide for a pat on his scrawny back. The young man in the shrunken, faded pajamas ushered him in and turned on the ragged floor lamp.

In the poor illumination Must's pale eyes ran over the piles of gun manuals and men's magazines stacked around the tiny hallroom. He nodded approvingly at the heavy German Iron Cross hanging over the bed. 'What's the good word, John?' Must sat down gingerly on the one available wooden chair. He would have to play out the farce with this callow puppet on sheer technique. He badly needed another drink.

'You were sure right, Mr. Edwards.' The young man's voice was flat and adolescent. 'She's a doctor and she's connected to the *University*.' He placed a special emphasis on the word, as if to suggest some vast subversive redoubt. Must feigned an admiring interest in Bottom's crackpot narrative.

'Yes, sir. I got a friend tracing her license plate, and two of my buddies in the SAO are gonna stake out her apartment.' The thin young man stood in his bare feet, waiting for another bone of approval from Must.

The SAO – Must kept a straight face. He would like to see Mr. Bottom's dog face if he were to tell him that the Secret Army Organization was not an ultra-militant offshoot of the Minute Men; that what the stupid SAO was was a gang of ex-Minute Men organized into a paramilitary unit by one Godfrey Howard – an *agent provocateur* working for the FBI! Oh, that would be rich, if only he could tell him. What he said instead was 'That is really good intelligence work, John,' in the special 'one patriot to another' soldier-of-fortune voice he reserved for what he considered lumpen proletariat scum like Bottoms. Don't ham it up too much, he cautioned himself.

'John,' he intoned portentously, 'we have penetrated a top-secret communist cell. Maybe even the brainwashing headquarters of the entire University network.' Bottoms stood there in his semen-stained pajamas, ready to die for freedom. 'Now, John, I don't want you to discuss this any further with your SAO boys. You know what I mean?'

Bottoms inclined his scraggly blond head in what he took to be a conspiratorial manner. 'Right,' he snapped huskily, imitating Must clumsily.

Must stood heavily. 'John.' His voice was as hamheavy and seductive as doom now. 'There's a shitstorm coming. We have to be ready. If this cunt is who I think she is . . . John, we may have to put her between the cross hairs.' Bottoms twitched with excitement as Must laid the code words like caresses on him.

'We could –'

'John.' The voice was paternal and somber. 'We don't want any of that bullshit in a case like this. You know what I mean – the little note with the cross hairs on it saying "We can put poison in your milk" or "There's cyanide in the meter man's fountain pen" or "The old news dealer on the corner *is one of us!*" You know, John. None of that horseshit.' Bottom's watery green eyes were bulging. Every time Must stroked him with the sound of his name, John's spine tingled like when he was masturbating. 'John, I've told *my people* that you're the man for this job – if the commies go for broke.' So far as John W.

Bottoms was concerned, 'my people' meant U.S. Army Air Force intelligence – A-2. 'So stay away from these pornographic-bookstore bombings of the SAO, old buddy.'

Must forced one hundred fifty dollars into Bottoms's pale, nail-bitten hand. 'No, you'll need it, and I'll get you a good silencer, John.' The two great patriots shook hands. Must took two steps to the door and turned stagily. 'John.' It was the voice of God. 'Watch the headlines. If the reds attempt in any way to subvert the election or any other of our free institutions, you'll hear from me at the dog fights.' Bottoms was breathing noisily through his mouth.

'John.' Must said it for the last time. 'We will need you in Chicago for the Democrat Convention this summer – to help prevent violence. Don't tell *anyone.* Just make your plans and wait for the word.' Must turned before Bottoms could salute or do anything foolish, and eased his thick shoulders out the door like a departing lover.

'Goodbye, Mr. Edwards,' whispered Bottoms.

Must's square, close-cropped head butted back through the open door. 'From now on, John, use only my code name – White. *Mr.* White.'

1:30 a.m. *La Costa, California*

Must's eyes were staring with fatigue as he headed toward the La Costa Country Club to meet his crime-syndicate contact, Eugene Brading. Brading had functioned in Dealey Plaza in 1963 as a lookout, and had proved his mettle by talking his way out of an arrest by an alert sheriff.

A wave of dizziness swept over Must, forcing him to turn off the freeway and park. He closed his eyes and felt better. Mentally he checked over the points he needed to make with Brading at their 2 a.m. meeting in the parking lot of organized crime's country club. Brading was a problem. Must's big face looked rancid with fatigue. He let his mouth hang open.

Tony Prince, Must's Teamster man, was technically in charge of running Brading, of making certain that the con man and soldier of fortune was at the Ambassador to back up Must's team if anything went wrong. Prince had passed on the simple instructions: 'If the little Arab gets cold feet and runs, you and your guys follow and take him out.' For that, Brading was now asking twenty-five thousand dollars and a fresh set of identification papers. Must searched the buzzing exhaustion of his mind for another hook.

Must sagged back and opened his eyes. He wondered if he was becoming the kind of 'burnt-out case' that had always filled him with loathing and contempt. Was his patriotism beginning to unravel? He stared at the cold gleam of the stars in the black sky. Interstellar space and gas, he told himself: no God, no judgment, no mercy, nothing. Just *nothing*. Sacks of meat, that's all he was, all any of them were. All the burning and killing he had done was the proof of that. He felt better, refreshed for the brief stock-taking and rest. The whiskey he reached out of the glove compartment burned his gut with reassurance. Dog eat dog, he thought, belching silently, remembering the carnage of the canine arena. Dog eat dog, power, will, winners and losers. He was himself again.

As he pulled back onto the freeway, the answer of how to control Brading came to him. Bobby Kennedy was going to reopen the JFK murder if he was elected; he would tell the hoodlum that he had picked up this bombshell on the Kennedy wiretap. There would be arrests, the Cubans would spill their guts, the Agency would dump it all on the mob. Brading would be picked up for questioning, and with his record that would be that.

Must lit a Marlboro and flexed his heavy shoulders. A vagrant theme of Dixieland ran through his mind – 'Buckets Got a Hole in It' – and he remembered Brown University and the combo he had played with his senior year.

The punk would shit green. He couldn't afford not to believe the RFK revenge story. Nobody dared doubt the possibility of that little ball buster moving heaven and earth to hunt down the men who had cut down his brother in Dallas.

Only Must, the super agent, and a few men above him were dead certain that RFK would *never* disturb the official mythology of the 'one lone nut' theory that had been peddled to the country. Must felt totally secure because he knew that any investigation would immediately reveal that the men, money, weapons used in Dallas that day were all part of a renegade assassination team that had been unleashed to assassinate Fidel Castro by the then Attorney General of the United States: Robert Francis Kennedy.

Renegades who had been available for the asking after the Kennedy brothers had vetoed any more invasion or assassination attempts against Castro's Cuba.

Bobby was smart, a political survivor. He would not take to the streets to smash his own dynasty by letting the Dallas genie out of the bottle. Because then *they* would bring him down too, finally. *They* would make the country know that Bobby Kennedy was ultimately responsible for his own brother's assassination. That the nigger that *they* had taken care of – Malcolm X – had been right when he said 'The chickens are coming home to roost' after JFK got his.

7:00 a.m. *Malibu Beach, California*

The red-faced retired Malibu police officer speculated as to whether the well-built, well-dressed black man who had joined him in his silent early-morning vigil was a Secret Service agent. But if he was an agent, the rent-a-guard wondered, what was the Kennedy sheepdog doing with the nigger?

Woods nodded to the asthmatic old man and told the dog to sit. The three of them stayed in front of the house, posed like subjects in a photograph. This election morning, the street was empty at 7 a.m.; no one in this wealthy beach community would vote for hours. Behind them the house of film director John Frankenheimer slept silently, and behind and beneath the house and the cliffs the ocean lapped below them as it had every morning since the beginning.

Woods checked his watch. He knew that in the dusty San Fernando Valley and Watts and East L.A. and Torrance, some of the working people were already casting their ballots in schools and garages. The guard, a longtime Nixon man leaning toward Wallace, walked over to his '58 Dodge to get at his coffee thermos, offering none.

Woods and the dog remained, immobile, where they

were in front of the house. The day would be gray and warm. The salt wind was rising.

9:00 a.m. *Pasadena*

'Saladin's' bedroom was dark, the shade drawn against the smoggy, thin sunlight. His lips moved as he wrote jerkily in the diary. Then he stared at himself in the dark mirror, his lips still moving. He did not move until he heard the sound of the horn.

The two Arabs were parked across the street in the dirty station wagon, waiting for him.

Three hours later, the scrawny Palestinian was still firing away with the Iver-Johnson .22 on the target range. Hundreds of spent shells were piling up at his feet. An old man wearing a World War II army jacket and earmuffs turned to watch Helen's convertible screech to a halt in the lot. The sound of the firing covered what one of the men in the old station wagon shouted at the well-stacked dame with the short lesbian haircut: 'Get the fuck out of here before somebody sees you!'

On the way home 'Saladin' insisted that the fat Arab's agents stop at Helen's apartment. As they walked out of the elevator on the third floor, he saw two moving men crating up the last of the furnishings in Helen's apartment. He stared at the flat, stripped of all its props; then he turned and walked back into the elevator with a look of loss in his dark eyes. The fat Arab's men were right on his heels.

4:00 p.m. *Malibu Beach*

The gulls circled. Judith pulled her rented car up in front of the Frankenheimer house. The radio news stated that the candidate had spent the day resting in the sun. Nobody 'rests,' she thought as Paul Woods came trotting, favoring his knee, across the yard to meet her.

For a moment they ventilated nervous energy by verbalizing about the voting patterns; 'tremendous numbers' in the ghetto and *barrio*, he told her; 'a lot of McCarthy workers will come over for Chicago,' she gossiped. He reassured her that the candidates had recovered from the extreme fatigue that had caused him to cancel the last San Diego speech the day before, 'if that was the real reason.' 'He's all right,' Paul insisted, detailing for her how Bobby had slept late that morning, then romped with the dog and six of his children, who had flown out for primary election day. After hours in the sun and water, the family was napping now.

Then he was quiet, and she knew he was troubled about asking her to do something. She was jealous of these rare quiet moments alone with him, so she temporized, before it could end, by asking, 'What's the schedule for New York?'

'Uh ... two days of rest here, then Niagara Falls, Friday.' She started to make a remark but he was rushing over the small talk now. '... Then Long Island that afternoon, then Manhattan, then, uh ... well, right through every one of the forty-one districts up to the election on June 18 ...' He took a deep breath and was silent again.

The sun was sinking; the gulls were screaming and circling; they ran out of words. 'Thanks for coming.' He leaned into the driver's window and lowered his voice. 'I have something – a *solid* lead. That FBI man I told you about?' She waited. This was why he had asked her to rent a car and drive out from the midtown hotel.

'He called me yesterday – I couldn't locate him till today – he's hanging out in a restaurant in Pomona, and he says a few days ago – when Bobby spoke there at a luncheon – he and the manager spotted a possible suspect – could be an Arab, he says, and –'

'An Arab?'

'An Arab, *maybe*. And a campaign worker here in L.A. saw *three* Arabs in the Wilshire Boulevard office *yesterday*.'

'Paul, all kinds of people come into –'

He straightened up, walked around to the passenger side of the car, and slipped in beside her, talking quietly from the bottom of his heart.

'They acted suspiciously, lady. The campaign worker that called understands Arabic. I have to compare the separate description of the two so-called Arabs, I'm meeting the campaign guy at the Ambassador. So you –'

'I don't know, Paul. Maybe you should just go to the Senator. I mean, if he knew, then –'

'Oh, he knows! He's a fatalist – like his brother. But yesterday, out in some little town, I *told* you, he disappeared for two hours . . . Hell, the family had a Scotland Yard report on the whole Dallas thing done in '64.'

'Why doesn't he say something in public, then?'

'Judy, I don't know . . . I just don't know. He *did* cancel the San Diego speech, but . . .'

She stroked the big scarred hand next to her on the seat. She touched his face, the eyes red with exhaustion, smoothed his brow with her fingers. How would it all end? Could she and Paul make a life together, no matter what happened? The questions hung between them. She massaged his eyes gently for a moment. He tilted his head back against the seat. The head and sculpted throat were classic Greek, or African? she wondered, finding the pressure points at his temples.

'Oh, yes,' he said, 'thank you, lady . . . No, he's not *going* to say anything in public. And I believe it's a mistake. Jack Kennedy did everything, used all his power to break up the out-of-control junta in the Central Intelligence Agency – I mean, he and Bobby did *everything* – fired people, raided Cuban and right-wing training camps, cut funds – *he did everything but go public*! That alone might have saved him.' She let him rest there a moment, his eyes still closed.

'What does he say in private?'

'He quotes Aeschylus.'

'The old Greek poet?'

He opened his eyes and laughed at her. 'Didn't they teach you *anything* at that school?' Then he saw that she had been teasing him, trying to cheer him, and he touched her face, smoothing the fine golden-brown hair. In front of them the sun was starting to go down in the gull sound. Paul's eyes caressed her face, then shifted, as if by their own volition, toward the horizon.

'He just looks at you and gives out that quote: "In our sleep, pain, which cannot forget, falls drop by drop upon the heart until, in our own despair, against our will, comes wisdom through the awful grace of God." I know it by heart.'

'Paul, have you told him about what you've found out on your own?'

'I can't do that to him without proof.'

In the house they could hear someone laughing. The dog barked. 'Maybe after the primary . . .' He trailed off.

She said, 'What do you want me to do?' and he knew she meant it.

'I can't leave on election night. I want you to go to Pomona, Bobbie's Restaurant. Here's the address and directions. We were there once – you'll remember. See if you can find the guy who saw the Arab – try to get a description.'

'What about the FBI man?'

'He doesn't want to get involved, you know.'

'The hell with that. He's in this thing now.'

'Right. There's his number, too. But he wants to stay out of it, if possible. Do you have enough money?'

Slowly, as if they had time, he wrote the information down on the pad, then kissed her a long good-bye. He waved as she pulled out. She looked back at his receding figure in the soft but still bright late-afternoon light.

Below, he could hear the tide coming in. His lips mouthed some words at the diminishing automobile.

'Be careful.'

6:00 p.m. *Los Angeles*

The H-shaped Ambassador Hotel's horseshoe driveway was clogged with cars, new and old.

By 6.15, Senator Alan Cranston's band was in full blare in the Palm Court Room. The rich, gilded lobby was filling up with Kennedy, Cranston, and archconservative Rafferty campaign workers and supporters. Added to these were sales executives of the Bulova Watch Company, General Electric, and Pacific Telephone, plus a conference of hospital administrators. Fire inspectors had already begun to circulate, checking exits.

Judy Royer, secretary for former California Governor 'Pat' Brown, was assigned to manage traffic in the anteroom and kitchen areas behind the Embassy Ball Room stage, where RFK would appear. She gave orders that no 'unauthorized people should be allowed in this area.'

6:30 p.m. *Los Angeles*

Must's apartment-hotel headquarters was across the street from the sloping terraced grounds of the Ambassador

Hotel. From his fourth-story window he watched the line of after-work voters as it wound around the corner from Wilshire Boulevard. The Americans waiting to vote looked like so many bugs to Must from his vantage point. He checked his watch and turned back to the activity in the room.

James Jerrold and two other men, who had come out from New York and Miami, respectively, to join Must, were in various stages of undress.

The man from Miami, a Cuban-American, had been a sharpshooter assigned to Must in Guatemala in 1961. They had sweated there in the secret jungle training camp, preparing the Cuban exiles for their doomed mission and trying to keep the various political factions from each other's throats. In the end, Must's aide had quit in disgust because the leadership of the invading force had been too far left and President Kennedy had vetoed Must's choice for the Command. The man from New York was an ex-convict on contract to the Teamsters, a colleague of Tony Prince's.

New York was zipping up the trousers of his security-guard uniform; Miami had put on a white waiter's coat; and James Jerrold was a long-wigged, beaded hippie.

Must's smooth face had broken down into planes of fatigue; there were purplish pouches under the pale blue moons of his eyes. 'I'll control on the scene. Don't anyone forget to plug in,' he said, stretching out his hand for the 'guard's' gun. He inspected the .22-caliber palm gun. The pistol had a thin plate flash-shield to protect the shooter's fingers from powder burns. 'Take off that ring,' Must ordered.

He handed back the gun. 'If you can't get the little Arab when all hell breaks loose, don't force it.' Then he turned to Jerrold, who was literally quivering with excited anticipation. 'You're on the outside,' he reminded his gung-ho Green Beanie. 'If he manages to slip through, go to your backup contingency.'

Must's mouth worked. He debated whether to offer them all a belt of bourbon. Instead, he chatted for a moment. 'Watch out for the Ace Guard Service people,' he reminded New York. To Jerrold he started to quote Machiavelli – 'If you strike at a Prince . . .' – but the

Special Forces man just stared back blankly. Well, thought Must, they won't miss, and for a moment he felt a protective impulse toward his little team of 'real men' of the Clandestine Service.

Must took a deep breath, heaving up his heavy chest and shoulders, and poked two blunt fingers under the rimless glasses to massage the small, watery eyes that had seen too much. He sighed. 'All right, let's go through it one more time.'

Below the conspirators, on the street, Americans were patiently standing in line to exercise their franchise that first colonists and then millions of other Americans had sacrificed and bled for.

7:00 p.m. *Pasadena*

'Saladin' walked stiffly toward the 1956 DeSoto parked in front of his house. For a moment his eyes focused on the memory of Helen's sleek convertible; then they went empty again.

From the station wagon situated across the street, one of the fat man's Arabs waved languidly to him.

'Saladin' did not know that they had tapped nail holes in his rear lights so that the white beam against the red glass would give his pursuers a constant trail to follow even on the crowded freeway.

The Arabs listened to their car radio as they followed their quarry toward the freeway. The sun was setting red in the smog's horizon. From time to time they glanced at each other as they heard reports that crowds had begun to assemble at the Ambassador by 6 p.m., a full two hours before the polls were scheduled to close. The computers were now predicting an 'unprecedented 72.4 turnout in Los Angeles County,' where the election would be decided. They looked at each other when the announcer talked about 'a flood' of black and brown Kennedy people voting in 'huge numbers.'

7:15 p.m. *Malibu Beach*

The Kennedys, the Frankenheimers, aides, guests piled into limousines. Sitting in his press car, waiting to bring up the rear of the short caravan, Woods winced as he watched the candidate walking in that soft treading way of his, giving the dog a good-bye tickle. RFK straightened up. The sea wind caught the chestnut hair; the sunburned, freckled face shone for a moment in the fast-coalescing twilight. Then, an enormous grin on his face, he plunged into the black limousine, bound for the Ambassador Hotel.

Following at fifty m.p.h. on the coast highway, Woods tuned in the first election coverage. After a moment he shut the radio off, too early. His thoughts were with Judith, on the Pomona freeway, fighting that unremitting evening traffic.

7:45 p.m. *Pomona*

Judith ran from the lot toward Bobbie's Bar. First she had to go to the restroom, then – The sign stopped her: CLOSED FOR ELECTION. But the adjoining restaurant was open, TV blaring election projections.

She hurried to the cash register. The thin, gray-haired cashier said, 'The manager doesn't usually get in until after nine – sometimes later.' And then: 'The pay phone is right next to the Ladies' Room.'

8:30 p.m. *Los Angeles*

The media mob seemed to Paul Woods to be growing geometrically. All of the campaign suites were overflowing into the corridors. Woods's press room was bedlam. Despite voting machines, the returns were coming in too slowly, and the television and radio brass were putting mounting pressure on their field reporters to feed them background and human interest stories. Woods had fed the insatiable maw of the media the last of his handouts, all the time trying to stay near enough to a telephone to take the call from Judith. She was at least two hours late calling in from Pomona, and he cursed himself for not having gone himself no matter what the consequences. What right did he have sending this girl ('I am not a "girl," I am a *woman* – you of all people should know that': He could see her serious, lovely face), this woman into the unknown?

Down the hall in the Royal Suite, the candidate and some of his family had been joined by senior aides like Fred Dutton, Stephen Smith, Charles Evers, writer Bud

Schulberg, athletes Roosevelt Grier and Rafer Johnson. They chatted nervously about Los Angeles and how the new Votoramic IBM data-processing tabulator *should* speed up the returns, but that there were bound to be 'mechanical problems,' and humorous comparisons were drawn between the new machines and the more dependable old Chicago Daley machine.

Precinct workers had started to pour downstairs, and a few, along with mini-skirted Kennedy Girls, had made the elevator ride up to the fifth floor to see the candidate. Pierre Salinger and Frank Mankiewicz turned back anyone without a press pass while Paul Woods held down the fort in the press room.

Woods's telephones were ringing constantly now. 'Tell the National Desk of *The New York Times* they can wait just like everybody else,' he called to his secretary, and tried to break away toward the phone bank. A TV camera swung in, blocking his way, and Woods found himself pushed into the no man's land of the corridor. He shook his head as they surged around him. Men and women who had come together, lived together night and day in the time capsule of the campaign; fighting deadlines, schedules, editors, deserted families; punch-drunk with fatigue, going on instinct and technique as the quadrennial ritual and blood sport ran down into the final hours.

The mass of press had backed up, jamming the corridor solid between the Royal Suite and the Presidential Suite. TV cables snaked around Woods's legs as he walked backward in the mass, like a black *Laocoön*, shouting, 'You're all invited, afterwards, to the Factory in Beverly Hills,' promising them a party with the Candidate at the chic discotheque.'

Back literally against the wall, he held up a placating hand. Only one face looked alive and sensitive among these grunts and shock troops of the Fourth Estate, his old friend Art Kevin of Mutual Broadcasting – so he talked to him while the ring of pressing flesh closed around him.

'. . . It'll be a hard, uphill fight. New York will be tough, but we have some tentative plans. First, a full page ad in Friday's *Times*, featuring closeup faces of Meany, Maddox, and financier Sidney Weinberger, and a little bit of type below asking if you want these three men to pick your next President – okay, Jerry, I'll be right in – a ten day trip to Europe – Rome to see the Pope, West Berlin, and then Poland. Then there is a chance to create a new primary by petition in Rhode Island in July, and dare Humphrey to enter. And then there will be exhaustive personal campaigning in all the nonprimary states that he had to neglect because of the demands of the primaries . . . See you later, gang.'

'South Dakota! *We won South Dakota!*' Henry Lord was hanging out the doorway. Now the press surged to the other side of the corridor as if the hotel were an ocean liner caught in a mighty wave. 'Call Judy,' Lord tried to pantomime to Woods. The media din escalated as transistors were flicked on to pick up the bulletin from South Dakota. Woods shook his head at Lord; he could not make out what the senior aide was trying to tell him.

8:40 p.m. *Los Angeles*

'Saladin', whose real name meant 'Wanderer' in his native tongue, parked his old car two blocks away from the hotel. He took his wallet out of his tight-fitting white denims and counted the few dollars, straightened his loose-hanging blue velour pullover shirt, and walked slowly toward the hotel.

He entered on casino level and stared at his reflection in the expensive hotel shop windows. The heat and humidity in the lobby were being driven up by the minute by the swelling crowd. He looked into the bar, open since 8 p.m., after the polls had closed.

Outside the Venetian Room he spoke to an electrician setting up a sound booth for the Rafferty party. 'Are you a Democrat?' The man nodded. 'So am I,' said the Palestinian. Twenty yards away the fat Arab's two men looked at each other and frowned. 'What floor does Kennedy stay?' The electrician grunted his ignorance. 'Saladin' turned and walked a few steps toward the two Arabs. His lips were moving silently.

In the packed lobby below, he signed his true name on the hotel register. His hand moved mechanically. The harried clerk handed him a key. Then he turned and stared at the backs of the two Arabs – did he know them? His eyes were peaceful again for a moment, and questioning.

The Arabs were leaving, following the fat man out the lobby door. The glimpse of the fat man's broad back started him trembling again. He could not remember why.

Then he walked slowly over toward the Colonial Room. He stopped at a Western Union machine. The operator looked up to see a thin, dark-complected youth in a loose blue velour pullover, his eyes vacant as he watched the keys tapping. The operator watched him turn and walk away into the gathering crowd.

9:10 p.m. *Los Angeles*

Fire Inspector Cecil Lynch decided that the Embassy Room had reached its 'safe and legal capacity.' Lynch ordered security guards to close the main doors and to maintain a 'one-in, one-out' routine. A few latecomers, tired of arguing with the guards, simply moved to the right, entered the kitchen pantry, passed around the ice machine and out through the anteroom behind the small stage where the Candidate was soon expected to speak, and found themselves inside the packed ballroom.

9:15 p.m. *Pomona*

It was full night. Judith tried to make William Thurman look away from the TV election coverage. When he did turn, she could see that his aging All-American face was reddening with drink.

'Look, I told you, I'm not getting mixed up in this. I told Woods what I saw – that's *it*.'

'But without you there to describe him, what good is it?'

Thurman shrugged and drained his glass, signaling for another. Then he pointed. 'There's your man. He's the manager – he saw him too.' The palpable commitment of this slim young woman made Thurman nervous, and for some reason he could not get drunk. The TV announced that the Kennedy-McCarthy contest was a 'horse race.'

9:30 p.m. *Los Angeles*

'Saladin' sat shivering in the single room. No sound from the election-night chaos penetrated the silence. The light knock at the door brought him up like a sleep-walker.

He stood with his hand on the doorknob looking emptily at Helen for a full thirty seconds. Finally she slipped in, and he closed the door slowly. She had on the long hair-fall that she had worn in Chinatown, he noticed, when he had failed at whatever it was that he had been told to do. He could not remember. He had not seen her since . . . He recalled vaguely the Violence Institute, late at night. She watched his unfocused eyes and wondered what he was thinking. She could still hear him screaming in the hands of the fat man. Then, in the silence, he gasped.

'Who was that man?'

'What man?'

'The man at the laboratory. Do you know what he *did* to me? He made me do *terrible* things. He hurt me.'

Her head was pounding as if with repressed tears, but she was dry-eyed as she moved toward him. Relating to him as if he were her and she were Must; the physical analogy sickened her. If I am becoming schizoid, she reminded herself, then slowly but surely I will lose my body image. She took another stiff step.

'It will all be over soon, Saladin.' She reached out and touched his brow. The eyes formerly so peaceful were like two open wounds. 'Soon,' she murmured, smoothing his temples, 'soon.' She folded $400 into his denims. Then she undid the top two buttons of her white-and-purple polka-dot dress and cupped her breasts, offering them to him this one last time.

10:15 p.m. *Pomona*

'This may be a matter of life and death.' She pleaded with the manager and the sketch artist she had finally located. Thurman watched from the bar, then walked over to their table. I could care less who wins this fucking election, he told himself.

The manager looked up at him. Thurman flashed the ID for the two men. 'FBI,' he said. 'Give her a break, for Christ's sake.'

10:40 p.m. *Los Angeles*

Helen walked past the public telephone. She did not notice Paul Woods, and could not hear, in the growing uproar of the night, the black man, with shoulders so wide they filled the glass booth, shouting into the receiver: 'Could you please page her – Miss Judith Shankland – *please!*'

She was able to single out her 'patient's' thin, hunched figure standing at the bar. For some reason, she could not fathom, he had ordered two Tom Collinses. She paid no attention to the 'waiter,' Must's man, standing next to her. Helen's eyes were fastened on the mirror hanging over the bar. She watched the dark youth watching himself in the glass. Then her eyes went out of focus – I have taken too much, she thought, I am no longer a free agent – and she began to imagine that she saw what he was seeing in the dark and beckoning glass.

Multiple, overlapping images of magnificent thoroughbreds racing in exquisite slow motion. Then the horses piling up, rearing, screaming, falling, their legs breaking under them – all slowly, slowly. The rocking, dying horses transubstantiated and stylized into the maddened beasts of Picasso's Guernica. *Under the plunging hooves, 'Saladin' rolling slowly like a child drowning under water. Silent and slow, the cruel composite of animals and man coalescing into the mirror's dark reflection. Knowing that from now on this primal scene of the horses of death would be her nightmare, forever, until she died, replacing and subsuming the image of her tortured father.*

She watched him watching himself. He sees Kennedy's head now, she knew, filling the dark screen of the mirror. Somewhere inside him, she knew, a voice, her voice, was commanding him to *kill.* Bigger, bigger, she saw him stiffen as if he might fling himself headlong into the glass. Then his shoulders drooped. Now, she knew, he was seeing only his own hated self fracturing into a sea of reflecting images in the glass, standing there in the worn blue velvet shirt with a Tom Collins in each hand, holding on, waiting to become 'Saladin' again.

Helen did not know that Eugene Brading was standing at the stairwell watching both of them, trying to catch 'Saladin's' eye in the reflected gold of the mirror.

A bellboy's call impinged on her fugue – 'Paging Miss Judith Shankland, paging . . .' – casually she felt under the hair-fall to check her miniaturized walkie-talkie cord. Thinking, he is not a computer. His brain cannot be turned off with the flip of a switch. His mind will never cease to function, day or night. That is the torture for both of us, she thought, our brains are like an infinitely repeated image in a hall of mirrors. My brain, she said, will never stop thinking about itself as it thinks about itself thinking about itself . . .

10:50 p.m. *Pomona*
Judith bought the sketch artist another beer and kept going, back to the toilet again. The FBI man had returned to the bar, the whiskey working on him now, mumbling, 'Embarrassed the . . . embarrassed the goddamn Bureau . . .'

The manager looked up. He hated to see a law-enforcement man getting sloppy drunk. 'Just a little more around the eyes, there . . .' He leaned toward the artist. 'Spittin' image,' he said, and walked away toward the kitchen. Judith handed the artist a $20 bill, carefully rolled up the sketch of the young Arab, started to speak to the FBI man, but instead raced for the parking lot.

10:55 p.m. *Los Angeles*
A Kennedy crowd monitor caught 'Saladin' as he emerged from the pantry to start slowly, deliberately into the Embassy anteroom, and turned him back.

She did not see the woman at the far end of the pantry in the white jersey dress with small purple polka-dots. As 'Saladin' retreated into the pantry, a busboy, 'Corky' Jimenez, passed the woman and entered too.

Jimenez turned to get an eyeful of the good-looker in the clinging polka-dot dress. 'Don't go, baby,' he called in Spanish, smiling in a friendly way at the other man, who was also looking after the woman. Then he continued, in Spanish. 'How are we doing? Has he won yet?'

The busboy was puzzled. Was this guy a Chicano or what? He talked funny, in English.

'Is Kennedy coming through here?' The kitchen worker shrugged. The big-eyed guy kept talking funny. 'Don't worry if he doesn't win. He's a millionaire. What's he gonna do for the poor people, anyway?'

11:00 p.m. *Los Angeles*
Must's New York man sat on a commode in the generous old-fashioned white-tiled toilet. While he defecated he studied his palm gun.

He heard someone enter and walk to a urinal; whoever it was had a transistor.

It appears now that Senator Kennedy's lead is irreversible, and, although there has not been a concession speech from his opponents, still . . .

11:40 p.m. *Los Angeles*

The crowd in the balloon-filled ballroom was building to capacity. Woods scouted the edges. Judith must have had mechanical trouble on the freeway, he cursed to himself. The press had given up on him; they were waiting for the Candidate to make an appearance now that he had pulled ahead in the returns decisively. People were pouring past Woods and the hotel security guards into the mounting frenzy, many of them, like Must's man, wearing love beads and sandals.

Inside they had begun to chant 'We want Kennedy,' and some 'We want Chavez,' and the singing rolled up and out: 'This land is your land, this land is my land, from California . . .' Singing the original lyrics now, signaling the end of the sectional primary campaigns and the commencement of the national crusade now aborning. '. . . This land belongs to you and me!'

11:55 p.m. *Los Angeles*

11:55: 'Jesus Christ!' Judith shouted in frustration, looking for a parking space in the lot behind the Ambassador. 'Christ, Christ, Christ!' There – she swerved in. Leaving the keys, forgetting her lights, she was running fast, through the darkened gardens, looking for a shortcut. So it was that she did not pass the man and woman whom she would have taken for a Mexican or Latin couple in any case.

Helen stayed in the shadow, watching the slight figure of her subject walk to her car, open the glove compartment, and take out the Iver-Johnson .22 the Arabs had taken away from him at the shooting range – none of which he remembered any more. He stood lost in the lot for a moment.

'Run!' She wanted to scream. But then he walked over and urinated in the weeds.

11:59 p.m. *Los Angeles*

The Candidate left the Royal Suite at 11:59 p.m., surrounded by exhausted but euphoric staff members. South Dakota and California meant 198 more delegates. They took the freight elevator down to the Embassy Room level, through the kitchen and the friendly reaching hands of the hotel workers, and on toward the last speech of the primary campaign trail.

June 5 *Midnight* *Los Angeles*

'This land is your land . . .' The Kennedy song rocked out into the street. The humanity jammed into the ballroom began to shake like a huge multicolored ball as the first RFK security aides hit the stage. Then the notables and state politicians, also all colors, the athletes, the senior aides, and the family – the crowd heaving, the sound rising and roaring beyond the capacity of the electronic media to encompass the decibels. A sea of fingers raised in the V for victory and peace.

There were another five hundred latecomers trying to force their way into the ballroom before the Candidate began his victory speech. Waves of people were literally hurling themselves against the barricades of flesh where the Embassy Room opened into the lobby. Buffeted and ignorant of each other's presence, Paul Woods and Judith Shankland pushed through the sea of people. Once she caught a flash of the noble black head above the crowd, but in trying to protect the rolled-up artist's drawing of the young Arab she was turned aside, into the vortex.

CBS announced that they were now projecting a clear Kennedy victory and that the California win 'coupled with the triumph in South Dakota, Hubert Humphrey's home state,' indicated that an RFK bandwagon was now rolling 'toward Chicago,' and the crowd roar went up by the numbers.

A mariachi band inched its way toward the speaker's platform to joi the Kennedy musical group The Sounds of Our Times in still another chorus of 'This Land Is Your Land,' the music smothered in the ear-splitting mania of the throng.

12:05
Must, in the linen closet, breathed into the handmike: 'On station in the pantry now. We are committed to the pantry now.'

In the throng, the 'hippie,' the 'guard,' the 'waiter,' and the woman in the polka-dot dress moved unnoticed through their secret agenda.

'Saladin' let himself be pushed along by Helen. He concealed his gun in a folded newspaper – the headline was KENNEDY WINS. Helen was half supporting him, clutching him around the waist. Whispering in his ear over and over, 'Saladin. Saladin.' The terrible inner monologue flowing from Must to her electronically, and from her lips into his ear, into his brain, into his nervous system and his soul: 'Saladin.'

12:07
The victory chanting finally leveled off, so that the vibrant, beaming man on the stage could be heard. The love affair was complete; the throbbing idiosyncratic voice and the little jokes were raised to the level of poetry for the lovers on this night of victory.

'... he pitched his sixth straight shutout tonight, and I hope that we have as good fortune in our campaign ... Cesar Chavez, Jesse Unruh, Paul Schrade ... Rosie Grier said he'd take care of anybody who didn't vote for me ...'

Judith could hear him introducing notables as she finally spotted Paul, within reach of the speaker's platform.

'... I want to express my thanks to my dog Freckles ... I'm not doing this in order of importance. I also want to thank my wife, Ethel ...' The pretty, sunburned woman on the podium laughed.

In the pantry, Helen was afraid that the boy was going to collapse and die in her arms. His trembling was beyond her reach and control now.

Then Paul saw Judith. He could not read her lips, so she had to hold up the artist's sketch.

'I think we can end the divisions within the United States ... We are a great country, an unselfish country, and a compassionate country. I intend to make that my basis for running. I'll take just a moment more of your time, because everybody must be *dying* from the heat ...'

Judith simply could not move past two large UAW delegates and a TV crew. Woods signaled to her to wait there, and he plunged into the crowd again.

'... I thank all of you who made this possible this evening. I was a campaign manager eight years ago, and I know what a difference that kind of effort and that kind of commitment can make.'

12:08
'Saladin,' she kept hissing into his ear now, gripping, embracing him like death itself, the two of them half lying across a steam table. The piercing voice from the ballroom rolling in as the pantry door was swung open by the excited kitchen crew, hoping that the Man would come their way.

'... Mayor Yorty has just sent me a message that we've been here too long. My thanks to all of you, *and on to Chicago. And let's win there!*', and made the V sign to them ...

12:09
The roar was complete sound and jubilation. The orchestra hit the downbeat: 'This *land* is *your* –' Sustained and terrific, the singing, chanting, roaring sound rose primitive, primal, atavistic, and somehow profoundly religious. The wooden floors and thick walls were shaking. Must could feel the sound waves where he hid, whispering hoarsely, without letup: 'Start the balloons. Not too fast. Balloons, balloons ...'

12:10
The exploding of bursting balloons could be heard now, accenting the group roar; Woods froze for a moment, cast a wide glance over his shoulder toward the stage, saw the candidate waving and laughing as he edged toward the steps, and continued his slow-motion balletlike ambulation toward Judith.

12:11
Pop. Pop. Pop, the balloons were still popping. The Ambassador's assistant maître d', Karl Ueker, held Kennedy by the right hand with his left, leading the vanguard of the

RFK party through the gold curtain toward the pantry. He would have preferred to take him directly to the Colonial Room, where the media were waiting, but he had been told by one of the temporary security guards that strict orders had been given to take the route through the pantry to the temporary press room, and he could hear another, authoritative voice calling now, '*This* way, Senator!' He saw the same security guard now, waving him forward, and two other uniformed guards trying to keep up with the entourage as they were all swept toward the open door. Ethel Kennedy fell behind in the crush.

12:12
Judith's sketch fell to the floor. She went down after it on her knees just as Paul reached her side. He retrieved the charcoal picture. Holding the rolled paper above his head, he half lifted her up and began to force a way through the mass with his swinging shoulders and forearms.

12:13
The first advance radio reporters hit the pantry, ready with their portable tape recorders to catch a few words from the Man. 'Saladin' was jerking in Helen's arms now; with her lips to his ear, he shook so convulsively that her teeth were jarred. But in the melee everyone was shaking, leaping, twitching, twisting, so that the dark kid and the woman in the polka-dot dress hugging him went unnoticed in their dance of death.

12:14
The Candidate was being pried apart from the security entourage by the people waiting to shake his hand or touch him or bless him, and the powerful bodyguards and close personal friends, Roosevelt Grier and Rafer Johnson, had started off in the other direction, ignorant of the new route through the pantry to the Colonial Room.

He was almost alone in the press of bodies, as if he wanted to make some direct, existential contact with them, unimpeded by the prophylaxis of attendant aides. 'Good night and thank you,' he kept repeating, touching all he could reach, letting them touch him one last time in California.

'Señor Kennedy, mucho gusto.' The line of kitchen employees in dirty busboy whites, high cook's hats, stained aprons, closed in toward him.

Pop, pop. The balloon sound was farther away now. Paul and Judith were within fifty feet of Bobby. But Must's men were in place only inches away from his head in the hot and malodorous kitchen.

'Here he is!' The workers milled around RFK as he crossed the pantry threshold. A sign taped to the wall read THE ONCE AND FUTURE KING. He reached out to touch them, and it was then they heard the wailing shriek:

'Kennedy, you son of a bitch!'

The Palestinian was transported, moving with explosive, kinetic physical commitment, with the tensile strength of half a dozen men. He stood shooting seven feet away from Kennedy. Fire blazed out of the .22, but none of the shots hit Robert Kennedy.

12:15

'Saladin's' gun arm was like a steel ramrod. Must's man put his hand gun three quarters of an inch behind Kennedy's right ear, and as the patsy's .22 began to spout fire, Must's man put a long-rifle hollow-nose slug into RFK's brain from point-blank range.

Twenty feet away, Paul Woods froze, knowing that these were not balloons or Chinese firecrackers popping now.

Kennedy threw up his right arm. And Must's man put two more quick shots into his armpit and back. Woods heard the scream of men from the pantry, like the sound of animals in the slaughter.

Karl Ueker had the Palestinian in a frantic headlock, smashing the gun hand again and again on the steam table. But 'Saladin,' with the strength of a madman, continued firing, the pistol flashing, squeezing off all eight shots, as it had 'been written.' The air was awash with smoke and what looked like tiny bits of paper. Paul Schrade, the UAW man, and four others went down. The tile floor ran brown-red with blood.

Woods, with Judith collapsing in his arms, heard the voice of a near-hysterical newscaster somewhere in the boiling, ear-splitting mayhem that blocked them from the murder.

. . . Could it be? Could it be? No, it can't be – *it can't be.* It is, oh, my God. It is . . . Oh, my God, my God . . . Get the gun, Rafer, get the gun . . . Get it – get his thumb – *break his thumb!* Look out, *his hand is frozen*! . . .

12:16
The woman in the polka-dot dress was clawing her way out the rear pantry exit as Rafer Johnson finally succeeded in wrestling the much smaller Arab to the floor, the pistol still flashing.

As she ran toward the fire escape, she could hear Must's mechanical panting through her fargo: 'It's a hit! Let him go! It's a hit! Go to ground. Last call. Go to ground!'

As she ran, Helen vomited out the words 'We've killed him, we've killed him . . .'

In the pantry door a TV sound operator sobbed to his cameraman, 'You've got to shoot, Jimmy! You've got to shoot!'

Paul left Judith crumpled against the wall, sliding toward the carpet, the charcoal drawing of 'Saladin' trampled under the feet of the insane mob of media, onlookers, and aides rioting in the narrow passageway.

Paul made his last move, exploding through the bodies in slow motion, his torso twisting and striated like a great stag at bay. As he fought hand to hand with guards and press, covering one yard at a time, his knee went out from under him. Weeping, cursing, he crawled like a wounded beast the last few feet through the shock waves of animal roaring. There in front of him, his eyes still open, lay his beloved Bobby.

Ethel Kennedy was crawling toward the ruined head from another angle. She heard her husband say, 'Oh, Ethel . . .' Blood poured out of his right ear.

Fists smashed into the Palestinian's face; his leg was twisted sharply at the ankle. They sat on him. He had fought off eight men, including the three-hundred-pound Rosie Grier.

In the Colonial Room, the press, still unaware, watched

the Huntley-Brinkley primary roundup on NBC, until a fat woman ran in and smashed the screen in with a heavy ashtray.

On the speaker's platform a Kennedy in-law begged hoarsely over the PA system, 'Are there any more doctors?'

Juan Romero, the pantry worker, was cradling the gallant and bleeding head in his arms, holding a crucifix down in front of the wounded, dimming blue eyes. Someone pressed a rosary into the dying hands and removed Kennedy's shoes.

Men screaming 'Doctor!' tripped and fell over the fallen, broken body of Paul Woods.

12:17

Kneeling there, like the eye in the whirlwind of the chaos, Woods began to beat the floor with his fists, a terrible prehuman sound forcing its way out of his throat. Where Judith lay, two Kennedy Girls, wearing red and blue ribbons and straw boaters, went down on their knees, praying brokenly. Above them a college student wearing the Peace symbol roared tonelessly at the top of his lungs, '*Fuck this country! Fuck this country!*'

On the fire-escape balcony, frightened faces focused on a woman in a polka-dot dress as she ran past them and down the steps, mumbling thickly something like 'We killed him. We killed Kennedy . . .'

12:18

The youth whose name in Arabic means 'Wanderer' was pinned to the floor under Kennedy loyalists. Someone had their hands around his throat. His eyes were blank, dead. Around him lay the wounded, bleeding and groaning.

Over the sobbing animal roar of the pantry, the California political power broker Jesse Unruh called out in his resonant orator's voice: '*Don't kill him! We don't want another Oswald!*'

12:19

Paul Woods swayed on his knees, hands hanging broken at his sides. His face was arched upward in a mask of immemorial pity and terror.

Juan Romero bent over Robert Francis Kennedy. The lips were moving as Romero tried to improvise the last rites: '. . . through my fault, through my fault . . .' Above them, the wife, Ethel, cursed and prayed in the whirlpool of the suffocating swarm.

The manswarm was sucking all the air out of the pantry. Stumbling toward the body on the blood-slippery floor, they hung over him, watching the brain dying in his eyes; hearing the last soft words break through the pink foam of his lips:

'Is everybody all right . . .?'

A few yards away the head of the young Palestinian was being pressed into the pantry floor. He panted silently: 'I can't, I can't, I can't . . .' His eyes stared in the direction of the dying Candidate. The eyes were open and peaceful.